HUNTER'S MOON

HUNTER'S MOON (VOLUME 2)

RAMÓN TERRELL

TAL PUBLISHING

RAMÓN TERRELL

HUNTER'S MOON

SEQUEL TO *RUNNING FROM THE NIGHT*

HUNTER'S MOON

ISBN: 978-1-9990903–1-9

Cover painting by Martin Maceovic
Cover Font by Nick Deligaris
Tal Publishing
Published by Tal Publishing Vancouver BC
e-book Edition: January 2017
First Edition: January 2011
Printed in the USA

For Tanya Terrell.
Your love and support means more than I can express.

CHAPTER 1

Humans. An oblivious species. So caught up in their daily lives, and working so hard to dull their senses to everything around them, that they almost always failed to intuit danger when it was right in front of them. Animals were different. The lower on the food chain an animal lives, the more wary they are. Even predators gave Remy a wide berth. Not humans.

Humans.

So fragile, so clueless. So *easy*. Not all, though. No. He had walked through crowds of people, even receiving the occasional flirtatious grin from a passing female. Remy had always thought it rather humorous, like a deer smiling at a passing lion. Some few actually shied away from him. On rare occasions, a human would glance at him with nervous eyes, knowing he was trouble but not really knowing how or why.

And then there were his current targets. Despite his firm belief that Yako's skills were lacking, evidenced by his failing to dispatch two humans, Remy still had to grudgingly admit that these two were more careful and more alert than most. Remy had always enjoyed toying with his prey. Oftentimes he would walk right by them, making kindly eye contact. Then he would walk by them again, on another street, then another, causing his target to become disconcerted, then panicked. The increased rush of blood flow gave it a more tangy, sweet taste.

The one named Jelani and his friend, Daniel, were somewhat … different. Remy had thought to play his game with them, and walk by on the street. Maybe he would even wink at them. Despite the fact that they were more wary, knowing someone was after them, they had reacted unexpectedly. One of them, Daniel, had noticed Remy as soon as he was within ten feet of them and alerted the other. They both had stolen several glances at him and moved to the other side of the sidewalk, all the time keeping an eye on him.

Remy had to admit he was at least a little impressed. In the middle of a crowd of people walking on that sidewalk, they had felt something out of place about him and moved to avoid contact. The Hunter had chosen to continue on and not give any show of recognition. There would be time enough for a little reunion.

He lifted his head and licked the blood from his lips. In his iron-like grip, a woman twitched uncontrollably. He glanced down at her with pale red glowing eyes. With a mind infinitely more focused than that of a frazzled human psyche, he managed to glean valuable information in bits, piecing them together into something resembling coherency. To be fair, he couldn't imagine anyone maintaining any kind of order to their thoughts and memories when being unexpectedly attacked.

"And what shall I do with you?" he hissed, though he knew she was beyond hearing. He had studied every person who worked in the department with one of his targets. There were twenty-two in total. This woman—Claire, her name was—had unfortunately been quite taken with the one named Daniel for over three years. After half a year of dating, they had mutually agreed to remain friends. Lovely Claire, here, had never quite gotten over her attraction to him. Apparently, Daniel loved the snow, hated the rain, enjoyed video games, and watching movies at the theater, as well as going for walks with his fiancée, Wen.

Remy smirked at her. Through the memories embedded in the cells in her blood—blood he now had in his body—he could feel the envy toward the other woman as if it was his own. Remy never understood how humans could become so devastatingly taken with one another to the point of depression when things didn't work out. There were over a billion of them walking the earth. Vampires accounted for a very small part of that population. Perhaps a shaquora could relate. Being a pureblood, Remy had no understanding of this aside from whatever information he gleaned from his occasional feedings.

"And what do I do with you?" he repeated, playfully tapping the poor woman on the nose with a finger. He had brought her to the *crossroad*, as vampires called it. He hadn't drained her to the point of death, but had not fully injected the vampiric essence that would seek to re-create her.

Remy rarely re-created a human, having no love for the hated turned vampires who had little or no control over the thirst and reveled in their newfound abilities. *Shaquora* were the primary reason Hunters were necessary. The woman convulsed and Remy gently stroked her sandy brown hair.

"Would you like to live forever or pass into the dark and the unknown beyond?" Her teary eyes were open, but the light inside them was fast fading. "Ah, well," he sighed, and bit into her again.

CHAPTER 2

Jelani drew in a deep breath. Deeper, deeper, deep into the stomach, the diaphragm, the groin. He blew out, until there was no air left inside him, then drew his breath in again. He became more aware of his body, his organs, the lungs that expanded and contracted with every long breath. He was aware of the steady beat of his heart, pumping oxygen-rich blood through his body while his mind steadfastly attempted to distract him, until finally it gave up and went quiet.

He visualized a single point in the upper center of his line of vision, a pinprick of light like a single star in a pitch dark sky. Jelani centered his mind on that tiny dot of light, then narrowed his focus into it. Slowly at first, the light grew bigger as he drew closer to it. Then he was enveloped in a soothing, white light that encompassed everything around him, everything in him. The light burned away all negativity, all worries and fears, angers or disappointments, or guilt. Enveloped in this light, he was able to forgive and be forgiven, and to forgive himself.

The light began to recede, and with it the energizing, blissful power that had cradled him in its warmth and love. Slowly, very slowly, he became aware of sitting on a mat. He became aware that the mat was on the floor in the living room of his apartment. His pinky finger twitched, and he was aware of it. Reluctantly, he opened his eyes.

For a while he sat, staring at the floor in front of him. Drawing in a deep breath, he slowly exhaled, letting his stomach expand and contract. Again, he filled his lungs and emptied them, and filled them once more. He blinked several times, then his gaze went to the clock on the far wall. Seven thirty in the morning. An hour and a half had passed. "Personal record," Jelani whispered to the empty room.

He slowly unfolded his legs and extended them out in front of him, placing them together and leaning forward to grab his feet, then gradually pulled himself forward till his face rested on his shins. The stretching felt good and got the blood circulating.

"Finally awake, hmm?"

Jelani looked up to see Alisha leaning in the doorway and smiling at him. She wore a pair of sky blue sweatpants and a workout bra. Well, the workout bra was underneath the matching shirt she was wearing, but since the bra was black, it was simply impossible not to notice. Just like it was impossible not to notice that her nipples were showing through two layers of material. No, he was not a pervert! How could he not notice? She should wear thicker clothes when she went out. There was no telling how many real perverts had been ogling her as she bounced ... *jogged*, down the street.

"Damn, do you see something you like?"

Jelani blinked. "Oh, no! I mean yeah, no, I mean ..." He took a breath. "I was just thinking you should wear something thicker. There's a lot of bad people out there, and you're quite pretty, you know, and ..."

She held up a hand. "And I'm going to allow you to stop talking now before you completely swallow your foot."

He stopped talking and smiled at her. Alisha was absolutely stunning no matter what she was wearing. Her alluring, smooth, dark skin contrasted with those amazing and piercing hazel eyes and that long black hair. Her dark, full lips stretched into a smile even as she frowned. She was irresistible.

"You look like you want to …" She stopped, holding up a hand again and shaking her head. "Never mind, I don't even want to know what's in that perverted head of yours."

"What do you mean by that?" Jelani leaned back on his hands. "I'm not a pervert!"

Alisha snorted. "You're not a functional pervert; I'll give you that."

"Functional?" Jelani frowned. "I didn't know there was more than one type."

"You're the kind of pervert that keeps his sexually charged thoughts to himself and rarely …" she eyed him, "… or should I say *barely* acts on them. The other kind is simply a womanizer."

"You sound like an expert on the subject."

"Every woman who has learned not to be taken advantage of is an expert on the subject."

"So you think I'm a nonfunctional pervert?"

Alisha rolled her eyes. "You have control over about every part of yourself except your eyes, baby."

He loved it when she called him that. Even though she wasn't his girlfriend, occasionally she spoke to him a little more affectionately when her guard was down.

"What are you looking at?" she asked, exasperated.

"Someone sexy."

"Will you quit staring at me?"

"You're asking a lot."

"You know I'm not going to have sex with you, so you're just torturing yourself."

"You waiting for marriage?" he asked.

"Familiarity. I don't have sex with someone who's not my boyfriend. You already know that."

"Your beliefs?"

"My comfort zone. People can 'get it on' after marriage or on the first date. Whatever is comfortable for them is their business. For me, I feel comfortable with someone I'm close to. And only my boyfriend or fiancé or husband, or whatever, can claim as much. You already know that, too."

He did in fact know it already. He just liked talking about sex with her, no matter how brief or fruitless the conversation was. He didn't care if he had to wait. Being in her presence was enough for now. Hopefully, things would move in a deeper direction someday. Jelani found himself drawn ever closer to her as the weeks passed. He could easily see something special between them. He wondered if she saw the same.

"You know," she said, breaking into his thoughts. "While my ego enjoys your fawning over me, I would advise you to consult your brain before your emotions activate your mouth."

"Huh?"

"Don't say something you can't take back, Jelani. I'm not feeling like jumping into anything committed right now, and you're a guy. I understand that. But my understanding stops at the point where you say I have your undivided attention."

He knew what she meant. She knew he had slept with Melinda on more than one occasion and was not bothered by it insofar as they were not in any kind of relationship. The moment he said that he wanted to focus only on her, they would still take things slow, but they would proceed with the intention of forming a lasting relationship.

He nodded, feeling guilty.

She laughed at him. "Jelani." Alisha crossed the room and wrapped her arms around his neck. "I know you better than you think. You've given me reason to trust you, and to a degree, I do. Just know that if, or when, you tell me you want more, I will have certain expectations."

"I know," he said. And he meant it.

The lock on the front door clicked, then turned, and the door opened. Daniel hobbled through, holding two bags of groceries in each hand. Alisha rushed over to help while Daniel pried his feet out of his shoes.

"I like a man that knows his way around a grocery store," she teased. "Wen better hurry up and marry you before I take the back door and beat her to it."

Daniel laughed casually, but the crimson stain creeping up his neck told a different story. Jelani held his laughter inside, knowing all too well what it was like to be on the receiving end of flirtation by Alisha, whether innocent or not.

"Where is my best friend anyway?" she asked.

"Went to work early." Daniel sat the bags on the counter. "They're designing a new building in West Van and everyone involved is being consulted. Gonna be some long days ahead, but payday will be big, and the recognition will be bigger."

"My girl is going to do some amazing things," Alisha said. "It comes so natural to her."

"Yeah." Daniel beamed. "I'm pretty lucky."

"You are," Alisha agreed. "You both are."

"Thanks." Daniel smiled. "So what have you been up to?"

"I went for a run," she indicated Jelani, "while the monk meditated for a few hours."

Daniel cast him a disbelieving look and Jelani patted the air in front of him, rolling his eyes.

"No, man. I wasn't meditating for that long. About an hour and a half. Time just flew."

"Not bad," Daniel said.

Jelani responded by addressing Alisha. "And will you please stop calling me a monk?"

She laughed, holding up her hands defensively. "Hey, don't snap at me. I call it like I see it."

He just sighed.

"Well, I'm off to my place to get cleaned up and head out to work." She went into Jelani's room and reappeared with a duffle bag. "Be good, boys."

"Of course," Jelani said deviously. She shook her head at him and gave Daniel a hug, then placed her hand on Jelani's chest and leaned forward on her tiptoes, giving him a gentle kiss on the lips. It was like he felt a surge of electricity whenever she touched him.

"Bye. See you tonight."

Daniel opened the door for her, and closed it again after she left. "So what's up with that?" he said, turning his brown-eyed stare on his best friend.

"Not much right now," Jelani answered.

"She still doesn't want to commit, or you don't?"

"It's a little bit of both, kind of." Jelani followed his roommate into the kitchen to help put away the groceries. "You bought a lot of food. How much was all this? A thousand?"

Daniel blew through his teeth. "Felt like it. Fill up one shopping cart in that place and you come out a couple hundred bucks lighter and a burning wallet." He pulled open the produce drawer and filled it with a variety of vegetables. "And don't change the subject. What's going on with you two? I'm an inquiring mind."

"Not much has changed," Jelani replied, handing him a couple packs of fish. "She's still not ready to do a serious, committed relationship so soon after her breakup. She says when it feels right, she'll open up to the prospect."

"And you?" Daniel asked, closing the refrigerator and following Jelani into the living room. They each sat down on one of the two couches, one facing the fireplace, the other facing the wall of window overlooking the boardwalk and the ocean beyond.

"I'm not gonna lie," Jelani said. "I really like her, and I want to go further with things when she's ready. She says she's willing to casually date, but not get serious."

"Which means you're seeing Melinda."

"That's where things are starting to bug me," Jelani said. "On the surface, it seems like there's nothing wrong with what I'm doing. Melinda made it clear that she wants to pursue something, but is enjoying the time we spend whether we get together or not. Alisha is fine with things the way we are, until I make it clear that I want to start dating her *for real*."

"So," Daniel said, his tone sarcastic, "you're gettin' it on with Melinda while you can, till you decide to make things serious with Alisha. Nothing wrong with that at all, dude. Nothing at all."

"You make it sound like I'm sleeping with the girl every other night. It's been twice." Jelani ran a hand over his clean-shaven head. "I know how it sounds. It's like I'm playing games, but I've talked with both of them and been honest about it. I haven't lied to anybody. And Alisha isn't ready to be serious anyway, remember?"

"You think that matters?"

"Possibly, possibly not."

Daniel rested his head his hand. "I don't have to tell you to do what feels right."

"I know."

"So?" he waved a hand in Jelani's direction. "What do you feel?"

"I really don't know. I can't say whether I'm right or wrong."

"Okay. Let me ask you this, then. What are you doing with Alisha?"

"Giving her the space she asked for," Jelani answered honestly.

"But she's interested in you, right?"

"Right. But she said she's not ready to do another relationship right now."

"Okay," Daniel said, nodding. "And what are you doing with Melinda?"

"Having fun. Enjoying her company."

"Is she expecting anything more from you than just enjoying your company?"

Jelani shrugged. "Expecting? No. Interested, yes. As far as she's told me on several occasions, whether or not we get together, she just wants to have fun and not worry over what may or may not happen. She just wants me to be honest with her."

"Okay," Daniel said. "After laying it out like that, is what you're doing outside the boundaries of what either of them expects of you?"

"Nope."

"Then how do you feel?"

"Thinking about it so plainly, I don't feel bad." Jelani said.

"Then you should be okay," Daniel concluded. "All I'm going to say is just be careful you don't cross a line and lose out completely. If something starts to feel wrong, stop doing it. You already know that."

"I know," Jelani said. "But it's good to have someone help put it in perspective."

"Well, here's another perspective we've left out. Saaya."

It was like a shadow settled over the room. Saaya. Beautiful and deadly at the same time.

"What does she have to do with this?"

Daniel gave him a flat look. "If you're about to sit there and tell me you don't think she's interested in you, I'm going to slap you."

"She's interested in me like a toy or something!" Jelani said, waving a hand. "She doesn't like me like *that*. The girl is just having some kind of fun with all this. I seriously doubt she's envisioning us curled up on the couch together in front of the fireplace watching TV and drinking tea."

"Okay, I'll give you that. But if you don't think she has something in mind, you're pretty damn naïve."

"Of course she's got something in mind, that's why she's still here. But what can I do about it? And before you say another word, consider the fact that we're still breathing is a direct result of her enduring interest in me."

Daniel bit his lip. "You have a very good point, my friend. A very good point."

"So what do I do, then? Tell the girl 'let's just be friends' and see how she reacts?"

"Well," Daniel thought for a moment, then shrugged helplessly. "I don't know what to tell you. If she decides she wants to do a few things with you in the bedroom, what are you going to do about it?"

"Here's a better question," Jelani replied. "What *could* I do about it? You know just as well as I do that if she decided she wanted to get it crackin', there wouldn't be a damn thing I could do about it."

"You know," Daniel said, frowning at him. "I'm not so sure I feel sorry for you. How many guys would wish to be in your situation?"

"Taking away the half-vampire capable of crushing you like a tin can element?" Jelani said. "Probably every guy in the world. But with that girl in the equation, no guy in his right mind would wish for it."

"Don't know what to tell you, brother," Daniel said, resigned.

They sat in silence for a few minutes before Jelani spoke again. "Personally, none of this is very high on my mental priority list. I'm still just a *bit* more concerned with not dying."

Daniel looked up at him and nodded gravely. "Can't disagree with that."

CHAPTER 3

S he could see far. Farther than any human, and in more detail. It was like the Hunter had been only a few feet away instead of half a mile. She had to admit that he was good at evasion. Twice, she'd tried to get close to him, and both times he had eluded her. Still, she'd gotten close enough to know it was a different Hunter than the three remaining from the last attack.

She'd seen him, but more importantly, she'd smelled him. That was the main reason she'd wanted to get close enough. Appearances could be deceiving, but no one, not even a vampire, could change their scent. And that one was not the Hunter of Japanese descent that had been hunting Jelani and Daniel.

The thought of the other Hunter drew him foremost in her thoughts. What had happened to the one named Yako? Saaya doubted his coven would have dealt him too harsh a punishment for his failure, considering her and Kafeel's involvement. Yet he hadn't appeared in over a month. After three weeks had gone by, Saaya had begun to think the Hunter had decided against pursuing the humans, perhaps returning to his coven and convincing the council he had put enough fear in Jelani and Daniel that they would remain silent.

She hadn't really believed that was true, though. It was unlike any Hunter to leave a matter like this to chance. Something had happened and Saaya was beginning to believe it would be in her best interests to find out what.

She was reluctant to ask her brother for help. Kafeel had little interest in the affairs of humans, and cared little whether they lived or died. He hadn't been particularly enamored of her interest in Jelani. He had no idea why she was wasting her time keeping two humans alive when they would die soon enough anyway. A large part of her could understand his thinking. The lifespan of the average human was not much to an immortal. Still.

Another part of her understood what it was like to live within the constraints of ephemerality. Although she would never know death's kiss unless she met with a violent end, the part of her that was human instinctively understood.

That hadn't been the reason she had plucked Jelani from death three times. She had gone back and forth with herself about it. Tried to explain to herself that it was mere boredom that led her to intervene. After decades of life without much excitement, she needed to have fun.

None of it was true. When she'd said as much to Kafeel, her brother had looked at her with those stony brown eyes and said nothing. He hadn't needed to. "Lie to yourself if you must" those eyes had said.

He was right, and there was no denying it. For the first time in more years than she could remember, Saaya found that she was attracted to a human, and it was maddening, as though both her natures were pulling her in opposite directions. There were moments when she wanted to feel his touch, his kiss, his caress, and merge with him. Other times she found him interesting in a passive and detached sort of way, like a human would regard a bird, or a cat. Cute and interesting, but not much else.

She sighed and turned her thoughts away from Jelani, focusing again on the matter of this new and elusive Hunter. Saaya didn't find his presence overly troubling, as she doubted there was much he could do to harm her and Kafeel, unless he managed to bring the whole of his coven down upon them. While that would be interesting, she doubted the prospect. Something significant had happened to cause the coven to pull the first Hunter away from the job and send someone different. Where Yako had been smart but aggressive, planning his attacks with a precision that would have surely completed the task if she hadn't interfered, this new Hunter was crafty. He was studying them.

She felt her brother's presence drawing near. "Your human lives," Kafeel said.

"You're disappointed?"

"I still find it interesting that you care."

"Since you do not."

There was silence for a moment before her brother spoke again. "Have you discovered a reason why I should care?"

Now it was Saaya's turn to be silent as she thought about it. "I wish I could tell you, brother. I truly wish I knew what draws me to him. It's like his blood speaks to me." Kafeel was silent and she turned to face him. "You've spent no time in his presence, or you'd have felt it, too."

Kafeel's steely features remained unchanged, but a tiny twitch of an eyebrow betrayed his incredulity at her suggestion.

"Doubtful."

"Why do you dislike humans so much?" she asked.

"I do not dislike them so much as tolerate them. They are like a species of animal that thinks to step outside their place in the world. The cattle think to rule the land."

"Not all."

"Too many."

"And me?"

He was silent again. "You are more than most, and less than few."

Saaya smiled and stretched up on her toes to put a hand on his

17

neck, pulling him down so she could give him a peck on the cheek. "My sweet brother. If you're not careful, you might actually issue an open compliment." A flicker of affection passed across his eyes. She tittered. "I love you, too."

She looked up at him and smiled. His long hair had been braided into cornrows that extended to his shoulders. It was a very becoming look. "I wonder how many girls would have fallen in love with you by now if you weren't so forbidding, big brother."

The corner of Kafeel's mouth twitched, the equivalent of a smile from anyone else. "What would I do with a human girl?"

"Anything you wanted, surely. You must admit that most human females are more interesting than vampire women."

Kafeel made a noncommittal sound. "She would wither and die in the blink of an eye."

"Not necessarily."

Kafeel's eyes narrowed. "I will not do that. I am not our father."

Saaya smiled sadly. Part of her understood why Kafeel was undecided with their father's decision not only to take a human as his wife, but also have a child, then re-create the woman. Not that he didn't love Saaya. As a child, her mother had often told her of how Kafeel had instantly taken to her, and how Saaya's birth had actually drawn Kafeel and her mother closer, even before she was turned. It was just that vampires as a whole had little to do with humans unless it was necessary. Purebloods less so, as they had no direct reference of what it was like to be human.

The human blood flowing through her veins gave Saaya the benefit of both perspectives. To a degree, she knew what it was like to be human and could more easily understand their foibles and perceived shortcomings.

"Love leads us down unpredictable paths, my brother."

"As you say."

Saaya gave him a sour look. "It's a vast world we live in, Kafeel. Why not explore it and enjoy the diversity it has to offer us? If you could learn to see the world through the ephemeral eyes of a human, imagine what that would be like."

"Rushing."

Saaya frowned. "Rushing?"

"Rushing to experience all there is before death takes you."

She laughed. "So grim. I won't expect you to understand, but there is more to them than you purebloods believe." When he didn't respond, she knew the conversation was over. Kafeel must be very interested in this business; he rarely spoke so much. Saaya wondered if Kafeel secretly felt what she did regarding the human Jelani. Something about him spoke to her on a blood level, and she suspected if Kafeel allowed himself to get close enough to the human for any measure of time, he would feel it, too.

"The wolf still plays hiding games," Kafeel said, breaking the silence.

"More fox than wolf," Saaya replied. "He nips at our heels, testing us." Behind her, Kafeel nodded. "He's studying us," she continued. "He plays a different game than the first Hunter."

Saaya looked upon the cloudy city. It started to rain and her shimmering black hair grew heavy, clinging to her head. "I can feel his presence, easier than the other. This new toy is better at evasion, but he is not as skilled. There's a manner to his tactics that belies his arrogance."

She knew Kafeel was aware of this as well, but as with most conversations between them, this one was one-sided and primarily Saaya voicing her thoughts.

"Hmm," she continued. "Arrogant, but not stupid."

"Does his presence sour the game you play?"

"On the contrary, Kafeel. It grows more interesting. I cannot deny my curiosity. What has happened to our first Hunter and his two remaining underlings? Why this new one, dogging our movements?" The rain started to intensify, and soon her clothes were soaked, plastered to her curvaceous form. She could have been a sculpted work of art, a depiction of all that was feminine and beautiful.

After a few minutes, Kafeel spoke. "There is something happening, either in one of the North American covens or in the High Council of Elders in Romania. This is inconsistent with how either of them operate."

"But what could that be, and why now?" A tiny frown creased her smooth features. "A solitary human witness could not have caused such a stir. And I won't believe that even our presence and aid to them would have caused this."

"You're right," Kafeel replied. "Neither the human nor our interference would have caused this. That first one, Yako, is possibly the most skilled Hunter I have seen in more years than you've been alive. His abilities are equal to most Reapers."

Saaya nodded. "I felt it. He is formidable … for a pureblood." She smirked. Although Kafeel was a pureblood vampire and she was a *dampeal*, a half-blood, their father was an *Ancestor*, a Count. The strength of the *Ancestors* was beyond what most vampires, pureblooded or turned, could imagine possible.

"You still do not think this is an unnecessary labor?" Kafeel asked.

"I cannot tell you why as of yet," Saaya answered, "but my feelings tell me that it's best to keep him alive. I didn't think so before," she added, sensing his doubt in her motives, "but I've a feeling there is more to all of this than we know."

Kafeel took a few steps back, standing under the cover of the roof. After a moment, Saaya also stepped back, standing close to her brother. He pulled one side of his cloak out and draped it around her. She closed her eyes.

CHAPTER 4

Seven hundred twenty hours. Thirty days. Four weeks. One month. One month he had now been detained in his prison in Romania. Of course, his accommodations had been dressed as otherwise. He had been declared a guest of the High Council, given a comfortable room, and free roam of the city. Free so long as his roam did not drift beyond the city boundaries.

Never once had he seen a guard shadowing his steps as he walked the night streets of Sinaia, mingling with the cattle. But he knew they were there. Only a fool would think otherwise. He couldn't be sure exactly why he was being detained here, but he suspected the cowardly Massius was at the root of it. If his suspicions were true, the devious Elder had sent his equally devious relative, Remy, to deal with the two humans and the vampire siblings in his stead.

What he hadn't yet figured out was how Massius believed Remy would be any more successful than he had been. Even though there was no way for them to know they were dealing with the son of an *Ancestor* and a *dampeal*, Remy wasn't a big enough fool not to realize he was dealing with something beyond him.

The night was crisp and freezing and snow fell in gentle

showers from the gray canopy above. He rounded a corner and made his way toward a park, seeking the quiet refuge only a wooded space could provide. Further down the street, on a corner between him and the park, stood a lone figure: a woman. He continued past her and she fell in step beside him.

"Only two shadow you today, Eldest," Mariska said.

"They are confident I will remain."

"Their confidence is well founded?"

"I do what must be done."

They crossed the street and entered the park, trudging through the ankle deep snow. The trees and benches and tables were white with the powder, making for a serene environment. Yako enjoyed that about snow, how it softened even the harshest environment.

"And what must be done?" Mariska asked.

"Nothing."

She cast him a questioning look and he elaborated. "Nothing, until our path reveals itself."

"You believe Remy will be unsuccessful?"

"I believe it would be a wonder if he is successful in surviving a confrontation, should he be fool enough to take action."

"There seems to be little alternative," Mariska said. "You are here and he is there."

"And there are those with a vested interest to keep things such," Yako agreed. "For now, we wait."

"I could travel back …" she trailed off when Yako shook his head.

"That is unnecessary and unwise. You're free to go where you will, but you are close to me. Your movements are watched no less than my own." He glanced sidelong at her. "And there is another who keeps watch."

"Another?"

She noticed they had stopped, and she looked around, turning a questioning look on the Eldest Hunter. When he didn't speak, she waited, knowing not to ask if he didn't volunteer. After a few minutes, a man of average height but heavily muscled, appeared in the distance, seemingly materializing in the middle of the gentle snowstorm.

Mariska frowned, watching the man as he approached. Once he was within ten feet, she hissed, reaching for a knife in her belt. Yako's hand whipped out in front of her.

"Hold," the Eldest commanded. "He's a friend, and it is already too late. He could have ripped your throat out before your stroke fell."

She looked at him, incredulous. "Friend?"

Yako flashed a rare smirk. "Ally, if you prefer."

"Oh, now that just hurts my feelings, Bloodhunter," the man said.

Mariska's narrowed eyes glowed crimson. "You would consort with that?" she said, disgust coating her tone. "A beast of burden?"

The man turned his head a bit to regard her with an expression of amusement. "I might ask that you mind your tone, little blood girl. Most among my kind are more ... temperamental."

Mariska narrowed her eyes.

"He is no enemy," Yako said, casting her a look that said he would not tolerate aggression.

"They are our enemies," Mariska said, never taking her eyes from the man.

"Only to those who know no better," Yako replied.

"'Tis true," the man said in an overly friendly tone. "My kind never initiated aggression with you. Ever have we simply wished to be left alone. It was you bloods who struck the first blow."

"Your explanation is rather simplistic and lacking in crucial details," Yako said evenly.

The man shrugged. "But true, more or less. And it is also true that I have forgotten my manners. I am Darren Lacey, at your service, my lady." He stepped forward and extended his hand.

Mariska bristled, eyeing him. "Put your paw back in your pocket."

"What are you afraid of?" Darren said.

"Fleas," Mariska shot back.

To her further irritation, he laughed. "Oh, little blood girl. So hostile." He turned his gray eyes back to Yako. "I wish my second in command was as vigilant. She compliments you well, Eldest. To Mariska's surprise, he bowed his head in respect.

"What news have you?" Yako asked.

"Let us walk," Darren replied. The snowfall had begun to intensify so that visibility was barely more than a dozen feet, and they would be up to their knees in it soon.

"You're right that Massius's little tool, Remy, has taken up the hunt. For the month that you've enjoyed your little vacation here," he smirked at Yako, who didn't return his mirth, "he's been stalking the two human males, and occasionally studying the brother and sister. A couple of times, I thought the little woman and her brother might catch him, but the little bat is quick and cunning. He's evaded them at every turn."

"I suspect part of it is their lack of total interest more than Remy's level of guile," Yako replied.

"Maybe," Darren said. "I have had one of the pack watching him. The little bat reports back to his coven sporadically."

Darren noticed Mariska's brow twitch whenever he referred to the vampire as a bat. "You seem offended," he said to her. "A lover of yours?"

She hissed at him, her eyes glowing.

"Peace, peace!" Darren said, laughing. "You really must develop a sense of humor, Second Hunter. I understand that most of you vampires take yourselves so seriously, but I mean you no insult. I would prefer your friendship than your enmity, I assure you."

"Not all wishes come true," Mariska replied in an icy tone.

Darren shrugged. "As you wish." He looked back at Yako just as they reached the end of the park. "I have a strong suspicion the little ba—" he stopped short, glancing at Mariska, "ahem, Remy, is planning a way to separate the siblings from the two humans long enough to kill them, but I can't be sure yet." They stopped and he turned to regard them. "I don't need to tell you that Remy is crafty, and is planning something. What I can say is that I am sure his plans involve making a show of accomplishing what you have been unable to and proving himself your better. I don't pretend to know the extent of your vampire politics, but I suspect that would be bad for you."

Yako remained silent. Darren was right, of course. If Remy managed to kill those two humans, and possibly the *dampeal* and her brother, it would cast a disfavoring light on Yako.

"Would you like for me to remove him from his task?" Darren asked.

"No." Yako stared at him. "You know as well as I that if it were discovered that one of your pack disposed of him, it could create conflict between our peoples."

Darren shrugged as though it mattered little to him. "True enough. I suppose I should leave you here, lest your escorts on the two buildings over there become suspicious." He jabbed a thumb over his shoulder as he spoke, indicating the four vampires that had been tailing Yako all night.

Mariska's eyes darted around, searching for the two followers she'd missed. Darren chuckled. "You bloods see well enough, but you really must learn to see better in the snow, and maybe learn to smell better also." He extended his hand to Yako, who took it in a firm grip, then they released each other. Darren looked to extend his hand to Mariska again, then smiled and shook his head, bowing to them both before turning away. Seconds later, he disappeared behind a curtain of snow.

They turned in the opposite direction and made their way through the less traveled streets. "Why would you trust one of them?" Mariska asked, openly disgusted. "He's an animal."

"We might appear so to humans, would we not?"

"That does not make us what they think we are."

"Indeed," Yako replied. After a moment, he looked at her. "There are some who would feed you a colored version of history, Second. Our biggest failing is that we don't ask questions."

"Questioning such a history would be disrespectful and ill advised, would it not?"

"Of course. But not all questions need be asked verbally. Ask yourself questions and seek your own answers, Mariska."

She nodded respectfully. "I cannot fathom how you bring yourself to trust a wolf."

Yako's expression never changed as he replied. "He has earned more trust from me, many times over, than many vampires I've known. And besides that, he could have killed you before you knew what he was." Mariska's eyes narrowed and Yako shot her a stern look. "Check your ego, Second. Think what you will of the wolves, but some among their number are more intelligent than our kind want to believe. They also have their own types of *talents*. Darren is able to hide his scent better than most, allowing him to get close enough to deliver a swift and deadly blow, if necessary."

Mariska snorted doubtfully. Yako glanced at her again. "I am fast. But I'm not faster than Darren. He could have snatched out your throat, and I would have given chase till he outran me. He's a friend, Mariska. And one I would recommend you respect if only for that reason."

"I will try, Eldest."

"I expect it," Yako said.

They walked in silence for a while, turning down the various snow packed streets, the sounds of the city muffled by the thick layers of snow that blanketed the environment like a white carpet.

"I've tried to find out how long they plan to detain you," Mariska finally said. When Yako didn't respond, she continued. "Meilana says that Massius has been particularly aggressive about your ineptitude regarding the humans. He refuses to hear any explanation as to why you were unable to eliminate them and steadfastly disregards your past achievements and service to the

High Council. His obvious hatred toward you has raised more than a few eyebrows, and I believe he has betrayed himself in this. If he had been more subtle, perhaps there would have been more inquiry regarding the situation."

"And that would have also worked against him," Yako replied. "Once a proper investigation was done, it would have been determined that the two who protect the targets are beyond what most Reapers deem a challenge."

Though his face was passive, Yako felt less so. The fact that Massius had succeeded in detaining him here for this long was irksome. He needed to get back to North America and quickly, lest Remy find a way to make things more difficult for him. The troublesome Hunter may think more of his skills than the true reality, but he was annoyingly crafty. If Yako didn't get back to Vancouver soon, Remy would likely find a way to achieve at least part of his objective. Any success by him would be a ding in Yako's reputation that would be greedily exploited by the likes of Massius.

"Your thoughts, Eldest?" Mariska asked when he was silent for a while.

"I need to know why Massius is targeting me. There's no logical explanation as to why he is so fixated on me. I am simply a Hunter. The fact that Remy covets my station is not enough of a reason."

"The serpent is ever wary."

"Of what, and why?"

"Would that we knew."

They turned onto the street that led to Peles Castle. The massive structure had been renovated and maintained by the country for many years. It was almost comical that humans had no idea it was the home of a coven of vampires and a focal point of their power. Yako found the town of Sinaia to be not without a good measure of charm, but the many human tourists were little more than tolerable. Though that very tourism extended itself to Peles, the High Council had limited it to only certain wings of the castle, and only certain times of the year, claiming that too much visitation and foot traffic would create wear on the historic grounds.

The fact that there were more than a few vampires in prominent positions of government around the world—Romania being no exception—this was a relatively easy thing to do.

Had he been here under different circumstances, Yako might have toured the town and the castle more. As it stood, he spent the majority of his time in the library or walking some of the streets of the town at night to get away from the whispers drifting through the walls of the castle.

"He will use his power and influence to hold me here as long as possible. I cannot allow this. One way or another, I need to get back."

"And eliminate the targets before Remy?"

Yako shook his head. "There is more to this than two humans witnessing a feeding. Massius's actions have made that clear."

"Then why not stay here to find out what the Elder plans?"

"I'll have to do that without being here. If Remy finds a way to succeed, my situation will be too tenuous for me to accomplish anything. I need eyes and ears here while I'm away."

"You would have me remain?"

"No. I need you beside me."

"Braggus?" Mariska looked doubtful.

"Braggus is a friend, yes. But he is also Eldest Reaper, and cannot move or speak against any member of the High Council without absolute probable cause. He aids me where he may, but it's a careful balance; one he has limited room in which to move."

He stopped and she faced him. "How well do you trust Meilana?"

"How well do you trust me?"

Yako thought for a moment. "Maintain communication with her that cannot be traced, and be assured, without a doubt, that her sister remains discreet. She knows the penalty for sharing information outside the Reapers' circle, but remind her nonetheless. It's not just her own uncreation at stake."

"Of course, Eldest," Mariska replied, and her eyes gleamed. Yako had just paid her a great compliment. "They rarely speak to one another when others are present, to maintain the show of rank difference, and none but the two of them and myself know about their mind bond. It is as much in their best interest as it is in ours for them not to be discovered."

Yako nodded, satisfied, and they continued. As they neared the castle, the *dampeal* and her brother came to the forefront of his thoughts again. He'd never met an *Ancestor* before, and he wondered how many still walked the earth.

"When do you think you will be able to leave?" Mariska asked.

If he'd had his way, Yako would have gone weeks ago.

"Soon," he replied.

CHAPTER 5

S o, how long did you know about this?" Daniel demanded, and gave Jelani a playful punch in the arm.

"Hey, concentrate on the road!" Jelani laughed.

"I can't believe you held on to that secret for a year!" Daniel said.

"They wanted it to be a surprise, homeboy," Jelani replied, still laughing. "You'd been going on and on for so long about how you'd love to have a character made after you in the upcoming game, they just kept telling you maybe, maybe not."

"So how did they do it? I didn't go into their mo-cap studio for any screen shots."

Jelani shook his head. "Doesn't work that way. The motion capture is faceless anyway. They just capture the body and facial movements of the actor. Later they can put whatever face on the character they want. In your case, they already had the actors do the motion work and they just pulled some photos from company get-togethers from over the years. The animators do their magic and alter your image to make it more cartoony, and there you have it."

"Sweet!" Daniel said, rocking back and forth in his seat. "So what's the deal with you, then? What new project will they have you working on now?"

"They haven't given me any details yet," Jelani said. "All I know is that it's an action adventure game. Third person."

"I bet it's that new one, *Indomitable*." Daniel turned his silver Lexus into the EA parking lot. "It's a kind of a twist on the other successful titles of the same kind. This one has the same death-defying, treasure-hunting aspects, and is also story-driven. The difference, though, is that it involves traveling to different countries and cities and actually talking to people, like in a traditional role-playing game."

"Really?" Now Jelani was curious. "An Indiana Jones type of game with RPG elements to it? Sounds like my kind of combo."

"It's been in secret development for three years now, with the team mostly working on the world, which is said to be detailed and pretty vast." He pulled into a parking slot and turned off the engine.

"I honestly believe that if they pull this off, we're looking at Game of the Year."

"That would be huge," Jelani said. Though he did a lot of voice work and motion capture for EA, he was not a direct employee of the company like Daniel. This kind of achievement would be more personal for his friend.

"Yeah, I know. And the fact that I've been working on the physics engine is a big plus on my résumé."

They walked along the architectural masterpiece that was the EA facility in Burnaby, BC. Complete with a soccer field and countless other options for employees to play, the building was sleek and high tech-looking. Daniel had told Jelani that the employees of EA worked hard and played harder.

They rounded the corner and stopped short. Further down the walkway stood Michael Shreeve, head of the physics department. He was speaking with two police officers.

Jelani and Daniel looked at each other, then continued on, figuring they would ask Mike what it was all about, later.

Michael caught sight of them, which drew the officers' attention.

"Gentlemen, would you wait a moment," the sandy-haired officer said. He was about Jelani's height, but much stockier built, and with icy blue eyes. "We'd like to ask you a few questions."

"Um, okay," Daniel said. He and Jelani glanced at each other. After a few more minutes, the officers finished with Michael and stepped up to them.

The second police officer was taller and leaner, but with a strong jawline and long thick arms. His small, bright blue eyes were equally as piercing as his partner's.

"I'm Officer Maddock," the taller cop said, "and this is Officer Neald."

"Hi. Daniel Ng."

"Hello. Jelani Shaudee."

"Are either of you men acquainted with a Ms. Claire McMahon?"

"No, sir," Jelani answered.

Daniel frowned. "Claire? She works in Human Resources." He swallowed.

Jelani looked at his friend and saw the rising panic in his face.

"Something hasn't happened to her, has it?" Daniel asked.

"Her body was discovered two days ago in the woods about a kilometer east of the facilities here."

Jelani only had a vague impression of how far that was. Though he had learned the metric system in school, the States had never adopted it, so he'd been learning it all over again.

"What!" Daniel's mouth hung open. "You're sure it's her? I just saw her three days ago …" he struggled for words. "This can't be right. There has to be a mistake. I … I can't …" He mumbled a few more words, then stopped and ran a hand through his hair.

"Were you close, Mr. Ng?"

Daniel nodded. "Yes. We dated for a while and have been good friends ever since. I can't believe ... Are you sure?"

"Yes. I'm sorry ..."

The conversation trailed off as Officer Neald led Jelani away.

"How do you know Mr. Ng?" the officer asked.

"He's my best friend," Jelani answered.

"When did you say you met Miss McMahon?"

"I didn't sir. Daniel knows her, not me."

"But she worked in the same building as you, didn't she?"

Jelani shook his head, then nodded. "No. Yes. Yes, she worked here, but in a different wing. I've never had a reason to go to Human Resources. I'm not an employee so I've never been to company functions where I'd have met her."

"Why are you here if you're not an employee?"

Jelani was starting to see why most people never got away with a crime. It would take a master of lies to fool a cop.

"I'm an actor, sir. I do voice work and motion capture on a project by project basis."

Officer Neald wrote all this down. "Have you seen anyone who looks or has behaved out of the ordinary?"

You'd give me a ticket for being a smartass if I answered that true. "No, sir."

"We may contact you again. You're free to go, Mr. Shaudee."

"Thank you, sir" Jelani said. He came back to the main walkway and cast a sympathetic look at his friend.

"Sir," Officer Neald said. "You can carry on."

"Oh, Jelani said. "I was just going to wait for my friend."

"You can wait for him inside if you want."

"Um, yes, sir."

"You said you saw her three days ago ..." Officer Maddock said as Jelani moved away. He continued down the walkway around the curving façade of the building, following the paved paths until he finally came to the building that housed the motion capture studio.

A person found dead in the woods. The woman had surely been murdered, and the fact that she was close to Daniel, that they had dated and remained close friends, was not lost on Jelani. He couldn't imagine why the vampire had chosen to kill a friend of Daniel's, but he knew there was something behind it. Perhaps Saaya would have some answers. Thoughts of the *dampeal* made him uneasy, though he hadn't seen her in nearly two weeks. He hoped she hadn't simply gotten bored and left the city, or just left him to his fate. That last thought had him feeling altogether vulnerable, and he was reminded once again how hopeless this situation would be if she had decided to simply leave him and his friends.

Now more than ever he hoped she would come to him so that he could get some answers about this. He stepped into the building and wiped his feet on the long mat, then continued on.

"Good morning, Jelani."

"Hey, Janet," he replied as he slipped off his coat. He glanced back out the doors, but Daniel was still talking to the cops.

He turned back to the normally cheerful front desk receptionist, who was in a subdued mood today. "You look like you've already found out," he said.

She dropped her head and nodded. "It's all people are talking about. They're going to do a write up on her in the company newsletter." She looked up at him with sad brown eyes. "I can't imagine why anyone would want to do something like this to her. Claire was so sweet." She dabbed a tissue at her eyes, sniffling. Jelani tried to think of something to cheer her up. He always felt uncomfortable when women cried. "How's Daniel taking it?" she asked.

Jelani glanced back at the doors again. "He just found out. The cops are talking to him about it now."

"Well, I hope they can find the son of a bitch who did this," she said, still sniffling.

For their sakes, they'd better not. "Me, too," he said aloud.

Janet sniffled yet again, and dabbed at her eyes. "They're almost ready to go. Just head on in."

Jelani glanced at the doors again. He'd hoped to see how Daniel was holding up.

"You should go," Janet said. "You know they take forever to get ready, but don't like to wait on anyone else."

Jelani nodded. "I know that's right." He didn't know what else to say, so he went around the desk and gave her a hug. She wrapped her arms around him tightly as the sobs came. "It'll be all right," he whispered. The words sounded hollow in his own ears, but he couldn't think of anything else to say. He patted her back. After a long moment, she released him and stepped back.

"I'm sorry."

"Don't be. I'm here if you need an ear or a shoulder."

She smiled. "Thanks, Jelani. You're a sweetie."

He forced a smile and waved as he continued down the hall.

"ALL RIGHT, JUMANJI," the director said from behind his computer screen. "Just do a couple test movements, maybe a kick or something."

Jelani started to correct him, but decided to just let it drop. The man had already butchered Jelani's name four times, and the effort wasn't worth it. He did a couple test punches and a kick, keeping his movements slow so they could follow. "That's good, that's good! Now go a little faster." Jelani complied.

Though punching and kicking the air slowly while dressed in a skin tight black body suit with tiny white dots all over his body was somewhat odd, the experience was always a blast. The past couple years, Jelani had proven to be an excellent voice actor as well as a natural at motion capture acting. It was like being paid to play at life.

Lately, the video game studios had begun incorporating both jobs into one, often having the actors play the entire role in an open studio with crude props that would later become various items and structures in the finished game.

"Okay, give us a second, Jumani, thanks."

"Jumani? For real?" Jelani frowned in disbelief, his mouth hanging open. He looked over at Paul, who worked the cameras. The cameraman responded with a slow shake of his head, a look of "just let it go" on his face.

Jelani sighed.

"Okay," the director said, and Jelani looked across the room as he approached. The director was a small man, around five feet four inches tall. The top of his head was bald, and two long patches of hair started on either side of his head and stretched around to meet at the back. It made Jelani think of the horseshoe-shaped laurel wreath that Julius Caesar wore.

He had an almost sideways rocking gate that seemed to make him take longer to traverse the same amount of space as anyone else. The mousy little man was altogether odd, but there was a likable quality to him despite his inability to properly pronounce Jelani's name.

"Here's what we need. Oh! And by the way, my name is Travis Barklay." He stuck out a stubby-fingered hand which Jelani accepted.

Wonder if I should accidentally call him Trevor or something.

"You're basically a wealthy anthropologist by hobby, and your passion is traveling the world and learning the customs and traditions of various peoples around the world. You also like to explore ancient ruins and caves and civilizations and all kinds of stuff like that."

"Gotcha," Jelani replied.

Travis Barklay nodded. "Okay. Since you've got all this money, and time, you've learned a bunch of languages, and also learned various martial arts, rock climbing, things like that. This is where your expertise comes in ..." As Travis went on to explain, Jelani noticed one of the technicians watching him. At first, he didn't think anything of it, but several times he'd seen the technician looking at him. At times, he could feel the man staring.

"… be lots of shooting while hanging by one hand, and stick fighting, too!" The more Travis explained, the more animated he became. It would have been quite comical if not for the unnerving feeling that technician was giving him.

Jelani shook it off and focused in on the director. *Just being paranoid.* It was early in the day and most vampires slept during the day. Besides, a vampire powerful enough to walk around in the sun wouldn't be concerned with him anyway.

After Travis was finished, he went back behind his desk. "Okay, Johnny. Whenever you're ready!" Jelani let everything else drop from his mind and went to task, creating the scene in his mind and miming the various actions he was instructed to perform.

Once the session was over, Jelani joined the director at his desk. "Mind if I have a look?" There were some directors that were completely unapproachable and some that were hesitantly friendly. Travis Barklay was on the far side of the latter, waving Jelani over to sit next to him.

"Sure, come have a look. Check this out. Right now, all we see are the various dots on your body connected by these simple lines. Later, it will be filled out and textured, and there will be an actual person there."

"I love this stuff," Jelani said, smiling like a child. "It's fascinating how all this comes together!"

"I see you're a gamer," one of the technicians said, still staring into his screen.

"All my life," Jelani replied. "Thanks for indulging me, guys. I'll let you get to your work. See you tomorrow."

"We'll see you tomorrow, buddy," Travis said.

Jelani started for the door and saw that same technician leaning against the wall in his path. Jelani's skin prickled as he moved to the exit, but he forced himself to smile and speak.

"You have a good day."

The technician winked one of his round green eyes. He had a passive, pale face beneath a shock of black hair. "Be careful the company you keep." His voice was a whisper. A dangerous whisper. "They leave a rather distinct scent on you." He wrinkled his pinched nose, and Jelani thought he saw a crimson glimmer flick across his eyes.

"I'll do that." He opened the door and stepped out. When looked back, the technician had already returned to his equipment. Jelani hurried down the halls. It was early evening, and there was only about two hours of daylight left. Daniel would be finished in another half hour and they could leave.

Once he made it to the building where Daniel worked, he found a place to sit and wait. He would have liked to deny that the guy was a vampire, but he'd have been a fool to do so. There was no subtlety in that threat, and the presence of the man was all wrong, like a predator in the guise of its prey. How could he be out in the day? Saaya had been adamant that not even all purebloods could endure the sunlight, and only Elders could bear the sun for any lengthy period of time.

Jelani couldn't imagine an Elder vampire or a powerful pureblood finding him worth their time to get a job as a technician just to kill him. A soft *ding* came from his phone, indicating he had a text message. Four unchecked messages. The first was from Daniel, saying he may be a little late finishing. That was the last thing Jelani wanted to happen after his encounter with that guy in the studio. The second was from Alisha.

"Hey there. I'm craving seafood, ambience, and a view. Lionel's on Grouse?"

"Damn skippy," Jelani thought aloud as he answered the text. *"Let's do it,"* he typed.

The third text was from a friend back in California he hadn't seen in three years. They'd always kept in touch, but he had only been back once, and had not the time to visit everyone he wanted to. He decided to answer that one later, and moved on to the last message. Melinda.

"Hello, love. I got your message last week, but I've been terribly busy. Maybe I should make it up to you?"

Jelani took a deep breath and blew it out. He needed to put an end to this, and quick. Regardless of what Melinda or Alisha said, his conscience was beginning to tingle. Melinda was a great girl and deserved more than a relationship that consisted of occasionally spending time together and the sex that followed. Not that he didn't enjoy either, especially the latter, but the longer this went on, the worse the situation was likely to get.

"Sounds cool to me," he replied. *"A little busy myself, so let me hit you up when I've got a minute and we can find a time to link."*

He sent the message just as the door across the hall opened and Daniel stepped out. His friend looked to have made a considerable effort at holding himself together to get through the day.

Jelani stood. "Hey man." They clasped hands and gave each other the customary shoulder-to-shoulder guy hug. "You all right?"

"As right as I can be under the circumstances, I guess."

They walked silently through the halls and Jelani let his friend be. Once they reached the car, Daniel started the engine and let his head fall back. After a few moments, he looked over at Jelani with tormented eyes. "Is this my fault?"

Jelani ran a hand over his head. "Only if you could control the guy who did it," he answered.

Daniel pulled the Lexus out of the parking slot. "I'm trying to tell myself that, but I'm having trouble believing it."

Jelani looked out the window. He had a good idea what his friend was thinking. As hurt as Daniel was about Claire's death, what if it had been Wen? He could only imagine what that would have done to him, and Jelani was still wrestling with his own guilt in the matter.

All of this was directly tied to him. He frequently had to

remind himself there was nothing he could have done short of not going for that jog that would have prevented all this. If he'd fled someplace far away, the Hunter would almost certainly have tracked him down, and the same results could have happened, only with strangers. People would be dead.

"What could he have gained by killing someone close to me?" Daniel said, a trace of anger creeping into his voice. "What could possibly help him get to us through killing a friend of mine?" He glanced at Jelani. "Why did you have to go jogging in Stanley Park at night, Jelani? At *night*. You know how dangerous that place can get at night. You know it, dude! You could have jogged all over the damn city! You could have jogged English Bay! Why the park?"

"I'm not psychic, Daniel," Jelani replied quietly. "There was no way I could have known this would happen."

"Common sense, man. *Common sense!*" The seatbelt locked Jelani in his seat when Daniel stomped on the breaks at a red light. "Of all the places to go for a fucking run! You have to do it in the woods, no lighting, surrounded by trees!"

Jelani put his hand over his face, then looked over at Daniel. "What do you want me to do? Do you want me to wish I hadn't gone jogging where I had? I do! You want me to wish all this hadn't happened? I do! You think a day doesn't go by that I don't think about how I got all of you involved in this by stumbling on two feeding vampires?"

Jelani checked his temper. How could he blame his friend for the anger he felt? "Look. If I'd known there were vampires walking around among us, trust me, I would have never gone out at night alone. If you feel like I'm to blame for all this, that's fine. I can take it. And if I thought for half a second that offering myself to that Hunter out there would take the heat off of all of you, I would have done it a long time ago. I was running for my life and didn't have a whole lot of time to think of the option before you got pulled into this.

"It may piss you off more for me to say this, but I'm sorry." He gave a helpless shrug. "All I can do is tell you I'm sorry, and I'll do my best to make this situation right, however possible."

Daniel's face softened, and he sighed. "I know. And I'm sorry for blaming you." He held up his hand to forestall the incoming rebuttal. "No. It was unfair of me to blame you for Claire's death. I'm sure the bastard has left a trail of dead bodies in his wake, and now Claire is one of them." They were moving again, taking the on-ramp to the highway.

"I don't blame you for any of this," he continued. I do wish you hadn't gone jogging that night, but I don't blame you."

"Dude, *I* wish I hadn't gone jogging that night."

"Yeah, but whether you had or not, that guy they were feeding on would still be dead, unfortunately."

Jelani looked back out the window. "Sometimes I still can't believe we've got vampires after us."

"Makes you want to go someplace where it's mostly daylight, doesn't it?" Daniel muttered.

Jelani looked at Daniel. "I think that may matter less than we think."

CHAPTER 6

I know, I know," Daniel said, patting the air with his hand. "There's day walking vampires that don't burn in the sun."

"Yeah, well, here's another thing for you to worry about," Jelani said.

"I'm so excited," Daniel replied.

"I think one of the technicians in the mo-cap studio may be a vamp."

"What? When did you find this out?"

"About an hour ago."

Daniel's eyes widened and he glanced at Jelani, his grip on the steering wheel tightening. "How is that possible? It's daytime, and I doubt one of those Elders or *Ancestors* Saaya was going on about would lower themselves to be technicians for a video game studio."

"I feel the same way. But I know what I saw, and he gave me a really bad vibe. Combine that with what he said to me—"

"What did he say?" Daniel interrupted.

"He told me to be careful of the company that I keep because they leave a distinct scent on me. Whatever the hell that means."

Daniel was quiet a moment. "Well, we got to the studio just

43

after dawn, and there are lots of people who work there in the predawn hours." He looked over at Jelani again. "He might have gotten there before dawn. It's not like they burn just because it's daytime. They have to be in the sun, right?"

Jelani nodded. "All he would have to do is stay away from a window to avoid the sunlight."

"So you think the Hunters are disguising themselves as employees and killing people close to us for some reason?"

Jelani shook his head. "No. I don't think that at all. And I doubt it was this guy who ..." he hesitated and Daniel finished the thought for him.

"Killed Claire?"

"I'm sorry."

"Don't worry about it, Jelani. It happened, and it's nobody's fault except the bastard that did it. I'm going to find some kind of way to make him pay for it."

Jelani believed him. "And you know I've got your back."

"So what about this camera guy?"

"Yeah," Jelani looked out the window at all of the trees and foliage rushing by as the car sped down the highway. "That guy is a part of the crew. I've seen him nearly every time I've come in to do mo-cap at the studio. I'd never really taken much notice of him, and we'd never spoken to each other or shared any kind of conversation."

"You think the Hunter has him watching you now."

"I really don't think so," Jelani replied thoughtfully. "It was like he just ... *noticed* me, or something like that. You know how you can see something a million times, but then there's something different and you take notice?"

Daniel pressed his lips together. "Well, based on what you told me he said, it sounds like he smells a vampire on you. That's just creepy."

"And the rest of this isn't?" Jelani said.

"Of course it is, but this just adds to it." He let out a long sigh.

"I swear if I had the kind of business you did, where I could work from anywhere, I would've already packed Wen up and made for the Caribbean or South America or something."

"If it was just me involved in this?" Jelani snorted. "You can trust me when I say I would already be sipping a drink with a tiny umbrella on it in a chaise lounge on some white sand beach right now, hiding in luxury."

"You still could."

"Yeah, right, man. You know damn well I'm not gonna burn outta here and leave my friends to deal with a mess that started with me. We handle this together. You know I've got your back."

They rode in silence for a while until Daniel's phone rang. Wen.

"Hey, can you pick that up for me?" Daniel asked. "Tell her we're on our way home?"

"Gotcha." Jelani answered the call. "This is the looooove master, and why have you called, you sexy thang?"

Daniel looked over at him as though he'd lost his mind, and the sound of laughter coming from the phone made the corner of his mouth twitch. Jelani bit his lip as he waited for Wen to recover.

"Okay, goofball, where is my fiancé?" she finally said.

"We're on our way home now. We shouldn't be more than another fifteen minutes or so."

"Okay. Alisha and I were thinking maybe we could all go for early dinner somewhere, or go see a movie. Let's just get out of the house for a while. What do you think?"

Thoughts of being alone at Lionel's with Alisha took wing and flew from his mind. Wen had likely suggested it and Alisha didn't want to say no. Jelani dropped his head and told her to hold on while he relayed the message to Daniel. "I don't know about a movie," Daniel said. "The thought of being in a dark place has me a little uncomfortable right now."

"They're not going to attack us in the middle of a theater," Jelani said, but Daniel shook his head. "I think maybe an early

45

dinner would work best. It's still pretty early, maybe we can all go for a walk or something afterward."

"We'll talk when you get home," Wen answered.

"You got it. See you in a bit."

"So, 'love master,'" Daniel said. "I'm guessing we're all having dinner today?"

"Dinner today it is." Jelani continued to gaze wistfully out the window. "You know, it sounds so strange saying dinner and today in the same sentence. It's just wrong."

"Could be worse," Daniel replied. "At least we get to see the sun. Vampires have to do everything at night. Imagine never being able to feel the sun again, or a cool breeze on a hot day ..."

"Or cheesy conversation with your best friend," Jelani added.

"Or being thrown out of a car and having to walk," Daniel countered.

"Why all the hostility?" Jelani asked, bouncing his eyebrows. That drew a laugh from his friend and Jelani relaxed. He was glad to be able to lighten the mood a little, given the circumstances. All too soon, however, things turned serious again.

"I think we need to talk to your friend," Daniel said.

"My friend?" Jelani said. "Last I checked, she's been watching over us both."

"The difference is that I'm engaged and you are not."

"And she looks at me like she's tempted to devour me."

"That she does," Daniel agreed, giving him a wink.

"I don't think it's a romantic thing," Jelani said dryly.

"I think it's probably both. Whether she wants to bite your neck or nibble your ear, she definitely wants to do something to you. Even you aren't so naïve that you don't see that."

"Yeah, well, you'll excuse me if I'm not excited at the prospect of drawing the interest of a woman who could quite literally snap me in half if she chose."

"Just make sure you keep her satisfied," Daniel teased.

"Like a good concubine." Jelani sighed and reached into the

side pocket in the door next to him, pulling out a water gun. "You know, I still can't believe that ingenious idea you had was filling some water handguns with garlic infused water. I feel like an idiot walking around with one stuffed in the back of my pants."

"You want a holster?"

"That'll make me feel much better," Jelani replied, rolling his eyes.

"The alternative is, what? Skulking around hoping we don't encounter one of them?" He held up the water gun. "With these, it's like carrying around a lethal handgun without a license. Hell, you could even walk around with it in your hand. You Americans are obsessed with guns, eh? How's that for open carry?"

Jelani narrowed his eyes at him. "Ya. True enough … *eh?*" Daniel glared at him. "Still doesn't make me feel any less ridiculous, but you've got a good point."

They exited the highway and passed by Rogers Arena. There were people walking around in their blue and white hockey jerseys with the hockey stick under a Native American inspired whale on the front. Everyone was smiling and talking loudly.

"Everybody's festive," Daniel said. "Canucks must've won. I think they have a genuine shot at the Cup this year."

"Maybe," Jelani replied. "This place will be one big party if they do."

"I have to admit," Daniel said, "I find it a little funny to see an African American from the States being into hockey."

Jelani shrugged. "It's the national sport, right? Everybody is obsessed with hockey up here. How could I not be into it, at least on a shallow level? Besides, there's black folks into hockey down there. Just not as many. I do miss my basketball, though."

"Hockey's the national winter sport, anyway," Daniel said.

"What's the other one?"

"Hockey is the winter sport," Daniel said, "Lacrosse is the national summer sport."

"Lacrosse?" Jelani repeated, surprised. "I didn't know Lacrosse was that popular here."

"It's pretty popular, but it's also of Native American origin."

"Oh." Every place and people had their faults, but as a non-Canadian, Jelani could appreciate the effort to retain Native American culture in the country. Whether that was through government benevolence, or the Native population making sure of it, he didn't know. Either way, he found it a nice thing.

Daniel steered his Lexus into the underground parking garage, the tires squeaking on the smooth concrete as he turned left, then right, finding his parking slot. He slipped the car into the slot and turned off the engine. They glanced at each other and Daniel reached into the glove compartment in front of Jelani, withdrawing his own water gun. Normally they wouldn't have bothered carrying them through the parking garage in daytime, since there was no sunlight down there, but after Jelani's encounter back at EA's offices, both were of a mind to take no chances.

Their silent path from the car to the elevator was quiet and uneventful. Daniel pressed the button on the elevator and turned around. He and Jelani stood on either side of the door and scanned the dimly lit parking garage. Several months ago, it had seemed like nothing more than a simple garage. Now, it felt more like a cavernous lair, its depths potentially housing predatory denizens with a hunger for blood.

The soft *ding* of the elevator door brought relief and an exhale of breath neither of them knew they were holding. The two steel doors opened and a very tall and elderly gentleman stepped out.

Upon seeing the two water guns in their hands, he frowned down at them with a confused smile. "A little early in the year and a little old in the age for water gun fights, eh?"

"Ah, well, you know," Jelani said, chuckling and having absolutely no explanation.

"Yeah, you never know," Daniel mumbled, also unable to think of anything that wouldn't sound foolish.

The old man shook his head and stepped out into the waiting darkness of the garage. "Have fun and don't catch pneumonia, then," his voice echoed as he continued on his way.

They shared a halfhearted laugh and stepped into the elevator, and Jelani pressed the number ten. The button lit up, and the elevator ascended.

"Gives me a new respect for birds and squirrels and such," Jelani said.

"What are you talking about?"

"Everything they do; they're watching their back in case something larger on the food chain comes creeping up on them."

"Good point," Daniel said, slipping his water gun in the pocket of his coat.

The elevator gave another soft *ding*, and the doors opened. They stepped out and turned down the hallway. At the door, they heard the sound of female voices in conversation. They frowned at each other and leaned closer to listen. One of the voices belonged to Wen, but the other ...

"... of course, now that your fiancé and his roommate have arrived and are listening at the door, we can continue this conversation without me having to repeat myself."

Saaya.

Jelani and Daniel eyed each other. With a resigned look, Daniel unlocked the door. "After you," he said, spreading his hand out.

"Thanks a lot," Jelani said.

"Hi, Jelani," Wen said. There was an uncharacteristic strain to her normal bubbly personality. The poor girl was no doubt trying her best not to appear uncomfortable in the presence of the *dampeal*. When Daniel appeared behind him, she visibly relaxed. Wen still hadn't fully grasped that ten Jelanis and ten Daniels would be little better than one of each, if their visitor decided to turn violent.

"Hey, Wen. Hi, Saaya."

"Hello, Jelani. Hello, Daniel." Saaya gave them an appraising look, noting the water gun in Jelani's hand. Her eyes rose to meet his, a questioning look. After a moment, she smiled. "Ah. I can smell it from here. Very clever, boys. Very clever."

"It was Daniel's idea," Jelani said. Daniel slowly turned his head to look disgustedly at him. Jelani looked back. "What? It was, wasn't it?"

Daniel shook his head and dropped his keys on the counter, scooping Wen up in a crushing hug and kiss.

"All right, all right, before I hurl over here," Jelani said, a look of mock disgust on his face.

Saaya giggled. "Don't tell me you're jealous, *jaan.*"

"Just nauseous," Jelani replied.

"If you're feeling lonely, I could give you a similar greeting." Her light brown eyes narrowed enticingly, and Jelani swallowed. The sound of someone clearing their throat broke the silence, and Jelani looked to see Wen, leaning against Daniel, staring at him.

"She's just joking," Jelani said helplessly. He turned back to Saaya. "Will you please tell her you're joking?" The *dampeal* gave him a pitying smile and turned to the couple.

"I was just telling your lovely mate here that I needed to speak with you. It seems fortune is with me, for here you are."

"It was quite the conversation," Wen said, still looking at Jelani, who wished he could think of an excuse to get the hell out of there before things became any more uncomfortable. The lock on the door turned and his heart sank into his stomach. *Too late.*

CHAPTER 7

M y!" Saaya said in a voice that none were sure was genuine or mocking. "It looks like my timing is perfect today."

Depends on who you ask, Jelani thought. Saaya turned her head slowly and gave him a look that made him wonder whether or not she could read his thoughts. Of course not. Whatever vampires or half vampires could do, reading minds seemed a bit of a stretch. She winked at him, sending tiny cracks into his reasoning.

"Weeell, it looks like Saaya is visiting us again," Alisha said, looking at Jelani. "Good afternoon, Saaya. How are you?"

"I am as I have been, ages come and gone, thank you. And how about you, lovely Alisha?"

Alisha smiled, and it was such a sweet smile, Jelani wasn't sure if it was genuine or not. The two had no reason not to like each other, and since Alisha had benefited from Saaya's help, she had even less reason to dislike their partially vampiric visitor. Still.

"I am quite well, thank you for asking. And what brings you here for this pleasant and unexpected visit?"

"I was just explaining to our friends here that I needed to speak with all of you about something important," Saaya said.

Alisha spread her arms. "It looks like all the friends are here now. Why don't we all sit?"

Jelani's pulse quickened. It was like watching two hyenas sharing pleasantries. There were wide smiles and bright conversation, but the teeth were still just as sharp behind those happy expressions.

"Indeed," Saaya replied. "I must admit that I wish I were visiting you under different circumstances, but as I'm sure you have already guessed, I am not." And so she told them about the absence of the Hunter named Yako, and that another had taken up the hunt. She told them that she suspected there was more to the situation, and that they should obviously continue to be careful till things settled, or became more apparent.

After she was done, Daniel told them about Claire McMahon, and Jelani added his experience with the technician. Alisha and Wen remained silent through the entire exchange. Neither had met the unfortunate woman, but they were no less disturbed by the news.

"He's gathering information," Saaya said. She looked at Daniel. "The woman was close to you, and that is why he targeted her."

"But if he wanted to gather information about me, he could have asked someone instead of killing her."

"I doubt anyone would freely give up information about you to some stranger," Jelani said.

"But don't you all have some kind of mind powers or something?" Daniel continued. "He could have just made her talk or something, right?"

Saaya favored him with what looked like an effort at sympathy. "You don't understand. Though some vampires can compel the mind, it is the blood that holds all the answers. The very cells in our blood holds every experience we've ever had, regardless of whether or not we remember them."

"Even among other vampires, the best way to obtain information is through blood. When one feeds, they receive all of the memories and experiences of the other. The more focused the person's mind, the better the information comes through."

"So by killing my friend, he now knows everything that she knew about me?"

"Not everything, but enough."

"What do you mean?" It was Alisha who asked.

Saaya spared her a sideways look. "This will sound insulting, but it is the truth. Most humans lack the necessary focus and mental stability to properly transfer information. Not all vampires are capable either. The *Ancestor*s are the best at it, and beneath them, the Elders. If an *Ancestor* decides to sleep through an entire age, upon waking they would immediately seek to familiarize themselves with the current time."

"Hence some poor unsuspecting human winds up dead," Alisha said.

"I'm speaking of an *Ancestor*, not a lowly turned vampire, or even a pureblood." Saaya looked at each of them in turn. "There is a difference, and it may help you survive to understand that."

"So what difference does it make whether it was an *Ancestor* or a regular vampire, then?" Daniel asked.

"Young vampires do not possess the necessary skill to feed on a human without killing them, or in some cases, turning them accidentally. *Shaquora*, our word for turned vampires, are reckless when first they are turned, and young purebloods are only a bit more disciplined. The one who hunts you is skilled enough to have gleaned a good deal of information from your friend."

Jelani felt the need to change the subject for Daniel's sake. "So this guy, Yako, is off the case, and another Hunter is on our trail." He slumped in the couch. "How much could it matter?"

"Does it matter whether you are hunted by a lion or a cougar?" came the reply. "One can kill you in a single blow but cannot climb a tree. The other is smaller, but would certainly climb up and pull you from your perch."

"So, all philosophical dialogue aside," Jelani said, "what's different about this guy that we need to know?"

"I do not believe he is as equally skilled as the other, but he is patient and elusive. I think he's motivated to strike quickly before the Eldest Hunter returns."

"Eldest Hunter?" Daniel asked.

"The one named Yako. He is the top ranking Hunter in all of the North American covens, the Eldest Hunter."

"So can we assume you'll be around," Jelani asked, "or did you give us this information so you can then sit back with ringside seats?"

Saaya's smooth brown lips stretched into a half smile, and a glint of light flickered across her eyes. "Your blood is too enticing for you to be so insolent, *jaan*." Despite the affectionate term she often used for him, there was a wisp of danger that floated on her tone.

Jelani felt the pit of his stomach go cold. "You know I was just kidding, Saaya."

"Of course," she said, coming gracefully to her feet.

The others stood as well. By the time they had all come to their feet, Saaya was standing directly next to Jelani. He tried not to jump. How could she be that fast? Everyone else flinched as well, and Wen gasped.

"Do try to keep those veins of yours intact long enough for me to figure you out, lovely Jelani," the *dampeal* said, laying a hand on his cheek. He struggled to keep his face passive, though the touch of her hand sent tiny jolts through his body. She leaned forward and looked up into his eyes. Then she glanced at Alisha, who rolled her eyes and looked away. Saaya gave his cheek a little pat and moved toward the door.

Jelani made to follow and let her out, but she held up a hand. "That is most gentlemanly of you, but I can let myself out. Thank you." Her smile was just as sweet as it was poisonous.

~

THEY SAT in silence for a several minutes. Finally, Jelani went and locked the door.

"Scared she would have heard you lock it and been offended?" Alisha asked.

"Nothing wrong with not wanting to offend folks," he replied lightly, attempting to inject a little humor into the tense room.

"You're such a gentleman."

"Hey," Daniel said. "So why don't we go get that early dinner? I could really go for some fish! How about you, babe?"

Wen didn't answer immediately. She cast a doubtful look at Alisha. "You still up for dinner, girlfriend?"

"I'm not particularly in the mood right now," Alisha said. "I'm thinking I might just grab something and go for a walk, or clean up at my place a bit. But you three go ahead and have fun."

"We're not going if you're not," Wen said, and Daniel seemed to sink a bit, though he tried to hide it.

Alisha laughed. "I think your man's grumbling stomach disagrees, Wen. There's no reason for you not to go eat and have fun. I'll see you all later." She forced a smile.

Daniel looked at Jelani. "What say you?"

Jelani shook his head. "You two go ahead. I'm going to get some work done. I'll get something later."

"You sure?"

Jelani sat down between Daniel and Wen. "Actually, it might be fun. Uh … that is, as long as you don't mind me sitting between you two like this? That way, I can talk to both of you!" He gave them each an exaggerated smile, showing bright white teeth.

Daniel shoved him into Wen. "Good God! Don't smile like that! You're too dark for those bright white teeth. You're blinding me!"

Jelani turned his cartoonish smile on Wen, who giggled and

55

pushed him back at Daniel. Finally, the couple rose from the couch and started for the door.

"You want us to bring you something back?" Wen asked them.

"You go ahead, girl," Alisha said. "I'll be fine."

"I'm good. You two enjoy." Jelani tapped a finger to his cheek. "Unless they've got fish sticks! I could really go for some fish sticks!"

"Ugh, Jelani that's gross!" Wen wrinkled her nose.

Daniel just laughed and grabbed his keys. "See you two later." Jelani didn't miss his worried look.

The door closed, and silence followed for a long while. Jelani tried to break the ice. "You're mad at me."

"Why would I be mad at you?" Alisha crossed her arms and stared at him. "It's not like—"

"—you're my girlfriend," Jelani finished for her, having heard it before. "Look. You know that girl is having fun with all this. I do believe she'll help us, but she's having at least a little fun with this, too." Alisha looked as though she weren't interested.

"Look," Jelani continued. "I really hope you don't think—"

"It doesn't matter."

"It does. To me it does." He ran a hand over his head. "Look. I want something more between us when you're ready. I'm not playing around with you."

"Your exotic little flower seems to enjoy you."

"Because this is all amusing to her, Alisha."

"Such wonderful company you keep."

Jelani laughed mirthlessly. "Alisha, she's over two hundred years old. Do you know what that means? Don't you think someone who's lived that long might find making you jealous amusing because it's so trivial?"

"Who said anything about me being jealous?"

Oops. "I'm not saying you are, but maybe she's having fun thinking she's making you jealous."

"I doubt someone two hundred years old would mistake whether or not that's the case."

"Well then, count me clueless. I don't know anything for sure." He moved closer to her, and to his relief, she didn't move away. "She may be playing games, but I'm not."

"We'll see."

"You already do."

She looked up at him, her hazel eyes peering deep into his. They were eyes you couldn't lie to. "What do you want, Jelani? Do you even know?"

"I don't want to hurt anybody. I just want to do what's right."

"I didn't ask you what you didn't want to do," Alisha said. "I didn't ask you if you were trying to ensure your canonization as a saint, either." He snorted and tried to pull away, but she held onto him. "I asked what you want."

For a time, they stood there while Jelani tried to figure out how to put into words what he wanted. He knew he was more drawn to Alisha than anyone else in his life, and he was becoming more and more certain she was the one for him. Yet he very much enjoyed the time he spent with Melinda as well. She was fun and light-hearted, and easy to be with. But Alisha brought out the best in him, he thought. She was also fun, and easy to be with, but she also complimented him in ways he still couldn't put to words. It was like a part inside of him felt complete in her presence. And then there was Saaya.

"You don't know, do you?" she asked him. "Truly?"

"I do know," Jelani replied hastily. "I just don't know how to put it into words ... at least not without sounding like an R and B singer, begging and pleading."

"Maybe that's what I need to hear."

Jelani just stared at her, his eyelids halfway down. "If I was that guy, we wouldn't be here having this conversation. You wouldn't have given me the time of day."

Alisha smiled. "True enough." She stared at him a while longer before she spoke again. "Okay. I'm going to give you a little while longer to figure out how to answer that question. The next time I ask you, have an answer for me. Okay?"

"Okay."

She stood on her tiptoes and leaned in, giving him a very long kiss. Her full, round lips were soft and warm, and he could have kissed her forever. One of the things that most drew him to her was her kisses. They were always soft and sensual and gentle, as if exploring him from that simple contact. Her hand slid to the back of his head and her other hand rested in the middle of his chest. Everywhere she touched him sent tiny sparks through him.

When at last they separated, Jelani opened his mouth to speak, but she placed a finger over his lips. "Don't spoil the moment, okay? And don't say words you don't know that you mean. Earth-tech is sending me to Alberta again for a week, possibly longer. Take your time and figure it out. When I come back, we will talk again."

"Okay," Jelani agreed.

Alisha leaned in and brushed her lips teasingly against his. "Next time we talk, have it figured out. If you find you're there, I may be there, too." The way her round lips stretched into that beautiful smile made him want to kiss her till he suffocated. Figuring she wouldn't appreciate such a macabre sentiment, he settled for hugging her.

"Okay, okay, now," she said, giggling as she pushed him away. "Don't get carried away with the body pressing hugs."

"What?" Jelani said innocently. "Hugs are a common form of human affection."

"Uh huh," Alisha replied. "Because it's not your way of feeling me up without using your hands at all." She slapped him on the arm and grabbed her purse.

"Since we're okay again, would you like some company?" Jelani asked. "Maybe go for a walk and get some dinner later?"

Alisha shook her head. "I'll have to say no to the walk. I need some time to clear my head and think. I'll see you tonight, though."

"Gotcha," Jelani said, understanding the unspoken words. He walked her to the door where she kissed him on the cheek, and left. After he closed and locked the door, he went and sat on the couch, and stared out at the water. Alisha had said more than her words indicated, but he understood. She, too, needed some time to think about things. She was probably trying to decide if she was ready for a relationship again, and how she felt about Jelani and the situation they were involved in.

He sank further into the couch, and thought that perhaps she was being more patient than he deserved. At that thought, he made up his mind to let things go with Melinda. He couldn't keep spending time with her in good conscience—casual or otherwise—knowing what his feelings were for Alisha. Just thinking about having made up his mind lifted a weight off his shoulders he didn't know was there.

"Well, that's that, then," he thought aloud. He was just about to change and go for a jog when there was a knock at the door. His heart raced. It could be a neighbor, but they rarely came by.

He moved across the room silently, and peeked through the spy hole in the door. And saw Saaya looking directly at him from the other end. She winked. With an audible sigh, he opened the door. The *dampeal* glided past him and went to the couch. Jelani closed the door, and lied to himself about not admiring the sway of her hips as she walked, or the way her slender waist bent left to right with each step.

She sat down on the couch as he locked the door and made his way into the living room. He started to sit on the opposite couch, but she threw him a wounded look and patted the empty space next to her. "You really must control that heart of yours," she said silkily. "It's racing so fast, I could likely hear it in the hall. Your blood must be flowing through your veins like a river."

"You know," Jelani replied, "it makes me a little nervous when you talk about my blood."

The tittering sound she made would have been more convincing had she truly been as delicate as she appeared. "I'm sorry, *jaan*," she said, using the affectionate term in Hindi, the native language of her Indian heritage. Her voice might have been coated in honey. "Have patience with me."

"How did you get in without me buzzing you in?" Jelani asked. "The building is pretty strict about that."

"I have my ways."

Jelani waited, but she said nothing else about it. "So what brings you back?" he asked, making a great effort at not sounding nervous.

"You've no need to be nervous with me."

Well, that's a fail. "Okay. So what brings you?"

"You, silly."

"Me?"

A small, thin finger trailed a path down the middle of his chest. "Yes, you." He started to reply, but she looked up at him with those light brown eyes and the words evaporated.

CHAPTER 8

Those hypnotic brown eyes held him transfixed, and he didn't know if it was her dazzling him, or simply the allure of the exotic woman. He decided that if he was able to ask himself the question, it must be the latter.

"Don't you enjoy my company, Jelani?" she asked innocently. "Don't you like to look at me? To touch me?" She was sitting so close to him now she was almost in his lap. "Am I not appealing to you?"

"Um, yes," he said dumbly, then shook his head. "Are you jacking with my mind?"

"I wouldn't do that," she said, and by the way she went rigid, he knew she'd meant it."

"Sorry. I guess now I should ask you to be patient with me."

"I'll forgive you if you cooperate with me."

"Cooperate." he parroted.

"You fight it so valiantly, *jaan.* I can practically feel your restraint, your mind screaming for you not to give in. The cute way you torture yourself about not wanting to betray those two sweet … women."

He knew she was about to call them little girls. Compared to her age, he guessed they would seem like such. He tried to use that as a defense against his growing desire, but that could only work if he were blind and deaf. Not only was the woman physically intoxicating, but the sound of her voice as she spoke in this way made all of his logical defenses melt away. It was like she was casually stripping every layer of his hesitance away, patiently removing layer after layer, taking her time with it, till he was bare and filled with nothing but a desire he could not deny.

He started to speak, but she spoke first. "Before you say another word, know that I am not here to listen to your moral dilemma. Torture yourself on your own time, my lovely Jelani. Right now is not that time." And she kissed him, long and soft and deep. Her tongue found his, teasing, probing, till finally he grabbed her by the waist and kissed her even deeper. Before he knew it, she had climbed on top of him. When they finally separated, she smiled in amusement as he gasped for breath. Maybe that thought about kissing till he suffocated was a little extreme, even if it was figurative.

"Okay, you need to remember to let me breathe—"

"Time's up," she interrupted, and her soft lips were on his again. She was still on top of him, and that tiny body that housed such strength, was so light that he easily lifted her and stood. Before he knew what he was doing, he was walking toward the door to his bedroom with her in his arms. He lay her gently on the bed, and straddled her, kissing the black dot in the middle of her forehead, then the bridge of her nose, then the hollow of her neck.

He'd gone no further than that, when she grabbed his shoulders and, in one motion, rolled them both over so that she was straddling him again. He basked in her gentle kisses on his face, her hand running over his head, then down his face, over his chest.

Where he had been gentle with his weight over her, she sat on top of him, smiling as his body confirmed his enjoyment of the contact. She pulled his shirt over his head and ran her fingernails down his chest, tracing each of the lines between the slanted square muscles on his stomach. She kissed him slowly, teasingly, then shifted her weight on him again, and he grunted. She grabbed his wrists and guided his hands to her thighs, her hips, sliding them up her waist and stomach, underneath her top.

He slid the top over her head and brought his hands back to her waist. She grabbed them and guided them higher, and she squeezed his hands as they massaged her bare, light-brown breasts. She leaned her head back and let out a deep sigh that flowed through the air. His fingers slid across her dark brown nipples, and she smiled when his body responded.

"Mmm," she whispered in his ear. "Not yet."

Jelani didn't know how much more he could endure. The way she swayed on top of him, the way she curled her body to unbutton his pants, then snake forward, sliding the erect nipples of her firm yet soft breasts slowly up his torso.

When she had finally removed his pants, she arched an eyebrow at him, then squeaked playfully when he flipped her onto her back. She closed her eyes and leaned her head back, enjoying the sensation of his gentle hands as they explored her body. Her chest heaved and her back arched when his hand slid between her thighs.

As she had taken her time with him, so he did the same until her hand shot down to grab hold of him. He grunted in pleasure, yet pain, and she lightened her grip, but just a bit.

She stroked him gently and he responded with a gasp, his body shifting with the rhythm of each stroke. He leaned down and she kissed him, lightly at first, then deeper, more urgent. Her tongue playfully explored his until finally she grabbed the back of his head and pulled him deeper. She stroked him with the rhythm of the passionate kiss, and when they released each other she looked into his eyes.

She saw his desire, the passion, the helplessness, and he knew that she could easily make him hers in a way no form of mind compulsion would. But she also saw something else. The flicker of doubt he was feeling, a shade of hesitance. He felt vulnerable to her, and she saw it.

She pulled him closer until her lips brushed his ear. "Join with me," she whispered, and the hesitation in his body melted away just before they merged.

As he rhythmically thrust to the sounds of pleasure from the woman beneath him, Jelani felt crackles of energy flowing from her in waves, enveloping him. It was all he could do to contain them, so intoxicating and nearly overwhelming, they were. She thrust her hips up to meet him, and he thought he would lose control. She shifted her body and rolled them over so that she was straddling him once again.

Saaya placed her hands on his chest and rocked her hips backward and forward. She gasped and arched her back, then curled down over him, her long black hair falling over his face. As she continued to rock atop him, her tongue explored his chest, his nipples, his neck. Then he felt the tips of her fangs sliding across his shoulder, down his arm, then up again.

He tensed when they found his neck, but a gentle pulse of warm energy flowed from her hand into his chest, and he relaxed.

On it went, and time slipped away until she whispered into his ear again. "Together."

She moved her body with more intensity now, rocking backward and forward, and Jelani was swept away. Sounds of pleasure and urgency escaped her, and along with the physical pleasure came flowing waves of crackling energy. Building. Building. Finally, she let out a sound that was between a sigh and a scream, but so high in pitch, that the vase on his nightstand cracked, then shattered.

Her body shuddered atop his, and together, at once, they

ascended. Jelani felt a tremendous release of energy that overcame him. She kissed him on the forehead, the cheek, the lips, lingering, tasting. Her eyes glowed in a lavender hue that pulsated with each wave of her retreating pleasure, like waves rippling gently over sand as they receded back to the ocean.

She lay beside him, running an elongated fingernail up and down the middle of his chest. "Not bad," she purred.

Not bad? I nearly shattered like that vase!

As if reading his mind, her eyes went to the broken pieces on the floor. "I'm sorry about that. Was it of great value?"

"Not against what caused it to break," Jelani said, and she giggled.

"Not bad," she said again. "For a moment, I almost lost control."

Jelani stared at her. *Almost* lost control? He looked at the broken pieces on the floor, then back to Saaya, her eyes still glowing in that lavender color that was both entrancing and unnerving. "And what would have happened if you'd lost control?" *Do I really want to know that?*

The only response he received was a titter, followed by the most welcome sensation of her tiny, soft hand sliding along his cheek. "I should go. I wouldn't want to upset the arrangement you and your friends have here, would I?"

She rolled out of the bed and stood, looking around the room for her clothes.

"Will you stop it," Jelani said, when she turned away from him.

"What?" she said, glancing over her shoulder at her still bare buttocks. "I'm sorry. Is this better?" She turned to face him. Jelani groaned, then nearly jumped out of his skin when she was suddenly right next to him. "No, you stop it," she whispered in his ear, placing a hand over his responding genitals, and running her lips along his neck. "Your blood is flowing at a very tempting speed, *jaan*."

And that killed it. Nothing could have more effectively killed the passion than that last statement.

She made a disappointed sound and poked out her bottom lip, stroking him once more before getting up. She took her time gathering her clothes, and Jelani made an effort not to watch as she made such a show of it. His body told him he was not successful.

CHAPTER 9

"What the hell am I doing?" Jelani asked himself for what had to have been the hundredth time since Saaya had gone. The door had barely clicked shut and he'd locked it before immediately turning on the shower and cleaning up the broken vase. The hot water and steam relaxed his nerves long enough to clean his body of the scents of sex.

Once he was dry and clothed again, the worries seemed to be right on the couch, waiting. He sat down and they settled gently and heavily back on his shoulders, like a familiar friend. "What the hell am I doing?" he asked himself again. He knew, of course. He knew, but he didn't know. He'd just had sex with a woman who was half vampire, dangerous on a level he didn't want to comprehend, and yet another complication in his situation.

As if on cue, the screen on his phone lit up. A text message from Melinda. *"I'm thinking about sushi in a little restaurant, across the table from a rather good-looking gentleman."*

Despite his situation, he couldn't help smiling. *"I'm thinking of how nice it would be enjoying sushi in a nice little restaurant, across the table from a damn good-looking lady."* A minute later, the response came.

"I'm thinking I would love to experience this tonight."

"I'm thinking I would, too ... if I didn't have a daunting workload. :-("

"Oh come on, love. You can't spare a little time for me? Just a little?"

"I can spare more than a little if you can wait a day or two."

A couple minutes went by and he thought perhaps she wasn't going to answer, when finally another message appeared: *"Oh well I guess so! :-)"*

Jelani answered again, promising to meet up in a day or two, then gathered up his keys and wallet. "I need to get out for a while," he thought aloud.

He stepped outside the building to cold brisk afternoon air, and made his way to the seawall. Spring was just beginning, and the cherry blossoms were blooming. He pulled out his phone and took a few pictures as he neared the rails overlooking the water. As always, numerous yachts were parked alongside the boardwalk, swaying lazily on the surface of the rippling water.

For moment, Jelani thought about what it would be like to live on the ocean in one of those floating mansions. Some of them had at least as much square footage as his and Daniel's condo. Surely their little vampire problem would be solved. He doubted if they discovered that he and his friends had taken to living at sea, they would pursue them to such an extent. *If I make a quick twenty or thirty million in a couple days, maybe we'll find out.*

So caught up in his thoughts and enjoying the fresh air, Jelani didn't realize that dusk had crept up on him like a silent predator. He looked around at the many tourists armed with high-powered cameras, chattering up and down the seawall.

Jelani set a brisk pace back toward his building. In his preoccupied state, he had wandered all the way to the convention center! If he walked quickly, he could make it home in ten or fifteen minutes. His phone rang.

"Yo, dude! Where are you?" Daniel's near frantic voice said through the phone.

"I'll be home in ten to fifteen," Jelani answered.

"It's almost dark, man. You need me to come out and meet you? Where are you?"

"I'm fine, Daniel," Jelani said. He couldn't help smiling at the sound of his roommate's concern. Before this whole situation came about, it would never have occurred to his best friend to call him just because it was dark outside. "I had some things on my mind and needed to take a walk. Time got away from me."

"Well, you better get a hold on that. You know they're watching ..."

Daniel's voice trailed away as Jelani's attention was drawn from the phone to a woman leaning against the rail in the center of the boardwalk. She was staring directly at him, a smirk on her face. When he was within a few feet of her, she closed her bright blue eyes and took a deep breath. When she opened them again, a hint of a red glimmer flashed across them, and she smiled at him. "Delicious."

"... Jelani? JELANI!" He was still staring at her over his shoulder when the sound of Daniel's panicked voice snapped him back into the conversation.

"Yeah, yeah. Sorry. I'm sorry."

"What happened? I asked you where you were and you didn't respond."

"I'll tell you when I get home. I'm all right, Daniel. I need to get off this phone and get home."

"All right, hurry up!"

"Believe me, I will." He hung up and walked as quickly as possible, careful to remain on the path with the most people around. After a few minutes, a man about his height, but slight of build came walking in the opposite direction. He slowed, staring openly at Jelani, his lips snaking into a half smile.

"Careful what company you keep," he said as they passed each other. Jelani continued to watch the man until they were a good distance apart. When he turned to face forward, another man, a little taller and with light green eyes and smooth black hair, gave him an interested look.

"You smell good enough to eat," a woman's voice said, close to his ear. He stumbled away with a start, and the tall thin woman glanced over her shoulder at him with a wink, flinging her bright red hair over her shoulder.

Around him, several people were stealing glances at him. The women's expressions ranged from curious to amused. The men's expressions were all the same: impressed. *I don't think I like all this attention,* he thought, as he smiled at a woman who was staring at him.

"I think she liked you," the lady said. She was older than he was, perhaps in her early forties. She had a somewhat portly shape, with a kind and loving face that was easy to like.

"Seemed like it," Jelani replied neutrally.

She chuckled, shaking her head. "You keep being so modest and you'll miss out on a lot of fun." She was from the States. He could tell by her accent, which sounded Texan.

"I'm sure you're right, ma'am. Have a great night." She smiled and waved, and he picked up his pace.

When he made the final turn, a stretch of about fifty feet of empty boardwalk separated him from his building. Jelani froze. It wasn't completely dark, but the sun was hidden by the tall buildings, and the boardwalk was shrouded in pre-nighttime shadow. *Better walk fast.*

He lengthened his stride, trying not to break in to a panicked run. His heart pounded in his chest as he closed the distance to the apartment building that stood mockingly close, yet so far away. He had closed half the distance when a figure came from around a tree. Before he could react, the man had grabbed his arm in a vice-like grip.

"Ah, ah," the man warned when Jelani started to struggle. "I'll make a quick deal with you. You don't struggle, and I won't crush your arm and knock you unconscious."

"You mind letting go, then?" Jelani growled. He could barely hear the response through the pounding of blood in his ears. His heart was racing.

"You're making it really hard for me not to drain you right now and deal with the consequences," the vampire said. "You're going to have to control that a little better." He tilted his head, seeming to remember something. "But then, it won't matter much longer, will it?"

"There's no business between us," Jelani said.

"I must disagree." A pale red glow crept into the vampire's formerly icy blue eyes. "You have a secret in that little brain of yours that we don't trust you with."

Jelani tried to calm himself, slow his heart rate so as not to further entice the vampire. He could see the hunger in his eyes, and he kept glancing at Jelani's neck.

"I don't have any intention of telling anybody about you all. You know all that would happen is me being put in a mental institute."

"That may be true, but you humans have a way of denying a reality in public, but believing it in private."

"What can I do to convince you otherwise?"

"Oh, my friend," the vampire smiled, revealing the tips of his elongating fangs. "You don't have to do anything at all. I'll do all the work. I'll take care of everything." He saw the defiant look in Jelani's eyes and laughed. "Don't make the mistake of thinking I'm like Yako and his inept little band. I'm patient. I'm better than he is. And I will kill you." His glowing red eyes flicked over Jelani's shoulder.

"But not today. Today, you get a reprieve. Good day." He released Jelani's arm and walked into the darkening shadows. "You better hurry on home before this boardwalk clears out, my friend," the vampire called over his shoulder. "Every moment is precious."

Jelani rubbed his forearm and half turned to see a knot of people moving in his direction. On the other side, further down the boardwalk past his building, a family leaned on the rail, staring out over the ocean and at the distant mountains. *I'd thank every one of them if they wouldn't think I was crazy,* he thought, for they had saved his life simply by being there.

∿

THREE CONCERNED FACES greeted Jelani when he opened the door. He held up his hands before anyone could speak. "I know. Believe me, I know. I've had a lot on my mind and dusk snuck up on me."

Wen looked truly afraid for him, Daniel looked incredulous, and Alisha looked as though she wanted to shake him.

"I just don't understand you sometimes," Alisha said, shaking her head. "You'd swear it was just some guy you were avoiding so you didn't have to give him back twenty bucks you owe, or something."

"I know. I got caught slippin' big time." He sniffed, then looked at the kitchen. "Something smells good."

"Oh!" Wen jumped up from the couch and ran to the kitchen. "We were so worried about you, I almost forgot about the chicken!"

"My baby's signature baked chicken," Daniel said, rubbing his hands together.

Alisha laughed at him. "Better than your signature cup o' noodles?"

"Hey, I can cook! It's just that cup o' noodles are so damn good, and convenient."

"You know your parents would have heart attacks if they knew you ate that stuff," Wen said, sliding the glistening baked chicken out of the oven. As if the aroma wasn't enough to elicit the growling from Jelani's stomach, she lifted the lid on a pot of steamed vegetables.

Dinner was delicious and satisfying, and a couple of hours later, Wen and Alisha dressed in their workout clothes and declared the boys could clean the kitchen since the girls cooked. At the looks on Daniel and Jelani's faces, they assured them that if no one else was in the fitness room, they would come right back. The fact that the fitness room was in the building did little to ease Jelani and Daniel's fears for the girls' safety. The memory of the attack in their own apartment was still fresh in their minds.

"This is what I want to know," Jelani said as he scrubbed the plates in the soapy water, passing them to Daniel who rinsed and dried them. "Why is it that when we cook, we wash the dishes and put them away as we finish with them, but when they cook, we have to clean up what looks like the aftermath of a tornado?"

"Dude why do you even waste energy over that?" Daniel replied. "As good an interior designer as Wen is, kitchen cleanliness has never been a strength of hers. I gave up trying to fight it a long time ago." He pointed a wooden spoon at Jelani. "You'll save a few gray hairs if you let it go."

"It's just not fair, that's all."

Daniel laughed. "And since when did fair have to do with anything?"

"Maybe we should start leaving the toilet seat up again."

Daniel gave him a warning look. "You do that and you're inviting misery into your life, my friend."

Jelani didn't disagree. "You know I was just joking about that. The toilet seat is like some kind of martial law with them, punishable by constant attitude."

"So you mind telling me what was on your mind that kept you out almost till night?"

They finished washing and drying the dishes, and started putting everything away. Daniel went to sit on the couch while Jelani poured himself a glass of water. "I had a little, visit, after you all left."

"Uh oh," Daniel said. "Melinda?"

"Nope."

Daniel's mouth dropped open. "Oh, no. Don't tell me it was your guardian angel?"

"This guardian angel has a very … passionate … side."

Daniel's head fell back against the top of the couch. "Please tell me you didn't."

"I could tell you, but it wouldn't be true."

"What are you doing?" his roommate groaned.

Jelani laughed, mostly because his friend had echoed the question he had been asking himself all day. "If I could tell you that, I wouldn't be in this situation."

Daniel leaned forward and stared at him for a long time. Finally, he threw up his hands and let them drop on his lap. "Okay. I can't deny that I want to give you a high five, so just tell me how it was."

Jelani smiled. "Oh, man. You can't even imagine. It was like there were waves of static energy wafting off her and flowing through me. And she really knows how to move—"

"Okay, you don't have to go into too much detail," Daniel interrupted, waving a hand.

"Well, I'll just say this. A guy could really get spoiled from that experience."

"So where does this put you with Alisha?"

"Well," Jelani said. He moved to sit beside Daniel, lowering his voice as though she might hear from the fitness room downstairs, "What do you think about this? Alisha is going away on business. Maybe I could have a little fun while she's gone. Get it outta my system and be done with it. When she gets back, no more. If she still wants to be with me, then that'll be it."

After a bout of incredulous laughter, Daniel said, "You plan to go on a sex binge for the entirety of Alisha's business trip, then be done with it and get together with her when she gets back? And no longer see the two girls you've been hammering daily for a week, maybe two? You think they would go for that? You think your conscience wouldn't work you over?"

Jelani fell back into the couch, deflated.

"I know the two of you aren't in a relationship," Daniel said, "but you should probably not do something like that."

"Yeah. I know," Jelani replied, almost whining."

"You really were thinking about doing it, weren't you?" Daniel asked, grinning at him.

"Well, maybe not to the degree of excess that I first said, but ..." Jelani looked at his friend, pleadingly. "Dude you don't understand! If you just knew what it's like when Melinda does that thing with ..." he trailed off. "Well, let's just say it's a real nice experience. And what it was like with Saaya practically demands an encore."

Daniel burst into laughter. "This is hilarious! I can't believe I'm hearing this from you of all people! These two must really be doing something to blow your mind for you to even be talking like this."

They went silent a while, then Daniel spoke again. "Okay, look, here's the best I can offer. Let's break it down like this." He held up one finger. "First. You know full well that Alisha wouldn't be overly accepting of the thought of you getting it on with these two girls as much as possible while she's gone, then wanting to get together with her. You may not be her boyfriend when this happened, but I know you're not naïve enough to think she'd be okay with it."

He held up another finger. "Second. Melinda is obviously interested in you beyond a physical relationship, whether she's rocking your world right now or not, she wants something more, and you know it. Ask yourself if she would be okay with this little plan of yours." Daniel's voice broke at those last words as he stifled his laughter.

"Third. Saaya may or may not have plans of her own with you. She's definitely got more experience on you, what with being a couple centuries old and all, and I don't even want to think about that. It's like a great, great, great grandmother or something—"

"Yeah, I get it," Jelani interrupted, waving his hand for Daniel to continue. "Let's just gloss over the age thing, will you?"

"Fine," Daniel said. "I doubt little things like sex and relationships are foremost in her mind, to tell the truth. But if she wants to continue having a physical thing with you, it could be a complicated thing." Jelani felt a chill at the truth of those words.

"Lastly, and this is my main thing for you." Daniel leaned back. "Everyone has their own business. Everyone, or at least most people, have a sexual past that's really no business of their current partner, right?"

Jelani nodded. "Yeah, that's real."

"Okay. And it only takes being in one relationship for a guy to know that telling your girl absolutely everything is a stupid idea. When we were dating, Wen asked the question they all ask."

"About your past girlfriends," Jelani said, shaking his head. "Why do they always ask questions they don't want the answers to?"

"Yeah, well, I knew better. If I'd had sex with a girl the day before we met, I would never have told her that, even though we never knew each other existed. It just wouldn't work.

"As for you,"—Jelani raised an eyebrow—"if Melinda is willing, and that's a big if, and Saaya doesn't do some kind of mind trick on you, would you do it? Would you feel guilty about it? Because I can tell you now, you don't handle guilt well. You don't have enough experience with lying. If you don't think you'd be doing anything wrong banging with Melinda and Saaya till the girl of your dreams gets back, then go for it. You're not together, and you're not even dating, not really. There's no exclusivity between you, only a possibility."

"And if she got it crackin' with some guy in Alberta, it's not my business because she's not my girlfriend, and we're not doing anything exclusive anyway." Jelani ran a hand over his head.

Daniel shrugged. "What you're saying is technically true."

"And also justifying."

"Could be. That's all I can do for ya."

Daniel got up and went for the TV. "While the girls are away, I think I'll sneak in a little video game time." He stopped when he reached the TV, his attention drawn to the window.

"What is it?" Jelani asked, feeling his stomach lurch. When Daniel didn't answer, he got up and went to the window.

A lone figure stood on the sidewalk, facing their building. It was the vampire Jelani had encountered earlier. He stood at ease, leaning against the rail by the water, and was staring directly up at them.

CHAPTER 10

Remy stared up at the two humorously oblivious humans while they stared down at him. He'd wondered how long it would be before one of them discovered him down here. The one named Jelani, whom he'd finally had the chance to speak with earlier, came to join his roommate at the window. He winked at them, though he knew they wouldn't be able to see. Surely they had to know how precarious their position was; that while they stood there foolishly staring at him, Remy could almost leap straight into that window and kill them both.

How easy it would have been to have killed Jelani right then, not far from the very spot where Remy now lounged. Unfortunately, there were others around, and humans always seemed to have this innate ability to witness things they weren't supposed to. The vampire smirked at the thought. That very fact was the source of his current target's plight. If Jelani had just gone about his business and ignored that often fatal instinct to help, his lifespan would be much longer than it was now. Remy cocked his head. Well, it would be longer, barring any unfortunate encounters with a hungry vampire on an empty alley or street.

"That's right, little rabbits," Remy said in a quiet voice. "Keep staring at the fox sitting outside your hole. Just keep staring." They were outside the reach of his hearing, but Remy could read their lips. They were talking about whether or not he could hear them talking, and if he would try to break into the building and come for them like Jacob had.

"Hardly," Remy responded, as though he were included in the conversation. He was nothing like that idiot, Jacob. On several occasions Remy had recommended that his coven do away with the filthy *shaquora*, take out the trash, so to speak. But they wouldn't. The coven would not uncreate any vampire unless they proved insubordinate or a dangerous liability.

Remy frowned at the thought. Unfortunately, one thing the Pureblood Council was not good at was recognizing a liability before it became one. Remy had seen, from the first time Jacob had reawakened, that he would be reckless and cowardly, that he would utilize little discretion when feeding. Despite several attempts to get the filthy grunt to at least supplement his feedings with the synthetic blood, which was, in fact, created from real blood and blood plasma, the fool would only drink from a warm neck. Such indulgences simply weren't always feasible. If every vampire thought like that idiot, the world's population would consist solely of vampires.

The two humans were still staring down at him, wondering what they should do. Remy gave them a big smile, prominently showing his extended fangs, and placed his two index fingers in the form of a cross, and held it up before him, pretending as though the sign of the crucifix was pushing him away. He staggered to the side in mock horror, then looked back up at them, still smirking.

They didn't seem to find it funny. Remy had to give them credit, however. They looked to have no intention of leaving that window until he was out of their sight. He wondered where their little girlfriends were. He would have to kill them, too, which was a shame. Both were very attractive, and Remy had been thinking of having a couple of wives to serve him. Perhaps, perhaps.

Finally having grown bored of the game, Remy turned his back on the building, melting into the shadows. Once in the concealment of the nearby trees, he looked to the rooftops. As he scanned every building, he had to be honest with himself about why he had hesitated to kill that human earlier today and why he didn't do so now. A ten-story leap was too high, for sure, but he could have done it in two: leaping onto a balcony, then another, from a sideways angle where they never would have seen him before it was too late. He would crash through the window, snap both their necks, and be gone before anyone knew what happened. But not while that pair of siblings was lurking nearby.

"Where are you, anyway?" he asked under his breath.

"You had only to ask."

Remy hissed, and whirled to face the diminutive woman who had been searching for him since he'd taken this task. She smiled, and it was a dangerous smile that Remy almost laughed at. The woman was clearly a *skiek*, a half-breed. Not a great deal stronger than humans, *skiek* were often preyed upon by purebloods. Even *shaquora* killed a half-breed on sight. The fact that this tiny girl felt confident enough to confront him without her towering bodyguard was humorous, but also made him a little wary.

"Well, then. I've asked, and here you are." Remy smiled and narrowed his pale blue eyes at her. To describe the woman as beautiful would have been a grotesque understatement. From her perfectly smooth brown skin to her long silky black hair and her body that curved in all the right places, she was a sight to behold. Interesting that she was dressed in such light material, as half-breeds felt the cold only a small degree less than a full-blooded human.

"I must say I'm a little surprised you would offer yourself up so freely here in the intimacy of this quiet, sullen night, with only the waning gibbous moon, and the blooming cherry blossoms to bear witness to our liaison."

"I hardly think this little encounter qualifies as intimate,

Hunter, and you and I both know that moon is more than just a partially full one."

Remy eyed her more closely. What was wrong, here? The girl seemed perfectly at ease, not even a bit concerned that a pure-blooded vampire was only several feet away from her, and during a Hunter's Moon cycle, at that. Was her brother nearby?

"Then tell me, little sparrow." He spread his hands. "What brings you into my company?"

He knew what the answer was, but he would play this game as long as she would. And of course, the answer came in the form of her gaze lifting in the direction of his two targets, no doubt huddled in a room discussing him even now.

"Of course. You're here to express your disapproval of my presence near your little pets."

"I'm here in a rare show of kindness to offer you your life."

This time Remy did laugh, but his eyes never left her. "Offer me my life? How so?"

"Go back to your coven and tell them your targets will never reveal our presence. I will see to that personally."

Remy was incredulous. "You intend to deal with them yourself?"

"I intend what I intend, which happens to coincide with vampiric law."

"I see." Remy rubbed his chin. "You seem rather confident about this. And by offering someone their own life, it could be perceived as a threat."

She giggled. It was a tiny, delicate sound. "Of course it was a threat, silly. But I assure you I'm being sincere. The fact that I haven't ripped your throat out already is in itself a show of good faith."

A bright red glow lit Remy's eyes. "You're tempting fate, *skiek*." His voice dropped into a hiss. She laughed again, and it set his blood on fire.

"Oh come on, now. What could you do, bite me, scratch me?"

Remy's anger reached its height, and despite the tiny flicker of warning in the back of his mind, he lunged at her. He thought to reach for her throat and rip it out and be done with it, but he only snatched at air. Twice more he slashed at her with his elongated fingernails only to miss her completely. Could he have been wrong about her? Was she a pureblood? No. She was a half-breed. He could smell the human blood in her! But how could she be so fast?

He snarled and came at her again, and to his frustration, she simply danced away as she evaded his every attack. Her arms slithered up over her head as she spun away from a slash that would have disemboweled her.

Remy hissed and leaped forward, reaching again for her throat. This time, she caught his wrist and bent it outward, forcing him to arch backward. The pain in his wrist was almost unbearable.

"I do hope you're done with this rudeness, vampire. This is no way to treat a lady, now is it?" Her tiny hand clamped down tighter, and Remy felt the bones in his wrist cracking. She leaned over him until her face was inches from his. Her eyes glowed in a soft lavender, and her fangs extended beneath her top lip as it curled into a smile.

"You really should leave those humans alone," she said into his ear. "And you should also leave this city and not come back. I feel no need to proceed with your uncreation, but I will if you persist."

A subtle twist of her hand and his wrist snapped at the joint. Remy's mouth opened in a hiss of pain. Her grip tightened, and the sound of bones snapping and grinding were loud in the quiet of the night.

"I think I'll just speak plainly," she said. Her casual tone suggested a relaxed conversation between two acquaintances. "If I see you here again, I will destroy you in the most savage way your tiny mind can imagine. If I see any Hunter pursuing these humans again, a similar fate will befall them."

She released his wrist and Remy fell to one knee, cradling his arm as the bones started to knit and reform. He looked up, but she was already gone.

"Don't forget, now," her cheerful voice said from behind him. Remy swore and turned to see her smiling down at him from a few feet away. She gave him a friendly wave and disappeared around the corner.

Remy winced as the bones continued to repair themselves. For a long time, he stared at the last place the half-breed woman had been standing. "Well now, something definitely isn't right about you," he thought aloud. "What are you, exactly? He stood and flexed his fingers, his wrist completely healed as if the injury had never happened.

He hated to admit to himself that she could have dispatched him with little effort. Never had he heard of a *skiek* with that much strength or speed. It wasn't possible. But there was no question that she was half human.

Remy made his way across the lawn, navigating between the trees that dotted the grassy mounds alongside the boardwalk. Should he report back to the Council about his findings? He didn't know if he could do it. How could he explain that he had been bested by a half-breed woman so easily? It was disgraceful.

He decided to keep this encounter to himself and do some research on his own. The best explanation he could come up with was that her vampiric parent must have been a particularly powerful Elder. But that would be odd considering Elders rarely had anything to do with a human aside from the infrequent desire to drain a human's neck of its warm contents.

The sound of heavy breathing drew him from his thoughts. About twenty feet away, a jogger came into view. Remy's lips drew back to reveal elongated fangs. His eyes glowed as the thirst overcame him. The runner was a thin man, just below middle years. The vampire could hear the rapidly flowing blood in his veins. Remy could practically smell it. The blood of athletes was rich in oxygen, and was thus more energizing.

In less time than the man could draw his next breath the Hunter bolted across the lawn, across the walkway, and snatched the jogger off his feet, leaping first on the rail, then into the air. His jaws clamped down and his fangs punctured the unfortunate jogger's throat. As they glided in an arc over the water, he drew the sweet rich blood from his victim. Far out, past the slumbering yachts floating on the rippling currents, they splashed into the water. Still, Remy held his twitching prey, jaws clamped over his neck, teeth still inserted as he continued to drain the lifeblood from his victim.

They descended gently to the bottom of the shallow seabed where Remy crouched over the jogger, siphoning the last ounces before finally releasing him. He pulled the dead jogger behind him, moving further out into deeper water. His fingernails elongated, and he slashed the body across the torso and, of course, the neck, biting repeatedly and tearing away chunks of flesh. Satisfied, he left the body to sway back and forth with the lazy current of the water, and swam away.

Remy swam below the surface until he'd finally reached the beach on the far side of Stanley Park. He emerged without a sound, and climbed the rocks, navigating them effortlessly until he stood alone on the paved walkway. Few people walked the Stanley Park seawall this late at night, and since the incident with Jacob, no one but unwitting tourists would dare.

The body would be discovered soon. Perhaps even tomorrow, but the police and coroners would have a fine time figuring out what killed him.

His thirst sated, and feeling much better since his encounter with that *skiek* girl, Remy walked across the sidewalk and leaped up the fifteen-foot high rock face and into the woods above. He still had several hours till daylight, so why not enjoy a nice evening stroll?

CHAPTER 11

T rapped. That was the only way Yako could feel about his situation. Yes, he was treated with the respect due someone of his station. Yes, he was afforded every luxury. Yes, he had free reign of Peles Castle and the nearby town of Sinaia. But that was where his freedoms ended.

His unseen escort shadowed his path, watched his every step whenever he ventured outside the castle. There was no possibility of his being allowed to return to Vancouver to finish his task, or to even return to the North American continent for that matter.

Any conversation he had in regard to his situation was held in quiet voices outside the castle. Braggus visited when he could and managed to slip him tiny bits of information through a joke or an offhanded comment. Mariska accompanied him on his daily travels to nearby Sinaia and shared what knowledge she was able to glean from the twins. In all, it felt like being a well-treated prisoner with contacts on the inside who carefully fed him information at the risk of uncreation.

Apparently, Massius had relented in his constant insistence that Yako be condemned to walk in the sun for his disgrace in not only failing to eliminate a human witness to a feeding, but also allowing the problem to exacerbate to the current situation of four humans needing to be eliminated. "A forest fire starts simply with a tiny spark," the Elder had said.

Yako stood on the roof of the castle and gazed at the beautifully lit town in the distance. The situation wasn't so simple, of course. Had it only been humans he'd had to deal with, the matter would have been resolved on that first night. But that's not what happened. Through a stroke of legendary bad luck, the human had happened across the path of a woman who'd, for whatever reason, decided to aid him. Not just a woman, and not just a half-breed, but a *dampeal*, and her brother, a pureblood descendent of an *Ancestor*.

Yako thought of the irony of the situation. In all his fervor to supposedly preserve the anonymity of the vampire race, and punish Yako for his unforgivable failure, he was sure Massius would have fallen just as quickly by the hand of either of those two.

It was only a matter of time before Massius's momentum slowed and Yako was allowed to give his full account of the events. No doubt, the craven Elder knew this as well, which was why he had been pushing for Yako's execution. He'd seen an opportunity to be rid of the suspicious Eldest Hunter and he'd seized it. Or tried to.

"Remy," he said under his breath.

Yako returned to the coven only when necessary because he had no desire to endure Remy's endless vying for power and attempts to manipulate Yako into taking the Trials of the Ancients to become a Reaper. Of course, this would clear the path for Remy to take the trial to become Eldest Hunter, a rank he would never attain as long as Mariska lived.

Deny it to himself as he may, Remy was no match for Mariska. But the writing was on the wall. Yako becomes a Reaper and is more closely under Massius's eye. Mariska becomes Eldest Hunter and Remy becomes Second. Betrayal is an easy thing when you are close to the one you seek to topple. With his conniving, it was only a matter of time.

But Yako had refused time and again, having no desire to ascend beyond his station. To shifty, power hungry minds like Remy and Massius, this was inconceivable. To their thinking, there had to be a motive behind Yako's refusal of the offer, and thus he must in some way know what they plotted.

He smiled, but there was no mirth in it. The truth was that before recently, Yako had no idea Massius and his lackey had been planning anything. In light of that thought, perhaps it was a boon that Yako had failed and had been detained here, otherwise he might not have discovered anything treacherous was afoot before it was too late.

And though he knew there was something going on with those two, he still didn't know what it was. Massius was no fool, and cowards typically were careful. Of all the Elders of the High Council, Yako never understood how Massius had not only survived as long as he had, but actually attained his seat. All of the Elders had earned their rank through their efforts to elevate the vampire species, whether through battle or politics. All were tried and tested. Massius, Yako was not so sure about. He was the only member of the High Council whose personal history was not fully accounted for.

Sure, there were recorded events of the Elder's prowess in the lycanthrope hunts. It was even recorded that he had participated in a real Hunter's Moon event. Despite his dour mood, Yako snorted. The thought of Massius leading warriors on a Hunter's Moon was so comical that he wondered why the other Elders had not questioned it. Thoughts for another time.

"What is your report, Second?"

Mariska, who had arrived a few minutes earlier, had stood silently, knowing the Eldest Hunter would speak when he was ready for her. "The High Council has held three private meetings, two at Massius's request. Your name has found its way across the lips of many in the castle." She paused before adding, "and the wolves are restless."

Yako continued to stare out at the night lights of Sinaia. Of course the wolves were restless. Given the history between vampires and werewolves, a Hunter's Moon cycle would doubtlessly put them on edge. Funny how lycans were most noted for their association with the moon, when vampires had their own special relationship with it.

"You spoke of three private meetings. Who called for the third?"

There was a pause before she answered. "Vicken."

Vicken.

This was unexpected. Massius was one of the most outspoken of the Elders, so his activity was not unusual. Yako would have actually been more suspicious if the duplicitous Elder had been quiet. But Vicken was not known for being outspoken or overly active in matters that weren't of utmost importance. The head of the High Council of Elders was the oldest vampire Yako had ever known, and he was very powerful. He had often been referred to as the closest any vampire could come to being an *Ancestor*.

"Do you know anything about this?" he asked, though he suspected the answer.

"No. Only members of the High Council were present."

"All members?"

"Yes."

He knew there was more. "What else?"

"There may be a formal hearing."

"How soon?"

"Possibly tonight."

"Possibly" meant there would definitely be a hearing tonight.

Yako considered his Second and the risks she and her contacts were taking to keep him informed. Vampires rarely established what one would consider a friendship, but circumstances had brought Mariska and the twins together in a rare friendship that began with mutual survival. Yako remembered the first time he'd seen her encounter a werewolf. Just the smell of it had nearly driven her mad with bloodlust. The memory of her family along with that of the twins being massacred by a pack of lycanthropes was forever burned into her mind.

Three pureblooded vampire children should have been an easy meal for the wolves, but the three girls had fled while their family members were devoured. The sisterly bond between his Second and the twins had been forged on that day and had endured ever since.

"Advise caution," Yako said, equally careful not to give away even the gender of their informant, who was in this case, Meilana. "But the information is appreciated."

"Yes, Eldest."

"The other?"

"I have not seen him personally, but there have been sightings of a particularly muscular and average-looking male, possibly from North America."

Given Mariska's history with lycans, Yako tolerated the disgust in her tone. Still, he couldn't afford any animosity between them. "It has not slipped your mind that he stands with us?"

"It has not, Eldest."

"Then adhere to proper etiquette."

"So it shall be done, Eldest. My apologies."

"Your apologies are unnecessary." He turned to face her. "And you are unnecessarily forgiven."

They jumped up and over the rail of the balcony of his room and stepped in. The room was a well-furnished chamber with antique décor and a fireplace that was unlikely to have been lit for years. The room could have been described as warm, but that was only in appearance, given that vampires had no use for it. Even the coats and warm clothing they wore was a necessary habit to maintain their human guise.

As soon as they'd entered the room, Yako's eyes fell upon a small envelop on the floor a few feet from the door. Inside was a simple note that read:

Hearing in one hour. All will be present. You are unaware.

It was unsigned, but doubtlessly from Meilana. How Tara had gleaned this information to mentally pass on to her sister, Yako could not know, but he appreciated the information. In a formal hearing, he was allowed to have one person stand with him if the other party was so inclined. Had he not known about the hearing, he would have sent Mariska out to watch the city.

"I would have you remain at my side, Second, though the choice is yours to make."

"That choice was made the day you named me Second."

Yako nodded and disposed of the letter. He would make a show of not knowing about the hearing by heading for the bridge to town.

As he'd anticipated, two guards stepped together to block them from crossing.

"Apologies, Eldest Hunter," one of the sentries said. He was skinny and pale, with blond hair that looked almost white. Bright blue eyes looked at him with a mixture of trepidation and determination. This young vampire would do what he must to stop Yako from exiting the castle, but he also knew it could mean his own uncreation. "We cannot allow you to leave the grounds by word of Vicken Drago himself, Head of the High Council of Elders."

Yako listened with amusement as the young vampire recited his orders to deny them passage. "Of course," he replied. "Have I committed some infraction that confines me?"

"No, Eldest Hunter. You are to report to Lemanda immediately. This is all I have been told."

"Of course," Yako repeated. They turned to leave, but the guard's voice stopped them short.

"I was told that Second Hunter is allowed to leave should she choose, as there is no matter that requires her presence."

"Of course," Yako said a third time.

"They wish me gone," Mariska said as they crossed through the front gardens.

"He wishes you gone from my side, and he thinks me oblivious."

"Insulting that he could so underestimate your intelligence."

"I am pureblood, yes, but I am not an Elder. And I have refused to take the Trials several times. In his eyes, I am foolish and dull-witted."

"What do you suppose the Lady Lemanda wishes of you?" Mariska asked.

"I have no idea, but if she dismisses you, leave without hesitation."

"Of course, Eldest."

For her sake, Yako hoped she listened. The Lady Lemanda was generally even-tempered, but her wrath was legendary, should it be invoked.

They crossed back through the courtyard and passed through the many halls and dens that marked an even more hedonistic than usual dwelling for a vampire coven. The occasional *shaquora* mingled here and there among their pureblood superiors, holding goblets high in toast and draining the crimson contents.

Yako didn't know what disgusted him more, the self-indulgent nonsense, or the lowly turned vampires lounging among their pureblood betters. The idiots didn't realize they were no more than pets, here. Elite pets.

They turned down a long corridor and followed it until it opened into a courtyard best described as a botanist's heaven. It was the first time Yako had seen the place, and he allowed himself to slow his pace long enough to take in the surroundings.

The gravel pathways that snaked in and out of the forest-like courtyard were narrow, but still wide enough for them to walk abreast. Overhead was a stained glass ceiling depicting various figures unfamiliar to either of them. Three were women dressed in flowing gowns. The figures on the left and right each had an arm extended, their palms facing up and pointed toward the central figure, who stood with one hand raised above her head, palm reaching toward the heavens.

It was magnificent, and they might have lingered to admire it further, but a creeping heaviness started settling over him. Yako glanced at Mariska and saw that she'd felt it as well. They continued on their way, and the heaviness continued to press down on them until they'd finally reached the other side of the courtyard and came to a set of tall double doors depicting the same three women. This time, the women on the left and right were half turned toward the woman in the center, who faced the viewer. All three looked outward, their thin lips stretched into half-smiles below narrowed, blood-red eyes.

The heaviness had greatly lessened once they stopped at the doors. The expressions on those three faces was at the same time mesmerizing and unsettling. Yako and Mariska shared another glance, and he had just decided to knock, when a feeling pressed upon him that he should just enter. The feeling was so irrefutable that he didn't think twice about simply opening one of the large doors and stepping inside.

The room was as large as the average house, and was the most atypical dwelling for a vampire that one could expect. Most notable was the existence of not one, but several windows in the room. Given that the overwhelming majority of the vampire population found the presence of sunlight fatal, it was an unusual thing to look upon the stars in the nighttime sky from inside the room.

The windows were high enough that one could still avoid the sun if they wished, but there would be few places the sun did not touch this room. A strangely lethal choice for a personal space.

A voice spoke from behind. "Does the Eldest Hunter approve of my dwellings?"

CHAPTER 12

The voice was smooth and elegant, and came from an indeterminable source. Yako's eyes darted in every direction, but he failed to find her. "It is not for this humble Hunter to have an opinion. It is for me to be honored in your presence."

"It is for you to be as I say, Eldest Hunter."

"As the Lady speaks, so do I act."

"And if I were to command you to stand where you are until the sun rises?"

Yako glanced at the position of the windows in relation to where he stood. The room was facing east, and when the sun arose, it would shine directly on him and Mariska.

"Then I would meet the sun's burning light and my own uncreation, should the Lady command it of me."

"Such loyalty and sense of duty."

Yako couldn't tell if the tone was mocking or sincere.

"We Elders often take for granted the level of devotion our warriors have for us." The voice was closer now, more substantial, and he knew that Lemanda was right behind them, though he dared not turn without her consent.

"Tell me, Yako." Her voice now close and coming around his left. "Given your level of devotion and loyalty, why are you here?"

"That is not a question I can answer with certainty, my lady."

"So formal." The Lady Lemanda came into view before them. She was easily a head taller than Yako, dressed in a similar flowing gown to the woman depicted in the middle of the other two in the art scenes on her doors and the stained glass over the courtyard. The central figure was undoubtedly Lemanda.

As soon as she came into view, they knelt to the smooth marble floor in deference. Yako heard an impatient sigh, and she beckoned with a thin-fingered hand for them to rise.

Her gown fit snugly at the waist and bust, as did the long sleeves that ended in finely stitched white lace. The lower portion of the gown hugged her somewhat narrow hips, then flowed outward. Yako admired the woman as discretely as possible, taking in her womanly form concealed in the midnight blue dress.

The Elder's thin red lips angled into a foxlike smile, emulating the narrow-eyed expression of her likeness on the outer door. Her long raven hair rested on both shoulders and down her back, shimmering as though with an inner light.

Beside him, Mariska cleared her throat, pulling Yako from his trance. Lemanda's lips twitched, and her crimson-eyed gaze flicked over to the Second. "Only a woman can be immune to a woman's charm. Is that not so, Second?"

"Only a woman can maintain the proper respect in the presence of another whose charms are undeniable to all," Mariska replied.

Lemanda arched an eyebrow. "Very well-spoken. I begin to see the value in Yako's choice in you as his Second. He is wise in keeping you at his side, so I will not move against his wisdom. Does this suit you, Mariska?"

"You honor me, Lady Lemanda."

"Come." She turned away from them and moved toward the curving stairs that traveled halfway around the circular chamber.

"So. I asked why you are here, Yako."

"You did, my lady. And that is not a question I can easily answer."

"I do not see you as an incompetent fool, no matter what Massius says." Her straightforwardness caught him off guard. "You are no fool, and I doubt you have spent your time here sight-seeing. I will ask you once more, and I expect your true answer, Eldest Hunter. Why are you here? Or rather, why do you believe you are here?"

Yako knew better than to even think of lying or omitting the truth to this woman, so he chose his words carefully. "I believe Elder Massius seeks to understand why I have failed in my attempts to eliminate the targets. I believe my ability as a Hunter is in question, and that it is the will of the High Council to determine whether or not this is the case."

Lemanda listened politely until he was finished, then laughed. "Very well spoken, Yako. And why do you think you are here, with me?"

"To that, I truly have no answer."

"Dispense with the formality. I hear it enough in the castle. So let us be done with the titles and speak with candor, shall we?"

Yako bowed in acquiescence. "As you wish, my lady ..." she arched an eyebrow at him, "Lemanda," he amended.

"Good. Now. I know full well your distaste for politics, and although I share your feelings, I am not afforded the luxury of separating myself from it. I can be sure this conversation will not endure beyond my lovely doors?"

"This conversation will not exist beyond your lovely doors," Yako assured.

"Of course not," the Elder replied.

They had ascended to the top floor of the huge room and came to a plush sofa with detailed flower and plant stitching. She gestured for them to sit.

"So let us get the obvious out of the way. Massius is a conniving and scheming craven. You know this. Your silent shadow sitting next to you knows this, and every other member of the High Council with the exception of Alicia, knows this as well." Lemanda seemed to think for a moment. "Or at least, she knows this, but is convinced that he may one day rise to power and she will rise with him." The Elder shook her head. "Foolish child."

Yako wondered how old this woman was, that she could refer to another Elder as a child. Who could be so much older than another Elder without being an *Ancestor*? "I believe Massius suspects I have ulterior motives for declining to take the Trials of the Ancients to rise to the rank of Reaper."

Lemanda nodded. "I must admit that such an interesting decision has not escaped our curiosity. Those of us who are not in possession of conniving minds do not immediately gravitate toward the possibility of subterfuge."

Yako was unsure whether or not he should speak his suspicions involving Massius and Remy. He didn't know any of the Elders personally, and was not at all confident that Lemanda had not simply called him here to glean information to use against him at the Hearing. No matter how well he did his job, Yako had no illusions that he was still a simple Hunter, pureblood or not, and to an Elder, that was a small thing.

Lemanda glanced from Yako to Mariska several times with those always-narrowed eyes. No matter how the conversation went, she always seemed to be amused by them. For a few uncomfortable moments, she studied them, tapping a long red fingernail on her cheek. "So are you prepared for the formal Hearing?"

Before Yako could feign surprise, she waved him off. "And do not insult me by insinuating that you don't know about it. I know a great deal more than you think I do, Hunter. Just because I have not put a stop to your little information gathering around the castle and in that charming little town down the way does not mean I have no knowledge of it." Yako was well practiced in keeping his features neutral, despite his alarm. If there was one scenario he greatly disliked, it was that of someone he didn't trust, knowing more about him than he wished.

Lemanda glanced at Mariska. "Tara takes a tremendous risk in feeding information to her equally at risk twin sister."

Beside him, Mariska shifted ever so slightly. For her, that was equal to a gasp. Yako remained still. Obviously, if Lemanda had wanted to crush them, she could have done it before now, or right now, in any way she chose. How many of the other Elders knew? Obviously not Massius, or Yako, Mariska, and the twins would all be dead by now.

As if reading his mind, Lemanda resumed tapping her fingernail to her cheek and smiling at them. "Rest assured that I alone am aware of your amusing little network of chattering birds. I would, however, recommend you choose your words very carefully in the Hearing. Massius is looking for the smallest slip to grab onto in his case against you."

"May I ask a question?" Yako said. The Elder nodded. "Why is he fixed on me? My existence is of practically no consequence beyond my station. I am no rival to him, nor do I live on the same continent."

"You already know at least part of the answer."

At that moment, Yako knew there was little point in pretending not to know.

"Remy."

Lemanda nodded. "His little sycophantic lackey is even now seeking to find a way to accomplish what you could not. The only reason I do not think of Remy as much of a disgraceful invertebrate as my peer on the High Council is because he is actually willing to take personal action, if hesitantly."

"And by declining to take the Trials, I have directly limited his ability to rise among the Hunter ranks."

She clapped softly. "And you've figured this out all out by yourself." She glanced at the still silent Mariska. "Or rather, yourselves." She looked back to Yako, and the humor in her expression was gone. "Five sit at the High Council, and three believe you an asset. Unless you become a complete fool between now and the Hearing, this will not change. And when Massius fails, he will switch tactics, but his goal remains the same."

"May I ask what his new tactic would be?"

She shook her head. "I don't know, but you won't like it." Her gaze once again flicked from one to the other. "And it's time for you to leave. Discretion would be the best option."

"Of course, my lady Lemanda," Yako said, returning to formality. "May I ask a final question?"

"As if I don't already know it," she replied, waving for him to speak.

"Why do you help me?"

The Elder stared into his eyes. "Two Reapers, a Hunter of the High Council, and your Second, have gone to great personal risk to aid you. Such loyalty among our kind is almost unheard of." She rose from the couch and they stood with her. "Besides," she said, the sharp-edged smile returning, "you hold Vicken's favor."

CHAPTER 13

J elani used the rigorous hiking trail as an excuse to distract his mind from the complications in his life and to not to have to talk. The Grouse Grind, it was called, and every year when the snow melted and the trail was dry enough to be deemed safe, countless hikers would come to the base of the mountain and climb to the top. It was a grueling and, in places, steep trail that took the average person nearly two hours to climb.

"Let's stop for a minute," Melinda gasped. "I haven't done this in years, so take it easy on me." She leaned against a tree, catching her breath. "I'm so out of shape."

"Right," Jelani responded. He used the moment to give her a head to foot assessment. "I don't know many people in better shape than you, Melinda. You just haven't done this particular exercise in a while."

Melinda looked at him with those sparkly green eyes. One of his biggest weaknesses was the eyes. You could see so much of a person through their eyes. It also didn't hurt that those beautiful eyes were looking at him with affection. He looked away.

"Are we not having fun anymore?" she asked, misinterpreting him.

"No, no. Of course I'm still having fun. Just got a lot on my mind."

"You worry more than any person I know. You've really got to quit that." She pushed away from the tree and started back up the trail, smiling and waving for him to follow. "You're not going to stare at my ass back there, are you?"

"Wouldn't think of it," he replied, staring at her ass.

"So then it won't distract you if I start bouncing up the steps?" She climbed the steep trail with more vigor, exaggerating each step and causing her more feminine dimensions to move.

"Watch it now," Jelani warned, now completely distracted. He quickened his steps and caught up to her, and they continued to climb side by side.

"You didn't enjoy the view back there?" She made a disappointed face.

"I didn't want to trip and fall and tumble back down to my death."

"I didn't know my butt had such power."

"Well, it can," Jelani said, pretending a grave tone to his voice. "It's a very dangerous thing you've got there."

She slapped him on the arm, giggling. They looked farther up the trail and sighed in relief at the sound of cheering voices. "Sounds like we're nearly at the top!" Melinda breathed.

"Sounds like it," Jelani said. "C'mon. Let's double-time it."

They quickened their pace, sometimes taking the steps two at a time, and several minutes later, the thick wooded surroundings gave way to a sunlit opening in front of the lodge. They took the last few steps, huffing clouds of brisk, chilly air. Hikers lay sprawled across several of the boulders scattered across the top of the trail. Melinda grabbed Jelani by the hand and led him to an uninhabited boulder, and they climbed on top of it.

"What a beautiful view," she said, and it was. Jelani looked out at the city of Vancouver, spread out below in the distance.

"I love it here," he said.

"I think you love it here more than many of the people who were born here," Melinda said.

"Sometimes you don't appreciate what you have till you don't have it anymore."

"True." She ran a hand through her sandy brown hair, leaning her head to one side. Jelani glanced at her, admiring her delicate-looking neck. He really wanted to kiss that neck. He looked away.

"Well, I'm all sweaty," she said. "I think we both need a shower, hmm?" She slapped the back of her hand on his chest when he didn't respond. "Hey. What's with you?"

"Hmm?"

Melinda frowned at him, putting her hands on her very nicely rounded hips that he tried not to notice every thirty seconds. "I just practically invited you to come have a shower with me and you answered with silence. That's really hard on the ego, you know."

"I'm sorry," Jelani apologized. "I know my company's been less than ideal. I've just had so many things on my mind. I hope I haven't spoiled the day."

The hikers started clearing out, going to the ski lodge, or to catch the lift car back down.

"You're sure to spoil it if you don't tell me what your deal is," Melinda replied.

Here it was. This was the moment he had been dreading, but he didn't want to do this here. Better to end things once he had seen her home, so they could part immediately with no uncomfortable ride back down together.

"Okay. But let's wait till we get back."

She shook her head. "Whatever your problem is, let's have it now." He started to argue and she just shook her head. "Nope. Come on. Out with it."

Jelani took a deep breath and let it out, visibly deflating. He sat down on the boulder, and she joined him.

"Look. I'm just going to be straight about it, okay?" She nodded, and he saw the concern on her face that turned to resignation. She knew what was coming. He hated seeing those beautiful eyes any way but happy, and he hated himself for being the cause of her unhappiness. "I can't do this anymore."

There was silence for a moment before she responded. "So you don't want to be with me. You want to be with her." It wasn't a question. It was a confirmation. Jelani nodded, unable to look at her.

"Yeah."

"When did you decide this?" Her voice sounded surprisingly steady.

"Couple days ago."

Silence.

"Well," Melinda finally said, standing and dusting herself off. "I can't say this doesn't hurt, because it hurts like hell." Jelani stayed silent, not trusting himself to not say something to make this worse. He stood up and finally looked at her. She was looking out at the city below. For a few minutes, neither of them said anything, just stood next to each other, staring in the direction of Vancouver without seeing it.

"Nothing to say?" she asked, looking at him. He looked at her and saw the moisture gathering in those beautiful hurt green eyes.

"I'm not smart enough to say something to make it better. I'll only make it worse."

She sniffed, then laughed humorlessly, running a hand through her hair again. She placed her hands on her hips and leaned her head back, looking at the sky. There was no joy in the nervous smile on her lips.

Jelani watched her, taking in her details perhaps for the last time. The freckles on her pink cheeks that always stood out after physical exertion. The shape of her ears, her slightly pointed chin and nose. He looked at her forehead, which now had lines in it from her saddened expression. His vision started to blur. She looked back at him and blinked away tears.

"Well, that's something I don't think I've ever seen," she said, sniffing again and wiping her eyes. "A guy who lets a girl go before having one last bang in the bed, then starts tearing up. Does that mean you really did like me, at least a little?"

"Way more than a little," Jelani said. "I haven't ever made a harder decision. And I hate that I'm hurting you. I'm sorry. And I mean it."

She turned to face him, then balled up her fist and punched him in the chest. She usually did it in a playful manner, but this time it hurt. He accepted the blow without flinching, and she punched him again. Then, before he could recoil, she grabbed his face with both hands and pulled him toward her, kissing him deeply. Her tongue found his and the kiss went deeper, more desperate, more urgent. Finally, needing to separate for breath, they parted. She let her hand slide down his chest and fall to her side.

"I really like you, Jelani," she said quietly. "And I really hope she's something special. I don't like you much right now, but you deserve someone special."

He opened his mouth to speak and she shook her head, waving him away.

"Just don't, okay? Don't." She looked back at the horizon. Voices came from the trees below. More hikers were arriving. "Can you just … do me a favor?"

"Of course I can."

"Just let me ride back down on my own."

Jelani couldn't agree more. How uncomfortable would it be to have to ride back down the mountain together? "Okay."

"Thank you. Goodbye, Jelani." She hopped off the boulder and walked away, not looking back. Jelani watched her leave, wondering if he would ever see her again.

"Well, I guess the only decent thing to do now is throw myself head first off this mountain," he muttered under his breath. Hearing the voices growing nearer and not wanting to be around anyone at the moment, he hopped off the boulder and walked up the hill, around the other side of the lodge. Where skiers and snowboarders had been sliding around the grounds just a month ago, now there was solid, dry ground.

Jelani made his way to the edge of the open ground and climbed downward into the trees. A few dozen feet into the woods, he found the perfect tree and sat down against it. He let his head fall back against the trunk and closed his eyes. He knew he'd done the right thing, but it felt terrible. He reminded himself several times that it would have been much worse for him to string things along knowing it would go nowhere. He would have hurt himself and Melinda even more than he already had, and the guilt would have been unbearable.

Time slipped by as he sat against the tree, thinking about how he would miss her ready smile, the dimples in her freckled cheeks, and the way she always playfully assaulted him with a slap or a punch. He thought about those bright green eyes, and how she looked at him before they kissed, after they kissed. When they were intimate. He didn't know if it was voluntary self-punishment or the strength of the experiences that made him think of the times they had been intimate together. He remembered the feel of her body on top of him, under him. The way she moved.

He gave himself a mental shake. It was done. Whatever pain he was experiencing from this, he was glad to have had the time he'd had with her, and he hoped she felt the same. Jelani stood up and allowed one more pang of regret at never experiencing Melinda's company again before he climbed back up the hill and out of the woods.

"Shit." He looked around. It was well past dusk, and night was not far away. As if on cue, his phone rang.

Daniel.

Jelani answered. "Yeah."

"Um. So you've got some sort of death wish, then?"

"Lost track of time, man. I'm on my way home now."

"How the hell do you lose track of time with vampires looking for you?"

"Just finished my talk with Melinda."

Jelani started toward the lift. There weren't many people around and he had no intention of being caught up here alone. For all he knew, the person operating the lift could be one of them. "It was kind of tough."

"So you went ahead and put an end to it then? Well, the Pimps and Players Club may not accept you, but I think you did the right thing, and you will definitely have earned some points with Alisha."

"Yeah, well, I hope so. The joke will sure be on me if she comes back with some 'let's just be friends' nonsense. I don't think I could handle that."

Daniel laughed on the other end of the line. "Don't even put the mental energy out there. Just hurry up and get home and we'll talk about it. Wen's making curry with vegetables and the left over chicken."

"Sounds amazing," Jelani said, suddenly hungry.

"It is. Just get home."

"See you soon."

Jelani stuffed the phone in his pocket and went up the stairs to the turnstile. He waited impatiently as the sun dipped below the western horizon just as the Skyride came swaying up to the station. Three more people formed a line behind him just as the door to the empty car slid open. The Skyride operator scanned his ticket as he passed. Once inside, Jelani and the three passengers waited silently while the operator held the door open.

"Just a few more minutes and we're off, folks."

Jelani glanced at the other passengers. Two women and a man. They stood on the other side of the car, rocking on their heels as the cold air whistled through the car. Finally, mercifully, the operator rolled the door shut and radioed the office at the base of the mountain that they were on the way down.

The Skyride car gently rocked back and forth as it began its slow descent above the evergreen treetops.

"To the front of the car you can see the beautifully lit city of Vancouver," the operator said over the intercom. "Do we have any visitors to the city?" The other three passengers raised their hands. "Well, I would like to personally welcome you to Vancouver in beautiful British Columbia. If you have any questions, I would be happy to assist you in any way I can."

"I have a question," the guy said. "Where can a guy go for a good drink around here?"

"There's a few pubs nearby," the operator said, abandoning the intercom. "Just down the hill and left on the main highway. Or were you looking for something downtown?"

"No, I was actually looking for something a little more sustaining."

Jelani's heart skipped a beat, but he continued looking out the window. He put his hands in his pocket, his left hand grabbing the small water gun.

"More sustaining?" the operator asked.

"Yeah," the man said. An unmistakable depth crept into his voice.

The operator didn't miss it either. "Um. I'm sure when we get to the bottom, I can help you find something."

"Actually," the man said, "I think he might know."

Jelani looked over his shoulder to see the man looking directly at him. A pale red glow smoldered in his eyes. The Skyride operator backed away, pressing himself against the side of the car. He reached for the radio, not taking his eyes off the other three. Suddenly, one of the women grabbed his hand.

"No need to go making calls right now." There was a sickening crack, and the operator screamed in pain. The female vampire released his crushed hand and grabbed him by the neck, easily lifting him from the floor, and hurled him at Jelani.

Jelani dropped to the floor of the car barely in time to avoid the Skyride operator's body as he went flying over his head to crash through the front window. The man's terrified screams grew fainter as he fell at least a hundred feet to his death. Jelani came to his feet, stuffing his hand back in his pocket. Without the driver to operate the controls, the car had stopped, and they now hung suspended high above the tree covered mountain.

"Whatcha gonna pull outta that pocket, big boy?" the female who'd thrown the poor operator taunted. Her crimson eyes narrowed at him and she smiled, revealing a set of elongated fangs.

"Yes," the other female said. "Whip it out and show it to us."

Jelani reminded himself that they were fast, but not as fast as that Hunter. He might be able to take one or two of them out by surprise. "What do you want with me?"

One of the female vampires sauntered up to him. He backed away until his back hit the side of the car. "Don't be so shy, love," she said. "I won't bite, yet." Before he could react, her hand snapped up and grabbed his neck. Her thumb slid under his jaw and forced his head aside. "I just wanna suck on it."

"And how are you gonna suck on it without biting first?" the other female asked.

"Good point," the one holding Jelani said, and her jaws stretched open with a hiss.

Jelani's hand snapped out of his pocket and he pointed the little water gun at her face, pulling the trigger repeatedly and shooting a stream of water heavily infused with garlic into her open mouth.

The result was instantaneous. The shrieking female released him and fell away, coughing and scratching frantically at her throat. No sooner had her hand fallen away, then the male vampire was on him. Jelani had just enough time to reach behind his back and pull out his silver blade. The vampire had grabbed his wrist and forced him to drop the water gun, but hadn't expected the second weapon.

Jelani slashed him across the midsection, earning a hiss of pain and a backhand across the head that sent him spinning to the floor. The Skyride car rocked dangerously on the cable. Jelani saw the burned flesh where his knife had found its mark. The vampire looked down at his midsection and looked back up at Jelani, fangs bared.

Those few seconds were foolishly spent, and by the time the enraged vampire had looked back up, Jelani had managed to retrieve his weapon. He pulled the trigger on the normally harmless water gun, and a stream of garlic infused water went right into his eyes. The vampire wailed and thrashed, and knocked into the now rapidly decomposing woman to his right.

Jelani whipped his hand around toward where the other woman had been standing, but she was gone. He looked around, but it was only himself and the two dying vampires in the car with him.

"Shit!" He moved to the center of the car, guessing that she was either on top of it, or had just jumped out. She must have slipped by while he was busy with the other two. Jelani looked out the broken window. The parking lot was a long way away. He had to get the Skyride car running again.

The window behind him shattered and the female vampire crashed through and slammed into his back. She lifted him and threw him toward the front window. Jelani dropped his water gun and knife, grabbing one of the poles as he flew by. His body whipped around it to slam into the side of the car, causing it to rock violently on its wire.

The woman was on him again, fangs bared, eyes glowing in that awful red. "I'm not so easy, baby," she taunted, picking him up from the floor.

Jelani threw gentlemanly decorum to the wind and punched her in the face with all his strength. Her head snapped back, and he punched her again. Four times he struck her, square in the face, but she never released him. Her head came back up and she winked at him, then tossed him to the other side of the car, causing it to bounce and buck unnaturally against the cable.

They heard static on the radio followed by the voice of the operator on the ground. "Everything okay up there? Why has the car stopped—"

The woman grabbed the radio, ripped it out of the box, and tossed it out the broken window. Jelani took that opportunity to grab his knife and send it spinning it end over end at her.

Through years of training or just plain luck, his aim was true, and the blade punched into her abdomen. She gasped and wrapped her fingers around the hilt, tiny wisps of smoke streaming from the burning wound. She fell to her knees, then struggled to rise. The already dangerously bobbing car, lurched backward, then forward. The sound of a huge cable snapping filled Jelani's ears and sent a chill of dread down his spine. The car lurched one final time and another piece of the thick cable snapped.

Jelani looked toward the sound, and he hit the floor just as a piece of the huge thick cable came shooting from further down the slope. It crashed through the car and whipped over his head, slicing clean through the female vampire's midsection.

She fell to the floor in two parts that began to rapidly decompose. Jelani scrambled to grab hold of one of the handhold bars as the front of the car tilted forward and treetops rushed up to meet him.

Jelani wrapped his arms and legs around the pole and held on. The top of one of the towering evergreen trees crashed into the broken window and shot past Jelani. For a moment, the car was suspended on the tree. Jelani took stock of the situation. The other two vampires had decomposed to little more than dust, and the last one was on her way to nothingness as well. His knife fell out of her shriveling abdomen and fell toward the window. Jelani snatched it out of the air and tucked it in the back of his belt.

He sighed in resignation when he heard the loud crack, followed by another, signifying that the top of the tree was no longer able to hold the heavy Skyride car. The groan and crackling of splintering wood was quickly followed by the car—which felt more and more like a box of death—leaning to one side. His arms and legs wrapped around the pole, Jelani looked out the window and immediately regretted it.

The car was leaning more and more over what looked to be at least a hundred-foot drop. "I'm dead. Oh shit, I'm dead." The car leaned a final time, and then the top of the tree snapped. Jelani tightened his body around the pole, hollering as the broken Skyride car tumbled downward. The car rolled and slammed into the trees, ricocheting from one massive trunk to another.

At first, Jelani was able to hold on, but then the car turned and spun, and the centrifugal force multiplied his weight and he was wrenched from the pole. He slammed into the roof of the car, then was thrown to the floor, then was thrown into one of the walls, then back to the roof.

On and on it went, Jelani's helpless body flying and bouncing inside the car as it tumbled through the trees on its violent descent to the sloping hills of the mountain below.

Glass shattered and he pressed his eyes shut, which made it even more terrifying. In shutting his eyes to protect them from the flying shards of glass, he tumbled in the car in total blackness until it came to a sudden stop. He opened his eyes and saw that the car had hit the base of a tree. Jelani groaned away the pain and took stock of the situation. The car had hit the base of the tree and been turned on its side, only delaying the plummet from the cliff it was now hanging halfway off of.

Jelani started to climb toward the opposite window. When the car tilted downward, he froze. "Fuck this," he growled, half crawling half running to the other side of the car. It tilted, then a little more, then just as Jelani reached for the broken window, it began to slide over the edge of the cliff. Jelani grabbed hold of the opening, ignoring the bits of glass that dug into his hands, and pulled, curling his body in and planting his feet on the outside just as the car slid over the edge.

With all the strength he could muster, Jelani jumped away from the car just as it slid over the cliff. He managed to hit the ground, but it was still a steep enough slope that he started to slide back downward. He scrabbled desperately for a handhold, but there was nothing but rock and dirt.

Just before he fell over the cliff, Jelani just managed to grab hold of a broken branch hanging low to the ground. The momentum from his slide caused the branch to swing him out sideways over the cliff, as though he were swinging from a rope over a lake. But the rope was a broken branch, and the lake was a thirty-foot drop to a nearly vertical slope.

Hanging by one hand, his legs dangling over the cliff, he had just enough time to see the Skyride cable car fall that thirty feet to slam into the slope and break into pieces.

The branch snapped at the same time the destroyed car rocked to its final stop at the base of yet another tree.

"Son of a biiiiiiiitch!" Jelani screamed, as he went flying sideways over the cliff. His voice was lost in the dizzying motion of his spinning body. The ground was up, the sky was down, the trees were sideways and upside down. Somehow, through the confusion, Jelani managed to catch a glimpse of a clump of evergreens that grew tightly together.

He just managed to prepare himself as they rushed toward him, and ignored the pain as his body slammed into them, breaking smaller branches and hitting and flipping over larger ones. He gritted his teeth and managed to grab hold of one, stopping his flight, but causing his body to swing downward.

Once again, the momentum of his flight caused his body to swing with too much force, and the tree limb was wrenched from his grasp. He fell downward, crashing through the snapping branches, earning countless cuts and bruises along the way. He saw, just in time, that he was about to fall on the space where the tree trunk and a limb as big around as his body connected.

The hit would surely break every bone in his torso, and just before the impact, he slapped his hands against the branch with all the power he could manage. He was thrown away just enough to miss the deadly *V*-shaped connection of the branch and trunk, and instead slammed into the trunk of a neighboring tree.

Still falling, he managed to grab hold of the thick branch he had fallen onto. His arms draped over the branch, his legs dangling beneath him, Jelani had no strength left in him to pull himself up. He strained to look over his right shoulder and saw that there was a series of crisscrossing limbs beneath him all the way to the bottom.

Slowly, he loosened his grip until he slid off the branch. Unlike before, when he was hurled chaotically through the trees, he was ready this time. As soon as his feet touched the first branch, he bent his legs to absorb the impact and lessen his weight on the branch. It still broke, but not immediately, which gave him the chance to grab another branch.

Jelani looked down again and sighed in relief. From this point, he could climb down. He reached down and grabbed a branch below, then recoiled. "Ah! Hoooly shit, that hurts! He inspected the bits of broken glass in his hands. "Urgh! I could use some more of that damn adrenaline. This shit *hurts*! He continued his slow, tedious, expletive-ridden journey down.

He dropped the last seven feet to the ground and fell forward in a roll. Fortunately, he had his feet in front of him and managed to stop his downward slide before slamming into a tree.

His hand burned, his body ached with a thousand large and small bruises, and every breath sent waves of pain through his side. The latter was more concerning than anything else, for it was a sign that his ribs might be broken or cracked. If he was lucky, they were just bruised, but he dared not hope for the best.

"Guess that's what I get for making Melinda cry," Jelani growled. "Karma's a bitch, ain't it?"

Jelani's phone rang and he shoved a shaking hand into his pocket, fumbling out his phone. The touch screen was cracked, but otherwise, it still worked. "Yeah," Jelani answered in a haggard voice.

"Uh, it's dark outside, brother. Where are you?" It was Daniel, of course. "And why do you sound like you just climbed out of a meat grinder or something?"

Jelani chuckled, then winced at the pain in his side. "You don't know how close you are to the truth."

"Dude, what happened? Where are you?"

With an effort, Jelani turned himself until his back rested against the base of the tree. He leaned his head back and closed his eyes. "Somewhere on the side of Grouse Mountain in the woods."

Silence.

"Hello?"

"Yeah, I'm still here. Why the hell are you still on Grouse?"

"Attacked by ... three vampires," he gasped. Don't know ... how the hell I ... survived that. Then the cable ... broke and the car fell."

"What the fuck?" Jelani rarely heard Daniel swear. "Okay, man. I'm coming to get you!"

"How are you ... gonna find me, Daniel? I'm literally ... in the middle of ... the woods on the side ... of a mountain."

"Activate the GPS on your phone. I'll be able to find you."

"I appreciate ... that." He winced at another wave of pain in his side. "But unless ... you've got mountain climbing gear ... handy ... there's no way ... you will get to me."

"Just do it anyway. If I can get to you, I will ..." Jelani was distracted by the sound of howling in the distance. He froze, staring at the ground, listening. Another howl, this one closer. "... *Jelani!*" He was startled back into the conversation.

"I'm here. Stop ... shouting."

"What the hell are you doing? Why didn't you answer?"

"I gotta go."

"No, man, stay on the line!" Another howl, this one even closer. "Was that a dog?"

"If it was ... it was a pretty damn big one."

"You've got to be kidding me."

"I wish ... I was."

"Be careful, bro."

"Not planning … to die on … the side of a mountain, homie." He hung up, and swore when he heard yet another howl coming from another direction. Oh, yes. The howls were definitely coming from the canine family. *Never thought I'd see the day I wished it was a Rottweiler or pit bull coming after me.* He groaned, trying to use his hands as little as possible as he stood. Another howl. Not from a dog, but a wolf.

CHAPTER 14

J elani started his less than graceful stumble down the slope, using the surrounding trees to stop himself when he picked up too much speed. The howls were still getting closer.

I swear, I can't think of anything that could go more wrong.

He stopped at a tree just long enough to pull a protruding piece of glass from his hand. After another round of gasping expletives, he continued.

He tripped on a giant root hidden underneath a bed of leaves and tumbled, growling against the wave of pain in his side. He pushed his elbows out and managed to straighten himself into a slide until he could use his feet to stop. Judging from the deadly view he'd had of the land right before plummeting into the woods, Jelani judged he was about a mile from the base of the mountain. Not normally a long distance to travel on foot, but his aching side, burning hand, and many bruises and cuts argued the distance to be a very long way. Add all of this to the wolves who were certainly on his trail, and that one mile might as well be ten.

Jelani forced himself to keep moving, stumbling and falling more than running as he navigated the dark woods on the mountainside. The only bit of fortune was that he knew he wasn't lost and wandering in circles, as the only way to go was down, and he knew to make his way left as he traveled. The howls started up again, so close that Jelani felt like he could almost hear the animals breathing.

He stumbled and fell again, sliding to a stop in an area where the slope was less steep. Cursing, he climbed to his feet and drew the foot-long blade from his belt, trying to ignore the burning pain in his hand. He heard growling from his right and shifted to face it, then adjusted his position when he heard another growl from his left. He continued to back away as the animals closed on him. A shadowed four-legged form came into view in front of him, and the two at his sides materialized from the trees shortly after. The wolves were big, at least as tall on four legs as his waist.

They barked at him, showing large, sharp teeth. Ironic that he would be killed by a sharp set of teeth that didn't belong to a vampire. "You might take me out," he said aloud, "but I'm taking at least one or two of you down with me."

The wolves closed in on him, and he held his blade ready, lowering his stance as he continued to back away. The wolves suddenly stopped and sniffed the air, then growled again, but not at him.

"What now?" Jelani muttered, still watching the wolves. What could make them hesitate? A bear? Surely they were around as well.

"Please let it be a deer or something that you smell, and go after that instead."

"I don't think your luck is good enough for that."

The voice came from above, and Jelani glanced up just in time to catch a glimpse of the speaker as he glided over his head to land between him and the wolves. For the span of several heartbeats, the wolves and the stranger squared off, staring at each other. The wolves barked several times, but appeared to have no intention of challenging him. After a few more moments, all three wolves reluctantly backed away and disappeared into the dark woods.

The man turned to face Jelani. He appeared to be a few inches above six feet tall and had muscle stacked on top of muscle. Jelani knew this because the guy wasn't wearing a shirt, only a pair of pants.

"Aren't you cold?" Jelani asked.

"No." It almost sounded like a growl.

"Must be all that chest hair, then," Jelani said, attempting to lighten the mood. The mood didn't lighten. "Thanks for helping me out. I can't think of a worse way to die than being eaten, especially alive."

"And what makes you think you've escaped that fate?"

Jelani looked at him. The muscled, hairy torso, the hairy arms and general rough and rugged look. He looked like everything a vampire wasn't. There also was the absence of the telltale glow that a vampire's eyes emitted when they were aroused.

"Aaaah, *fuck*!" he shouted at the sky. "Can I not catch a damn break, here? I mean really! A fucking werewolf? A *werewolf*?"

The man stood there, half laughing half growling, his massive shoulders bouncing as he patiently waited for Jelani's tirade to end. "You know," he said. "I kinda like you. If it weren't that I'm hungry at the moment, I might have actually let you go."

"Come on man! You just let three wolves go."

The man frowned and wrinkled his nose in disgust. "Since when was cannibalism acceptable? That's just disgusting."

Jelani was thunderstruck. "You're talking about eating *me* right now!"

"And?"

"I'm human!" When the werewolf looked at him as though he still didn't understand his point, Jelani indicated the two of them with his hand.

"Oh. I see what you mean." The big man smirked. "I don't think you understand." He took a step forward. Jelani took a step back. "I could see what you mean if I were to eat you while I'm in human form, but I don't. I don't hunt that way, you see."

"Of course not," Jelani replied, heart pounding. "That would have given me too much of a fair chance."

"Not really. Even in this form, I could easily catch you before you took three steps."

"Of course you could," Jelani said. He remembered the silver blade in his hand. Would it be enough? The wound it inflicted on the vampires caused their skin to fester and burn rapidly. Would this guy be affected the same way?

The werewolf's eyes took in the blade in Jelani's right hand, then he looked back up at him. "I smell silver in that little pocket knife of yours," he said, taking another step forward. Jelani noticed his voice growing deeper, more bestial. "I'm not so sure you could take me down with that before I managed to either rip off your arm, or snatch out your throat."

"Might as well give it a go."

The big man shrugged. "Suit yourself." A low, long growl rumbled from his chest, and Jelani didn't know if it was the darkness of the woods, or his imagination of what would happen, but it looked like the muscle and bone beneath the man's skin was shifting. It was a grotesque and terrifying sight. A sight that stopped before it had fairly begun.

Before he had fully committed to the change, the werewolf stopped. He sniffed the air and made a sound like a bark that sounded like it belonged to the largest dog on earth. Jelani wondered what bigger problem could befall him. Maybe a larger werewolf? An entire coven of vampires? Godzilla?

A cloaked figure dropped in front of him and towered over both Jelani and the werewolf. "You have no business with me, blood," the werewolf growled in an agonized voice. Maybe stopping at the beginning of the change was painful.

"This one is not for you," the deep voice replied. "There is plenty of prey. Find it."

The werewolf looked past the cloaked man at Jelani. His gaze alternated between the two of them several times before deciding

Jelani wasn't worth the trouble this new threat would give him. With an angry howl, the man turned and disappeared into the trees. After a moment, the towering cloaked figure turned toward Jelani. As he'd suspected, it was Kafeel, Saaya's dour older brother.

Jelani tucked the knife back in his belt. "Man I cannot tell you how gla—" his sentence ended with his consciousness.

MUFFLED voices slowly came into focus in Jelani's cotton-filled mind. He opened his eyes, and his hand went to touch his aching head. His vision gradually came into focus, and he saw that his hand was bandaged. He went to sit upright, and a wave of dizziness overcame him.

"Whoa, there! Easy, buddy." A set of strong hands pressed his shoulders back to the bed. "You got banged up pretty bad." It was Daniel's voice.

Jelani opened his mouth to speak and found that his throat was dry. He croaked out a response.

"Hold on a sec," Daniel said, and disappeared. Jelani heard water running from outside the room, and then Daniel was next to him again.

"Here, have some water."

Jelani sipped carefully, feeling the water sliding down his throat and moisturizing it. "You've got Wen to thank for the bendy straw. She figured you wouldn't be able to sit up right away, so she went and bought some."

Jelani swallowed. "Tell her I said thanks."

"You can do that yourself," Daniel said, and called into the living room. "Hey babe, wake up! He's alive again."

"Real funny," Jelani croaked.

Wen came tiptoeing into the room, took one look at him, and burst into tears. She flew right past Daniel, nearly knocking him over, and wrapped her arms around Jelani. He hid his wince, not wanting to be ungrateful for her concern.

"Oh, my! I'm sorry, you're still sore of course." Wen leaned away, inspecting the bandages that crisscrossed Jelani's torso.

"I hope you would be this concerned if it was me lying there," Daniel grumbled.

"Oh, be quiet," Wen snapped, never taking her worried eyes off Jelani. "How do you feel? Other than the soreness, that is?"

Jelani didn't try to sit up, but he moved his arms, experimenting with his ribs. They ached, but they were well wrapped, and he didn't feel them moving. "I think I'm fine. My head hurts, though."

"I still can't believe you survived," Daniel said. "I thought you were dead, man." Jelani heard the concern in his best friend's voice.

"You gonna give me a big kiss and tell me you're glad I'm all right?" Jelani said. Wen giggled till Daniel gave him a playful shove, causing Jelani to wince again.

"Daniel stop it! What's the matter with you?"

"He deserved it."

"He's in pain!"

"He'll be alright." Daniel looked at Jelani, trying to ignore his angry fiancée. "You've got a sprained ankle, severely bruised ribs, and a bunch of superficial scratches and cuts and bruises all over your body. Other than that, you're alright."

Jelani's eyebrows rose. "And who, may I ask, found all these cuts and bruises all over my body?"

"Definitely wasn't me, my friend. We're buddies and all, but my medical care for you stops at the waist."

"Why are boys so stupid?" Wen said, shaking her head. "Your friend could have been dying and you were worried about seeing him naked."

"I knew he wasn't dying, babe."

"Oh, be quiet." She turned back to Jelani again. "After that

Saaya girl's brother brought you in, I called my cousin, who is a doctor. I told her you were hiking in Linn Valley and went off the trail and fell a long way. She said to take you to the hospital, but I told her you weren't that banged up. She owed me a favor anyway, so she was the one that fixed you up."

At the mention of Kafeel, Jelani remembered why his night ended so abruptly, something to do with the back of a fist to the side of his head. "I'll have to pay her something for that."

Wen shook her head. "Just get her a bunch of tulips in a nice planter. She loves them."

"Done." He blinked. "Hey. How long have I been out?"

"Two and a half days," Daniel said.

Jelani wasn't really surprised. He felt like he could sleep two more.

Daniel went and grabbed a chair for Wen, and then sat back down and leaned forward. "So what happened?"

Jelani told them of the events of the day, starting with his telling Melinda he couldn't see her anymore, the attack on the Skyride car, and everything that followed.

Daniel whistled through his teeth. "Wow! Too bad there wasn't a film crew to get all that. It could have surely been a movie." His expression then went serious. "I know I shouldn't be surprised at this point, but are you absolutely sure that guy was a werewolf? I mean, my brain still has trouble making sense of vampires, but werewolves now?"

"I know what I saw, and the conversation I had with the guy would have made your hair stand on end. It was the most unusual and terrifying exchange I've ever had. Try imagining talking with a lion or a tiger before it eats you, and you'll have the general idea."

"So we've got vampires *and* werewolves walking around, now? This just gets worse every day."

"I think I want to move." Wen had been so silent they'd forgotten she was there. "I want to get out of here, out of this city."

"Babe, we've had this conversation before. They're everywhere."

"I know! But at least if we moved, they wouldn't know who we are, there. We could just move someplace far away, maybe the UK or France. I love it there."

"Babe—"

"No!" She stared at him, her hands knotted into tiny fists. "I don't want to hear why we shouldn't move, and I don't want to hear that they'll hunt us down! We could at least try." Tears filled her eyes again. Jelani studied the ceiling to his left, in the opposite direction. "We could at least try," Wen said again, her voice tiny and deflated. She whirled and ran out of the room.

"Sorry about that," Daniel said.

"I'm the one who should be sorry."

"We've already been down that road, buddy. It could have easily been me, if I was walking to my car at night, or walking to the store and took a side alley, as I used to do. I don't blame you, and neither does she."

"Thanks, Daniel. That means a lot." Jelani frowned, rubbing his head again. "By the way, did Kafeel tell you why he knocked me out before bringing me here?"

"What do you think?"

Jelani didn't bother to answer. "Guess I'll have to ask him next time I see him."

Daniel smirked. "You really going to do that?"

"Nope," they both laughed, and Jelani winced.

"I'd better go get her before she has all our things packed up and books one way tickets to Aruba or something."

"That wouldn't be so bad."

"Yeah, but the commute wouldn't be very economical." Daniel stood up. "I still can't believe you survived that crash. All that twisted metal scattered down the slope."

"That bad?" Jelani asked.

"It's been all over the news. Air coverage and everything,

you'll see." Daniel turned away, then stopped at the door. "Oh, and you might want to give Melinda a call. She phoned you so many times, I had to call her back for you. She was nearly frantic."

Jelani felt his heart skip. Daniel read the look on his face. "Don't worry. She didn't call the police. I told her you got sick and have been sleeping for the past two days, dead to the world, and that's why you hadn't called back."

"Thanks."

"Yup." He left and Jelani drifted back to sleep.

The next time he awoke, it was eight o'clock in the morning. He'd slept for another half day and his stomach was complaining about it. He carefully sat up and swung his legs over the side of the bed. He sat for a couple minutes, breathing in and out, then slowly and carefully stood. Whether from the rest he'd had or his slow movements, there was no dizziness, for which he was glad. The pain from his many cuts and bruises had dulled, but his ribs remained tender.

He looked at his bandaged hand. It was newly wrapped. A pair of black house slippers sat next to his bed, and he slipped his feet into them. The warmth and softness made him wonder why he'd never owned a pair.

He walked to the dresser and found a shirt to put on, then slowly made his way to the door. Alisha was curled on the couch, asleep. *What's she doing home?* Careful not to wake her, he went quietly into the kitchen. He opened the refrigerator door and gritted his teeth at the sucking sound it made.

"Jelani?" a tired voice said from the living room.

"Didn't mean to wake you," he said, smiling at her. In seconds she was next to him. Concerned hazel eyes looked up into his.

"Go sit down. I knew you'd be hungry, so I made some chicken and noodle soup."

"Sounds great."

She turned on the stovetop. "It is."

Alisha guided him to the couch, sat him down and wrapped him in a blanket like a newborn, then went back to the kitchen.

"You know I'm just a little beat up, not sick," Jelani said.

"You're a little sick in the head, if you ask me," she said from the kitchen. Once the soup was heating in the pot, she came in and sat down next to him, one of her legs tucked underneath her. Jelani always wondered how girls could sit like that. It looked painful. "What on earth were you thinking being out at night on Grouse Mountain?" she asked.

"Daniel and Wen didn't tell you?"

She shook her head. "When Wen called me and told me what had happened to you, I jumped on a plane as soon as I could. By the time I got here, they were asleep, and when they got up to go to work, I was asleep."

"That was sweet of you," he said.

"I know," she said, patting him on the leg. "And the reason better be a good one, other than how stupid you were to get caught up there at night. I saw the news." She shivered. "I still can't believe you're alive."

"Neither can I."

"So?"

For the second time, Jelani told the story in full. When he was done, Alisha's beautiful hazel eyes had welled with tears. "You must have liked her a lot," she said. "For you to have gone some place and drifted off, losing track of time like that."

Jelani didn't know what to say. "I really hurt her. It wasn't a good feeling, but my mind was made up."

Those beautiful eyes softened, and through the calm demeanor and indifference, he saw that she had been waiting to hear him say those words. She leaned in and kissed him. The sensation of those full, soft lips pressed against his sent a flood of warmth through his body. He didn't regret hurting Melinda any less, but in that moment, he knew he'd made the right decision. Alisha made him feel more alive in a way he couldn't explain to himself, only that it just felt ... right.

She pulled away from him, and placed a hand on his chest to stop him when he leaned forward for another kiss.

"Wouldn't want things to get out of hand while you're still hurt." She winked at him. "You'll be hurt enough when I'm done with you." The injuries he's suffered weren't enough to stop Jelani's body from responding.

Alisha glanced at his lap then back at him, a seductive grin splitting those delicious lips. "Down, boy," she said, giving his leg a little pat, then leaving to check on the soup.

Some time later, after three hearty bowls of chicken noodle soup, Jelani reclined on the sofa with Alisha curled up next to him. They had just begun to drift off to sleep when his phone rang. Alisha picked it up and looked at the cracked screen, rolled her eyes, then handed it to Jelani. He didn't have to look to know it was Melinda.

"She's just calling to make sure I'm okay."

"I didn't say anything," Alisha replied.

Jelani sighed and answered the call. "Hey, Melinda."

A familiar voice responded. "Good guess, but wrong."

CHAPTER 15

"Y ou get one more guess who this is and you win the grand prize."

Jelani's blood went cold. Beside him, Alisha sat up and stared at him. "What is it?"

He didn't hear her, only that sinister voice on the other end of the line, taunting him. Jelani wouldn't forgive himself if something happened to Melinda. "She has nothing to do with this. There's no reason to involve her."

"Well, what else was I supposed to do?" the voice said on the other end of the line. "You wouldn't cooperate, so I had to get your attention somehow. Seems to me this was the best way. I mean, you human males just eat up that whole damsel in distress thing."

Jelani closed his eyes to control his rage. "Okay. You've got my attention loud and clear. What do you want to do?"

"Oh, come on, now. If you were that stupid, you'd already be dead. You know what I want."

"To kill me."

There was silence on the line for a few seconds. "Well, when you put it like that, it just sounds cruel. I assure you it's nothing personal. Think of this as like you witnessing something the American CIA was doing. They would likely make you disappear, not out of some personal vendetta, but because the potential for you to open your mouth about it is too dangerous. That's about the same situation we've got here."

"Look. Who am I going to tell?" Jelani made an effort to hold his patience. "I keep hearing this same thing. You all don't want me to go and blab about your existence. But people would put me in a mental institute if I went around telling them there were vampires in the world."

"Compelling words that I've heard so many times I could have said them myself. You humans are nothing but predictable. You beg and plead because you don't want to die, professing your absolute word of honor that you will never speak of it. The truth is, just a simple whisper. Just a word spoken, and the seed is planted. Why would I take that chance? When the mouse is in your house, do you trap it and put it outside that it might come back in? Or do you set the trap that snaps its neck?"

Jelani sighed. He was so tired of this. "Okay. Fine, you win. What do you want me to do?"

"I want every last one of you to come visit me—"

"I'm going to go ahead and stop you right there," Jelani interrupted. "I'm not bringing everyone up here to line up for the slaughter."

Jelani gnashed his teeth as he struggled to control his voice. *Man how I'd like to kill this guy!* The realization that he wished he could kill someone, vampire or not, did not sit well with him.

After a bit of silence, he heard chuckling. "Fair enough. I didn't really think you would be that stupid, but I thought I'd try."

"What do you want me to do?" Jelani asked again. Beside him, Alisha had a tight grip on his arm.

"I want you to deliver a suitcase of three hundred thousand unmarked bills to …" Jelani stared at the phone in disbelief. "Heh, heh, just kidding. If there's one thing I don't need, it's your stupid money. Okay seriously. How about you just get in your car and drive up to Grouse Mountain. Go for a little hike and we'll meet up. I take you to the backcountry and dispatch you and leave you there. All this after we've left your attractive little friend in a safe place to wake up, of course."

"Of course," Jelani replied. "You mind letting me know she's still okay?" A moment later, he heard Melinda's voice.

"Jelani? What—" her voice was gone and the vampire was back.

"Okay, that should be sufficient. I know you may have no reason to believe it, but she will remain safe as long as you meet me as I've said. You don't have a choice anyway."

"What time?"

"I'm sure you are aware that it's daylight right now, so I'd prefer to get a little shuteye. I will call you when the night has returned and I awaken. Fair enough?"

"Fine."

"Don't be so curt. It's business, nothing personal."

Jelani clamped his eyes shut, struggling with his self-control. Melinda's life depended on it. "I'll be waiting for your call," he said evenly.

"Oh, and just one more thing," the voice said, just as he was about to hang up. "I know about your little exotic half-breed guardian angel and her brother. If they are anywhere near the place we meet, or if I even suspect you are trying to involve them, I will leave a trail of your friend's smaller parts to lead you to the rest of her. Understood?"

Jelani took a deep breath. "Understood," he said in a steadier voice than he felt. The line cut off. He sat frozen with the phone still up to his ear until Alisha's voice broke him out of his trance.

"Jelani, what is it?"

He turned his glassy-eyed expression on her. "He's got Melinda. The vampire has Melinda and is going to kill her if I don't meet with him."

"But he'll kill you."

"That's the plan."

"You're not going to actually meet with him, are you?"

"I have to. I can't just leave Melinda to die. It's bad enough she's involved now because of me."

"So you're just going to meet up with him and let him kill you?"

"Hell, no."

Alisha looked confused. "Didn't you just say—"

"Oh, I'm going to meet with him," he interrupted. "But I'm not just going to walk up and let him kill me." Jelani sat his phone on the coffee table and leaned forward. "He must think I'm stupid. He kidnapped Melinda and just had a full conversation with me about vampires with her right there. She knows they exist just like we do."

"Which means he will kill her, too," Alisha said, catching on.

Jelani nodded. "He'll keep her alive long enough to get to me. Then he'll kill us both and come after the rest of you."

"Are you going to take your little vampire friend with you?" Alisha asked. Jelani knew she wasn't particularly comfortable with Saaya, and only partially because of the other woman being a half-vampire.

"He will definitely kill her if he thinks I'm bringing Saaya."

"So, what, then? I know you don't plan to just walk up and meet him alone."

"No. I'm going to have to be slick about this. I definitely want her and her brother there, if she agrees."

"So how are you going to pull it off?" Alisha asked.

Jelani thought for a few moments before his face brightened. "I think I've got an idea."

JELANI AND ALISHA walked casually along the dirt and gravel path through the middle of Stanley Park. With spring in full swing, many different trees were coming into bloom, and the dogwood and cherry blossoms were amazing. Mostly, though, this far into the interior of the park, were the giant redwoods and various maple and fir trees sporting coats of vibrant green moss along their trunks and limbs.

They walked slowly, as Jelani was still in pain from his nearly fatal hiking adventure several days ago. They spoke casually about the warming weather, and how it would be nice to go bike riding more than they had last year. Several times the conversation turned to the situation at hand, when there was no one in earshot.

Finally, having reached Beaver Lake, one of Jelani's favorite places to go, they stopped at one of the few benches around the small body of water and sat. Jelani reached into a shopping bag and pulled out a sack of corn, and Alisha pulled out a small bag of feed. As they had agreed back in the apartment, Alisha tossed the feed to her left, attracting the ducks and pigeons, while Jelani tossed corn to his right.

As they'd hoped, the waterfowl and pigeons were more interested in the feed, whereas the crows favored the corn. After a few minutes, they had accumulated a good number of avian visitors, and Jelani and Alisha continued to talk idly about nothing important. After a while, one crow landed close to Jelani and snatched up a few pieces of corn, then looked directly in his eyes.

Crows were very intelligent, but there was a level of recognition in that gaze that seemed to reach a little farther than normal. "If you're watching right now, please say something," Jelani said, feeling just a little foolish. The crow threw its head up, cawing at him. Jelani smiled. "I think this is a hungry one," he said to Alisha. He tossed a few more bits of corn to the crow, then tossed a big handful past it to the others, so that they would not interfere.

When he spoke again, he kept his tone casual, as though he were speaking to Alisha, even looking at her from time to time. But his words were specifically for the crow, or rather, the *dampeal* who was listening through the crow's ears.

"The Hunter who is after us has a friend of mine. He wants me to meet up with him or he'll kill her." He smiled, pointing at a Canada goose that came waddling out of the brush to partake of the free food. "I know he'll just kill us both and then come after the rest of my friends."

He tossed some more corn to the other crows, then a few bits to the crow nearest to him. The black bird pecked up the bits one at a time. He didn't know what was more eerie, speaking so conversationally with a bird, or the fact that the bird was actually listening.

"If he even suspects you will show up, he'll kill her." He glanced at Alisha and gave her leg a pat. She nudged his elbow, tossing out some more scratch. "I know you have no vested interest in whether my friend lives or dies, and still might not have made up your mind about me, but I'm hoping you'll help." The crow cawed at him several times, throwing its head up and down. He wished he knew what it meant.

He heard the argumentative cry of a seagull overhead and knew he would need to be fast. The larger—and frankly, more aggressive —birds would chase off any smaller ones, or at least force them to move farther away.

"I hope you'll find it in your heart to help me with this, and see that it would be of mutual benefit to be rid of this guy. He has a good friend of mine, and she doesn't deserve this." He couldn't think of anything else to say. "I hope you'll think about it."

He tossed out the rest of the corn and stood, Alisha rising with him. She emptied the last of the scratch and they made their way back through the wooded trails. "Think it worked?" Alisha asked under her breath.

"She heard every word," Jelani said. "Let's just hope she feels inclined to help."

"Some friend you've got there."

Jelani looked at her. "Who said she was a friend? To tell the truth, I don't know what to call her."

Alisha clicked her tongue at him. "I really wouldn't buy your cluelessness, if I didn't know you as well as I do."

"What does that mean?" Jelani asked, suspecting he knew what it meant.

Alisha looked at him as if to say she'll play this game as long as he does. "Whatever, Jelani. You know that woman wants you. I'll give you credit for trying to pretend you don't see the way she looks at you. Still doesn't change the fact that you know it."

"Then why do you call me clueless?"

"Because you don't really understand it. You interest her in more ways than you should be comfortable with, and quite frankly, it makes me uncomfortable simply by being near you."

"Why would—"

"Jelani," she interrupted. "Use your imagination and think about what it would be like to stand between a lioness and her intended mate."

"Lionesses are only one of a pride of female mates to the male," Jelani replied, not following.

"All of them by their own choice, and led by a single dominant matriarch," Alisha countered. "Not that we're getting off subject here. Just answer the question. What feeling do you think you would have if you were standing in between a lioness and her intended mate?"

"I'd want to be anywhere but in that spot," Jelani answered.

"And there's my point," Alisha said.

"You think she wants me as her mate?" Jelani asked, frowning.

"Mate? Maybe not. But she wants you. And there's little anybody could do to stop her."

"I don't think it will come to that."

"Why not?" Alisha asked. "You don't think she could let Melinda die, easily make me disappear, get rid of that thing chasing you, and have you for herself?"

"She wouldn't do that," Jelani said, surprising himself at his defensiveness of the *dampeal*. "She's not as amoral as you think."

"Which is why you're not entirely certain whether or not she'll help you, right?"

Jelani sighed. "She's hasn't let us down so far."

"She hasn't let *you* down, so far."

She had a point. Still. "You may be right, but what choice do we have?"

"What if she names a high price for her help?" Alisha continued. "And don't tell me she won't ask. I know better, even if you don't."

Jelani leaned his head back and looked at the looming treetops, and the sky beyond. "Again. What choice do I have? I think this whole situation is beyond my ability to handle on my own, or even with Daniel."

"So if she tells you to stay away from me?" Alisha asked.

"I'll make her promise to get rid of the Hunter and any of them that come after us." He hesitated, then added. "And I'll stay away from you."

"Just like that? You'd just walk away?"

"I would walk away from a living Alisha instead of holding onto a dead one."

"How chivalrous you are."

Jelani grabbed her hand and dropped to one knee. Alisha glanced around, looking at him as if he'd lost his mind. "Chivalry is born in the deed, not the blood, milady," he said, kissing her hand and touching it to his forehead.

Alisha snatched her hand away and rolled her eyes. "Don't try to lighten the mood, I'm serious." She still giggled. "Will you get up already? Someone might see us." Jelani stood and they continued. "If it's all the same, I think I would prefer being alive and not restricted against who I can be with."

"Does that mean you want to be with me?" Jelani asked.

Alisha looked up at him. "It means I like you a lot. It means I can see something in the future for us. It means that I want to be with you, but I never make emotional decisions."

"Oh, so you're a calculating one," Jelani said, snapping his fingers as though he'd figured her out.

"Yup," she said. "Cold, conniving, and calculating. I'll eat your soul."

"Sounds like a succubus to me," Jelani said, taking a step away from her.

"No. That's what you're hoping will help you."

"Damn, girl. That's a little unfair, don't you think? She can't help how she was born."

Alisha sighed impatiently and started walking faster.

"Hey, hey, don't get mad, girl. I didn't mean anything by that."

"Okay, fine," Alisha said, not looking at him. "But I think I'm okay with not talking about your exotic blood sucking friend for a while."

"She doesn't ..." he saw her lips press together and held up his hands. "Okay. You're right. Sorry."

They came to the end of the wooded trail and crossed the street, making their way around the lost lagoon and toward Coal Harbour. Tourist season seemed to have come earlier than usual, evidenced by the milling tourists snapping photos of the puffy pale pink and white cherry blossoms and tulips that had begun to bloom. They walked by two girls sitting on a bench, taking careful pictures of the cinnamon bun on the plate that they were about to share.

"No matter how many times I see it, I will never understand why people take pictures of the most mundane things." He nodded his head in the direction of the girls. "I could see if it was an exotic pastry or some wildly colorful or unusual dish, but it's a cinnamon bun."

Alisha shrugged. "Maybe it's their first one. Maybe there are no cinnamon buns where they're from. Maybe this is the first vacation they've ever been on, and the first dessert they're eating since arriving here. It might be mundane to you, but not to them."

Jelani looked over his shoulder at the girls, snapping a picture and talking rapidly in a foreign language, giggling excitedly. "I guess you could be right about that. You never know what another person's situation is, do you?"

"No. That's why you don't go judging people."

"Hey, I wasn't judging them. I just thought it was weird."

"Sounded like you were judging to me."

"What? Over a cinnamon bun?" He looked at her, and saw the barely restrained smirk. "Having fun?"

She elbowed him. "I can't help it, baby. You're just too easy."

Jelani thought her calling him "baby" was a good sign, but he thought it best to play it cool and not acknowledge that his heart gave a little leap after she'd said it. "If you say so," he replied.

They walked in silence for a while, enjoying the crisp, almost warm, spring day. If there was one thing a Vancouverite would never miss, it was a sunny day. It seemed like every resident who was not at work was outdoors enjoying the weather.

"As much as I hate to bring her up again," Alisha said, her tone turning sour. "How are you going to figure this out with her?"

"I can't let him see me speaking with her, so I'm hoping she and Kafeel will figure something out."

"Why not just meet in the day, like now? That Hunter is a full-blood vampire, right? He can't be in out in the day."

"That's only part of it. Remember what I told you about that session at EA? One of the camera crew was absolutely a vampire, but he was there, in the daytime. I think it's the sun that they have to avoid. Whether it's daylight or not doesn't matter as long as they don't let the sun touch them."

"So much for them having to sleep during the day," Alisha said.

"From what Saaya told me, they do have to sleep during the day, but how frequent they do this depends on the strength of the vampire. They also are less powerful in the day, so that's why a lot of the time they just sleep it through."

"I wonder why that first Hunter didn't do what this one has: kidnap someone close to you?"

Jelani thought about it. He'd encountered the first Hunter on three occasions, and although he'd been on the business end of his sword every time, there was something different in the eyes of that one versus the Hunter who stalked him now. There was an obvious deviousness to this new Hunter that suggested nothing was off limits to achieve his goal, whereas the other Hunter never showed any intention of involving anyone else to get to Jelani. He wondered if there was a significance to this which might be used as leverage in some way. He decided to bring it up if and when he met with Saaya again.

Jelani's phone gave a soft ding. Daniel had sent him a text message. *"I think you should get home ASAP. You've got a visitor."*

CHAPTER 16

J elani reached the front door to the building just as Wen was coming out.

"Hey Jelani," she said. The normal cheer in her tone was strained.

"Hey, Wen. Heading out?"

"Yes. I figured it would be best to let you three talk. Besides, it's a beautiful day. You never know how long it'll last, right?"

"Yeah." There was an awkward silence between them that had become more frequent since Saaya had first appeared in their apartment. Daniel had told Jelani that Wen really wanted for him and Alisha to get together, and she apparently saw Saaya as a threat. Given his most recent encounter with the *dampeal*, he couldn't say it was an unwarranted concern.

"Actually," Alisha said, "I think I'll join you, if it's okay?"

Wen raised her eyebrows. "Oh! Sure, girl. Let's go grab lunch."

Alisha turned to Jelani and gave him a tight hug and a kiss on the cheek. "I'll see you later."

Jelani smiled at her. "You know it. I'll see you two later tonight, then."

Wen looked at him with those kind brown eyes, filled with concern. "You be careful, okay?"

"I'm doing my best."

Her cheeks dimpled when she pressed her pink lips together. "See you later."

When he stepped through the door, Jelani found Saaya lounging on the couch opposite Daniel, the two engaged in seemingly lighthearted conversation. Jelani took off his shoes and hung his jacket in the closet, then joined them in the living room. He stopped and looked at the space on the couch next to Daniel, then the space next to Saaya. The latter was resplendent in her usual short top that stopped at a *V*-shaped point, well above the navel, and long skirt that flowed down to her delicate-looking ankles. The colors were a stunning blend of red, gold, and green. The clothes would have complimented any Indian woman splendidly, but on Saaya, the effect was that of an irresistible dark angel. *Maybe I'll just stand.*

Daniel seemed to read his mind. "I don't mean to be a couch hog, but you're not snuggling on this one with me, dude."

Jelani guffawed as he sat on the couch, as far away from Saaya as possible.

She looked at him with a hurt expression. "I have no contagious germs for you to avoid, Jelani." When he didn't respond, she asked, "What's wrong? I won't bite … right now." She winked at him. Daniel closed his eyes and slowly shook his head.

"I just like to lean on the arm of the couch," Jelani mumbled He glanced in the direction of the kitchen. "You want something to …" He nearly jumped out of his skin when he looked back and saw that Saaya was now right next to him, nearly on top of him. Across the room, Daniel had backed all the way to the other end of his couch, nearly falling over the arm, with his foot up in the air. Saaya laughed at them. It was the first time he'd heard her outright laugh.

"Girl, would you mind not doing that?" Jelani said, forcing his heart to stop thumping in his chest. "You nearly gave me a heart attack!"

"Mmm. All this blood pumping in the room. You two are trying to make a girl hungry and intoxicated at the same time. Do us all a kindness and try to calm down?"

Daniel and Jelani looked at each other, Jelani seeing the barely concealed fear in his friend's eyes.

"It would be a lot easier if you didn't do things like that," Daniel carefully said.

Saaya tipped her head. "Fair enough." She looked back to Jelani. "You know, if you don't make up your mind soon, I may just have to sneak your friend away from his little butterfly."

The corner of Jelani's mouth twitched and he looked at Daniel, who looked horrorstruck. "I'm sure you could find more interesting guys than either of us," Daniel said. Jelani had to give it to him. It was a valiant attempt to deflect.

"You're interesting to me right now. That's all that matters. Later is in the future, so it doesn't exist." She winked at Daniel, whose mouth opened and closed several times before he'd recovered enough to deflect her attention back to Jelani.

"Okay, so you came here to talk to him, right?" He nodded at Jelani, who glared at him.

She looked back at Jelani again, those light brown, almond-shaped eyes probing into his soul. Damn, this girl was hard to look in the eye!

"That was my impression," she said. "Unless you were actually having a conversation with the crow and not with myself." She smiled at him. He tried not to want to devour that delectable smile. He found it impossible.

"Yeah, I was talking to you. And I think this is a risk, meeting right now. He could see us."

"It's daylight, silly."

"I met a vampire in the daytime not long ago, though it was inside a building."

"Ah, that's right." She nodded in understanding. "It may comfort you to know that even though vampires can walk in the daytime if they avoid the sun, most cannot function for long before the need to sleep overcomes them. I recall telling you that the stronger ones can remain awake in the day for as long as a few days before needing to sleep. The one named Remy, who stalks you now, is not so powerful. He is crafty, and that makes him dangerous, but he is not as skilled or powerful as Yako."

"Oh," was all Jelani could manage.

"It was cute, how you thought to attract my attention by so cleverly feeding the crows," she said. Her tone suggested she might pat him on the head.

"Yeah, well, I didn't want to take any chances," Jelani said. "He called me in the morning ..."

"And probably went to sleep shortly after," Saaya finished for him. "He is a pureblood, yes, but not so powerful that he could move in the sunlight. And there is a lot of sunlight between here and that lake in the middle of Stanley Park." Jelani hadn't thought of that. "Still," she continued, "it's good for your little female that you are careful."

"My little female?" Jelani glanced at Daniel, who shrugged.

"So you wish me to help you to save this girl. You have chosen to be with her?"

"No," Jelani answered. "I don't know why this matters, but no, I've chosen not to be with her."

"Then why is this a concern?"

Jelani looked at her, genuinely puzzled. "Do vampires have any sense of friendship at all?" he asked. "And being half human, don't you?"

She tittered, draping an arm on the head of the couch behind his back. The move placed her considerably closer to him. Now Jelani knew why Alisha and Wen had chosen to be anywhere but here. "What you would call friendship is a little different to us," she said. "Vampires do form friendship-like bonds so long as it suits both parties. In some rare instances, a friendship in the definition you relate to can happen, but it is rare."

"That's kinda cold," Jelani said, and Saaya shrugged as if it didn't matter. "Well, just because I don't want to be in a relationship with the girl doesn't mean I don't care about her."

"Fair enough, but your situation has a complication."

"Which is?"

"*I* don't care about her."

There was a moment of silence. Neither Jelani nor Daniel knew how to respond to that. Saaya just smiled pleasantly as she waited for them to speak again.

"Well ..." he started.

"Hmm?"

"Well," he repeated. "I was hoping ... is there any sense of ..." he threw up his hands. "All right I don't know how to come at you, then. I was hoping for some kind of sense of decency, but you don't seem to have it."

"I don't seem to have it to you because I don't fit into your rationale of what is decent? You humans are but a small thing in this world, your lives a flicker of an instant in the grand scope of creation. If your female should die, in time she will live again, perhaps."

Jelani frowned at her. "Are you speaking from a spiritual sense, or a"—what was that word again?—"re-creation sense?" Saaya shrugged, but didn't elaborate. "Do you care about me?" Jelani asked. It was the right question. For the first time, he appeared to have stumped her.

"That is not something I can say for certain. You know that."

"So the other day—"

"When we merged?"

Jelani's mouth fell open and he glanced over at Daniel, who burst into laughter. Saaya looked at the two of them as though she had missed some joke between them.

"Um. Yes. When we, *merged*."

145

Daniel recovered, snorted, then fell into another round of laughter.

"By the way," Jelani continued, "could you please not speak so openly about things like that?"

"As you wish."

"So that other day meant nothing to you, then?"

"How could it have meant anything, *jaan*? It was a merging of the body, not the heart."

"Seemed different to me."

"Do you wish it otherwise?"

She had him then. It was a well-placed question and he had been baited with his own hook. "Okay, let's start again. You don't know that you care about me, yet you've helped us out on several occasions. Be it out of boredom, fun, adventure, attraction, whatever, we're grateful. But if there is even a small amount of you that cares about me, would you not help me save Melinda because it would make me happy?"

Saaya didn't hesitate. "What would I gain, should I take action? Do you wish to explore life with me if I choose to have you? Is it me that you wish to companion yourself with?"

"Companion myself with?" Jelani had a bad feeling he knew where this was going. "Well, I wasn't planning on that. I just want my friend safe."

"So," Saaya replied. "You wish me to help you save your female, but have no intention of having any kind of interaction with me? If Kafeel and I were to completely eliminate every Hunter that stalked you, would you then cast me aside and never wish to see me again?"

"Of course not!" Jelani responded, and he was surprised that he actually meant it. "I'm not like that. I won't lie and say you don't make me uncomfortable more often than not, but you seem like you could be a good friend."

Saaya stared at him for a long time. For what must have been the millionth time, Jelani admired the smoothness of her skin, the way her eyes angled upward ever-so-slightly, the glittering diamond stud in her right nostril. She arched an eyebrow at him. "What a kind, if hesitant, compliment."

"Saaya," Jelani opened his hands and shrugged. "You've made it clear that this whole thing has attracted you more out of curiosity than any sense of moral obligation ..."

"Well, we've been down this road enough times already," Daniel said. "Let's just lay it out on the table. You know we need your help, so what do you want? In exchange for your help, what do you want?"

Saaya tapped a finger on her cheek. Daniel sighed impatiently and Saaya glanced at him, the nail on her finger elongating as she held his gaze. He held his hands up, palms outward. "Sorry. I'm sorry." She threw him a lazy smile and continued to think. A few seconds later, the fingernail retracted.

"Honestly, there isn't much that a human could offer me that I want. The two of you may or may not live long enough to come to understand what is truly meaningful in life, but it is not material wealth of any kind."

"So what does the sage Saaya consider meaningful in life?" Jelani asked, sure to smile warmly so that the *dampeal* wouldn't take offense.

She leaned forward until her face was only a few inches from his. "Life experiences," she said seductively. Her sparkling light brown eyes flicked over at Daniel for a second, then back to Jelani. "I find myself in the presence of two handsome males. Surely there are a great deal of life experiences to be found in this situation."

Jelani glanced nervously at Daniel, whose mouth was hanging open again in a mixture of desire and terror. Jelani understood the feeling. Then the terror melted away, and the desire strengthened. It felt like a quilt of longing was settling over his shoulders, warming him inside, drawing him in. Jelani didn't have to look at Daniel to know his best friend was in a similar state.

He clamped his eyes shut and pushed the feeling away. It was like trying to push a truck uphill. Inch by inch, he pushed against the feeling until he hit what had to have been a wall. The feeling grew stronger, pushed back until it enveloped him. He drank it in, breathed it, drowned in it, absorbed it. Just when he was nearly lost to himself, it was gone. The absence was so abrupt it might have never been. But it was. The resonance was still there, the ebbing passion and longing, beating like a slowing pulse.

Jelani shook his head, trying to clear his thoughts. Finally, he looked at her. Saaya hadn't moved, but through her lidded eyes, Jelani saw the truth. She desired his company in the same way it had been the night they'd coupled. Those brown eyes told him that she could certainly have him, both of them, if she desired, and there was nothing they could do about it. She had also let them know, through the abruptness of their release, that she didn't intend this. Not at the moment, at least.

On the other couch, Daniel gasped. Jelani felt a pang of pity for his friend, having forgotten that this was the first time he'd been subjected to Saaya's powerful will. Did his roommate realize how completely she could dominate them if she chose to? Not the best feeling to have.

"Well, then," he said, clearing his throat. "Now that that's cleared up. What can we agree on? You know Daniel is engaged, so it would be a very bad thing for him to be involved in anything more than friendship—"

"And as unfortunate as that is for him," Saaya interrupted, "so available is my lovely Jelani.

Gee. This is going to be a lot easier than I expected. "Um. You know, Saaya, if this had happened maybe a year earlier, it wouldn't be an issue, I assure you. No guy in his right mind wouldn't want to get-it-crackin' ..." he trailed off when she arched that eyebrow at him again. "Well, I'm being truthful, here."

"You have an interesting way of articulating things," she said.

"Yeah, I get that a lot. But anyway, I'm pretty invested in someone already."

"Of course you are referring to your other female?"

"My female?" Jelani laughed. "She doesn't belong to me, Saaya."

"I would say otherwise. She belongs to you in heart and soul, but not yet in body."

"Then you know we can't repeat what happened between us before." Jelani was starting to allow himself to be hopeful.

"Why ever not?"

The hope shriveled. "Well, I just told you—"

"That you and your female belong to each other yet you are not bonded? Yes, I understand that."

"Not bonded?"

"You have not yet merged. You are not bonded."

Jelani glanced at Daniel who silently mouthed the word back at him. *"Merged?"* It would be really nice to have this conversation without a third party present, best friend or not. "Just because we haven't had sex yet doesn't mean we're not bonded, as you say."

Saaya tittered condescendingly. "So much to learn," she said, half to herself. "I admit that I have not yet come to understand why so many humans treat physical intimacy as though it were a poisonous serpent. The physical bond is a part of the whole, Jelani. Without it, you are not bonded as you would have me believe."

"Okay …"

"I will help you, *jaan*." She said suddenly. "Unless you have changed your mind about enlisting my aid," she said when they fell silent.

"Oh, no, no! We haven't changed our minds," Daniel said.

"It was just unexpected," Jelani added. "So what's your price for this?"

"I haven't decided yet."

And back to square one we've come. "I think we should probably get the terms of service out of the way before we come to an agreement."

"What does it matter?" Saaya asked. "If I do not help, all of

149

you will perish. Whatever my conditions are, you will have preserved your life and that of your friends."

She was right, of course. Whatever she might want with him, it was worth his friends' lives. If that meant he had no future with Alisha, better that than she have no future at all.

Saaya looked at him, reading his features and perhaps, his mind. "Stop worrying about a future that doesn't exist," she said patting him on the leg. "You are too sober for your own good. Humans typically live sixty years? Seventy? Perhaps eighty or ninety? Such a tiny spark in time to have so many concerns. I have forever to name my price of you, Jelani. It doesn't have to be now."

That admission made him feel somewhat better. Maybe she'd wait a few years then ask him for an Easter basket or something. "Sounds fair enough. So while there's still daylight and that guy, Remy, is still sleeping, maybe we should plan this thing out, then?"

"What is there to plan?"

"Well, he's got werewolves and other vampires involved." When he saw the uncertain look on her face, he recounted the night in full when the vampires nearly had him in the Skyride, and the werewolf a while later in the woods. He took special care to make sure she knew about Kafeel's little backhand that sent him into darkness and waking with a nice headache.

"I see," she said. "Knowing Kafeel for as long as I have, I'm guessing two things. He decided you would object if he threw you over his shoulder to bring you here, and he could get you here faster by carrying you."

"What's the second thing?" Jelani asked.

Saaya looked as though she would laugh. "He doesn't like humans."

"Ah," Jelani said.

"As for the other situation," she continued. "I think you just ran into some bad luck, partially my fault. Daniel told me about your encounter with those other vampires at dusk last week. It is my scent that draws them to you."

"Your scent?" Jelani thought he might laugh if the urge to go someplace and lie down wasn't stronger. "What do you mean about your scent? Like you've left your mark on me or something?"

"No. Every living thing leaves a scent. By being as near as we are to each other now, our scents are intermingling, and a vampire would smell you on me, just as they smell me on you. What they smelled was probably what they perceived to be a *skiek.*" Jelani remembered that word. It meant half-vampire/half-human, in the vampiric language.

"Since half-bloods are not common, this would attract them to you. It was only a matter of time. I'm impressed with your ingenuity. The garlic water is a fine idea."

"Thanks, it was Daniel's idea. So why didn't you tell me this before?"

"It slipped my mind."

"Of course it did," Jelani replied, swallowing his irritation. "And the werewolf?"

"Just hungry," came the casual answer.

"But won't he be coming after me now, since now I know that *they* exist?"

"I don't pretend to know how the world of lycanthropes functions, but in this case, he would assume that Kafeel took you for himself."

"So werewolves are actually weaker than vampires?" Daniel asked, surprised.

Saaya chuckled again. "Vampires stronger than lycans? Don't be simple. In human form, they are formidable. In their lupine bodies, they would tear a vampire apart."

"But you just said—"

"That he let Kafeel take Jelani. That is because he smelled the blood of an *Ancestor* in my brother's veins."

"So the *Ancestor*s are stronger than werewolves, then?" Jelani surmised.

"They have a mutual respect that is largely nonexistent between the two populations. And yes, the wolves know well not to challenge an *Ancestor* or the child of an *Ancestor*."

"Well, at least I'm not being hunted by another monster. I think I would probably have just slit my own wrist."

"That would probably have been a good idea," Saaya said. "Unlike we of the night, a lycan might simply kill you quickly, whether day or night."

"Okay, so I'm not hunted by giant wolves, great news. The vampires that attacked me weren't enlisted by Remy, more good news. Remy is not as skilled as the other guy, Yako, but he's sneaky. I'm not sure whether to be comforted or not. Guess it doesn't matter. So how are we going to get Melinda away from this guy?"

Saaya smiled. "How indeed."

CHAPTER 17

Yako stood in silent attention in the middle of the Hall of the High Council of Elders, where for the first time in his life, his eyes looked upon the marvelous portraits of the five most famous *Ancestor*s in vampire history. Behind him, on the wall above the entrance, was a thirty-foot tall hanging portrait of a tall, slender man with curly blond hair and icy blue eyes. He wore a silver shirt and doublet, and matching trousers that fit snugly to the legs. In his left hand was an intricately carved cane that held a sword sheathed within. Count Targis Mair.

On the far left wall hung a portrait of the same type, this one depicting a short but regal woman wearing a sleeveless, shimmering black gown. Her strawberry blonde hair fell in wavy curls down to her ankles. Her skin was the same milky cream color as Targis, but with a flawless sheen that came right off the canvas. Most notable were her cold, pale blue eyes—the telltale eyes of Countess Tevina Lyss.

A portrait on the right wall depicted another female, taller than Tevina, but not by much. She wore an ankle-length gown with long sleeves, tight against the arm, and a snug bodice that pushed her cleavage upward just enough to distract the eye, but not too much.

Her gray eyes were stark against her olive colored skin and shoulder-length black hair that flared out at the sides like the long black feathers of a raven. A slanted grin stretched the corner of her lips—Countess Lycia Trevaghna.

On the far wall hung a longer and wider portrait depicting not one, but two figures. The figure to the left was very tall, perhaps over seven feet, and solidly built. His skin had a similar tint to it as Lycia's, but where her eyes were gray, his were almost purple. His blue-black hair fell over his shoulders, blending so perfectly with the cape hanging from his shoulders that it looked as if they were one and the same.

Count Drago Rayne.

Beside him, half turned toward Drago was a female figure nearly his height, but where he was built solid and muscular, she was curvaceous and hypnotic. In the same manner as Drago, her scarlet hair fell well below her shoulders, blending with her equally brilliant red gown. Her pale, slender-fingered hand rested on Drago's chest, and she stared out at the viewer with matching, blood-red eyes that were both awe inspiring and fear inducing. The Countess Miriana Khova Rayne, and Count Drago's wife.

The histories hinted that there was a sixth *Ancestor*, a Count of incredible power but of more shrouded identity. Being well-versed in vampiric history, the scholar in Yako had always been curious about the identity of this sixth *Ancestor*, and where he might fit within the hierarchy of the other five.

"Eldest Hunter Yako." It was the rumbling voice of Elder Vicken who interrupted Yako's thoughts.

"My lord Elder," he responded, dropping to one knee and bowing his head.

"Second Hunter, Mariska."

"My lord Elder," Mariska replied, kneeling beside him.

"Rise."

They complied, and stood silently as the five Elders of the

High Council scrutinized them. "We have met before, but not in the Hall of the High Council."

Vicken, though not as imposing as the *Ancestor*s depicted on the walls, was nevertheless an impressive figure. With close-cropped black hair and glacial, light grey eyes, the Head of the High Council of Elders was a force.

Yako briefly met his eyes, then averted them in respect. "Yes, my lord Elder."

"Concern has been expressed over your ability to perform the duties required of Eldest Hunter. What say you?"

Yako didn't miss the subtlety. He knew the Elders never pulled their words or hid their intentions. If it was of concern unanimously or even to a majority of the council, Vicken would have expressed it as such, not speaking in neutrality.

"As Eldest Hunter it is my duty to perform the tasks and fulfill the duties of my station without fail. I have succeeded in working to the best of my ability, but my best has failed."

"The admission of your failure displays your admirable integrity and saves the High Council a considerable amount of time in determining your fate." The thin, gravelly voice belonged to Massius.

Yako's gaze darted to the short, unremarkable, gray-haired Elder, and he had to remind himself to avert his eyes and maintain respect. It was difficult to respect a craven who could be easily dispatched, should Yako have his sword and an opportunity. The thought briefly passed through his mind that he might be fast enough to behead the troublesome serpent before the giant Braggus, standing against the right wall, and another Reaper he didn't recognize on the left wall could bring him down. He banished the pointless thought from his mind.

"Elder Massius, my best has indeed failed, but it is my belief that extenuating circumstances have been the cause."

"An excuse you have already listed that need not be heard again."

"So says Massius, representative of the will of the High Council?" Lemanda challenged.

Yako looked at her as long as was respectful before averting his eyes. The similar nose and expression. The same deep black hair. There was no mistaking the likeness between her and the portrait of Lycia Trevaghna. Could Lemanda be directly descended from the bloodline of the Countess? Looking at her now, it seemed a possibility.

Massius narrowed his tiny black eyes at her. "One would think you have a vested interest in the accused Hunter, Lemanda."

She waved his words away with a causal hand. "It is no secret that I have a vested interest in the truth, Massius. This cannot be had until we have heard the tale in full."

Massius opened his mouth to argue but Vicken stopped the exchange. "There will be no bickering in this Hall. We are above pettiness, are we not?" He looked to each of the four faces to his sides, all masks of calm. Yako took that opportunity to quickly assess each of the Elders' expressions. Of Massius's stance, there was little doubt. Lemanda had gone out of her way to speak with him about this meeting and had given at least a small measure of support to him so far. To the far right from Vicken's seat, Stavros was unmoved. He was known to be fair, but swift and harsh with judgment.

Opposite Stavros, on the other side of Vicken, was Alicia. Mariska had said that she was close to Massius. Despite her cool demeanor, that fact alone made any word she uttered suspect. When his eyes fell upon her, he found that she was looking directly at him. What he saw in those vicious pale red eyes made Yako doubt if Massius truly knew with whom he'd aligned himself. Was Massius the most dangerous enemy here?

"Lemanda speaks truly, Massius," Vicken said, bringing Yako back to the moment. "We have not yet heard Eldest Hunter Yako's tale in full. Would you pass judgment without complete knowledge?"

"What worth is this knowledge against the fact that the result is the same, and not one, but several humans now know of our existence. Any excuses this Hunter can conjure are meaningless."

"All knowledge has value," Stavros said. His voice was low and deep, as commanding as Vicken's in fact. "It is for us to determine the depth of that value, Massius. Let the Eldest Hunter speak."

Vicken nodded, still looking at Yako. "Alicia?"

Yako could feel those red eyes boring into him. "I am interested in what portrait the Eldest Hunter would paint of his possible inadequacy for his mission." The words were plainly spoken, but Yako heard the meaning. His story would grant him a leniency, or the rope with which to hang himself.

"I gather your position is also in favor of the facts, Lemanda?" the leader of the High Council asked.

"It is."

"Speak, Eldest Hunter," Vicken bade Yako, and he did.

He spoke about the *shaquora*, Jacob, who had been recently turned, whom Yako had been monitoring. When the human had seen Jacob feeding, he'd intercepted the *shaquora*, dispatched his friend, and went after the human, figuring to eliminate the easier target first.

Then, he reached the part when he'd encountered the *dampeal* and her brother. Time passed as he relayed the entire mission, and by the time his tale was done, he had the rapt attention of every member of the High Council. Despite himself, even Massius had leaned forward in his seat.

"You are absolutely certain of this?" Vicken said. "A *dampeal*?"

"Yes, My Lord Elder."

Having finally recovered, Massius scoffed. "A remarkable, if creative, tale. And when was the last recorded birth of a *dampeal*, might I ask?"

"About twelve hundred years ago," Lemanda answered, "More or less. In South America of all places."

"So rare. Do you suppose this could be the same creature?"

"She is not, Elder," Yako answered. "The *dampeal* from South America is male."

Massius nodded. "Do you think it possible that perhaps you have created this little half-breed in an attempt to save face at being bested by a female *shaquora*, and eluded by a human?"

If he'd had his sword, Yako might have made an attempt at the fool, Elder or not. To question his honor was an unforgivable act. Yako now considered Massius an enemy, not just an annoyance. Eventually, one of them would die. "No, Elder. I have not created a fictitious enemy in order to save face. It is against everything I am and have been trained to do. I live or die with my honor intact."

"So you say."

"May I ask permission to speak, My Lord Elder?" It was only the second time Mariska had spoken since their arrival.

Vicken nodded.

"I was not present when Eldest Hunter first encountered the *dampeal*, but I myself have fought her." That got their attention.

"You, Second Hunter, fought a *dampeal* and are here to speak of it?" Vicken looked back and forth between them. "Does your prowess so eclipse your Eldest?"

"It does not, My Lord Elder. The *dampeal* woman toyed while I fought. It pains me to admit that she could have brought about my uncreation at her will."

"Yet she chose not to," Vicken said.

Mariska nodded. "She fought both Steja and me, and together we were unable to overcome her. Whatever her motives were, she did not finish us, as she well could have."

"And this brother of hers?"

"He is as Yako said. A full-blooded spawn of an *Ancestor*."

"It's convenient this so called *dampeal* and her brother defended two humans against you, and then allowed you to live to make yet another attempt." Massius flicked his hand at them in disgust. "I'm having difficulty finding merit in your words."

Vicken nodded. "I must admit that I, too, find your words difficult to accept, yet I have never known you to lie about anything, Eldest Hunter. Never once have you failed us, and your Second has proven herself to be equally competent." Yako and Mariska bowed in unison.

"Should your words be true," Vicken continued, "this situation is far more complicated than we would otherwise have believed." To Vicken's left, Massius's mouth tightened until tiny wrinkles appeared. Farther to the left, Alicia's pale red gaze bore into him. A tiny smile that held no mirth rested on her lips. He held that gaze only for a second, then looked away. Lemanda had called her a foolish child, but there was nothing childish or foolish about that one.

The thought of the Elder caused him to glance in her direction. She was watching him as well, although not with the same predatory intensity of Alicia. Lemanda only spared him an instant to catch her eyes before looking away. Yako didn't take Lemanda for a person who could easily misjudge someone as she had seemingly misjudged Alicia, so what was he missing, here? Vicken's voice pierced his thoughts.

"We should have a report of what goes on across the ocean shortly. Remy's account of the situation may well bring credence to your report."

Damn it, Yako thought. He could practically see the hungry grin behind Massius's placid features. Oh, yes. There would indeed be a report soon, and regardless of what Remy discovered, it would be the opposite of whatever Yako had said. Massius would see to it that the Hunter was properly coached before giving his report.

"My lord Elder." He received a silent nod to continue. "I am familiar with the *dampeal* and her brother's actions and, somewhat, the relationship between them and the targets. With a small contingent, I could use the targets to draw them out and obtain proof of my words."

"And why would we have confidence in you after your most recent multiple failures?" Massius challenged. Never mind his sword, Yako's hand itched to snatch the Elder's heart out of his chest and let him watch it cease to beat.

"Unlike before, I understand my enemy. Had I known those two existed and intended to preserve the targets, for whatever reason, I would have adjusted my tactics."

"We are not interested in your excuses," Massius snapped.

"Yes, Elder," Yako replied, placing just enough emphasis on the title that it could be interpreted as insult.

"If Massius is content to dispense with the sparring," Stavros said, "we might continue?"

Yako respectfully bowed in the Elder's direction. "I would ask again that the High Council allow me to return and redeem myself."

Vicken must have sensed the forthcoming reproach, for he raised a hand and silenced Massius just as he was opening his mouth. Vicken sat in his high-backed chair for a long time, studying Yako and Mariska. Finally, he spoke.

"There is no perfection in this world, not even among the immortals. You have served us well and faithfully Eldest Hunter Yako. As to your return across the sea, you will be granted passage, after you have completed a task that I've seen fit to appoint to you." Yako knew better than to allow even a flicker of disappointment to show on his face. Vicken may hold him in favor, but that meant little if he angered the powerful Elder.

"Perhaps it is good fortune that brought you here when it did, for Hunter's Moon is upon us, and the wolves become restless." All Yako could do was listen as the net of helplessness settled around him. Not only would this delay him from returning to deal with Remy and the human targets and those troublesome siblings, but the fact that he was being commanded to lead a lycan hunt during the Hunter's Moon cycle was an added blow. He would need to communicate with Darren, but how? The leader of the Shadow Pack, as they were known, may have already left. The last thing that was needed was another open conflict between the two species.

But then, in his wisdom, Vicken threw Yako a glimmer of hope. "There have already been reports of several attacks in one day. I wish to avoid open war with them, but I'll not stand for the careless attack upon the human population. Their identity revealed upon the human masses would only briefly precede our own, and that is a problem we will not allow to occur."

"What is your will, my lord Elder?"

"Though I see little need in it, you may attain the redemption you feel you must. Take your Second with you and assemble a team to deal with the lycans. Do what you must. This situation will be ended through truce or attrition, but it will end."

Yako and Mariska bowed in obeisance. "Yes, my lord Elder," they said in unison.

Vicken raised his voice to address the others. "Does the High Council have anything to add?" Silence answered. "Then this hearing is adjourned. Go, Eldest Hunter Yako and Second Hunter Mariska. Find success in your task." It was as much a warning as it was a wish of luck. *Do not fail in this,* that was the unspoken command.

The two Hunters bowed and exited. For a time, they strode the many hallways and corridors in silence, following twisting and turning paths through the massive castle. Mariska had worked with Yako long enough to know that he would not wish to speak until he was certain no other ears would hear.

They turned down yet another open, spacious hallway just as a short, athletically built woman rounded the corner. Upon seeing the two of them, her eyes immediately went to Mariska, and the two exchanged eye contact. The woman continued down the hall and around the bend. They came to a spiral staircase and descended to below ground level, then continued on. The halls were growing darker as they moved ever downward, and soon they were surrounded by not granite or marble or worked stone pillars and walls, but solid rock. Having descended to the deepest level beneath the castle, they came to a thick stone door. With one hand, Yako opened the door that no two humans could have easily moved, and Mariska stepped inside. Yako glanced down the hall in both directions, then closed the door.

Finally, alone and secluded, he spoke. "Your assessment?"

"The Reaper on the far wall opposite Braggus was Tara," Mariska answered. Not until Yako nodded and turned his back, did she allow herself a quick glimpse around the room. Every wall and a good portion of the stone floor was covered with books as thin as a short novel or as thick as a tome. Some of these books looked as if they would disintegrate at the slightest touch.

"Then that was her twin, Meilana, that we passed above," Yako surmised. "Continue."

"I believe the hunt is a test. Perhaps one or more of them suspect you have dealings with the wolves, and suggested you lead the contingent to deal with them."

"And Vicken made his own amendment to the task in allowing me to seek less violent means to settle the situation if possible."

"That is my belief."

"Lemanda?"

"I do not believe she has betrayed us, but I believe she underestimates Alicia. There is a danger in her eyes that makes me wary."

Yako couldn't have agreed more. It may be whispered that Alicia had aligned herself with Massius for whatever reason, but she was clearly the more intelligent and formidable of the two. She'd spent the entire meeting watching the proceedings, listening to all that was said without offering any perspective, without tipping her hand one way or the other.

"Lemanda does not strike me as one who could easily underestimate anyone, but I'm sure we would be wise to tread carefully.

The situation with the wolves is not a timely one. I would deal with this quickly and decisively, and return to Vancouver. The longer Massius can delay us here, the more time Remy has to figure out a way to undermine me."

"You believe he's behind your being appointed to this hunt?"

"Yes, but not directly. Massius wouldn't have made the decision to place me in command."

"Yet if you were to fail ..."

Yako got her point. If he was to fail, then there would be nothing to stop Massius's claims that he was unfit to lead the Hunters. There was still something missing about all this. It didn't add up straight. Why all this trouble to discredit Yako and elevate Remy's station? Why were those two so bent on discrediting Yako? As was often the case, Mariska and Yako were of one mind, and she voiced his own thoughts.

"It escapes me why Massius needs your reputation tarnished," Mariska said.

"That's why we're here," Yako answered.

"An ancient library," Mariska replied, skeptical.

"The histories regarding the Elders are all clearly accounted for, except for Massius. Whatever was recorded, I suspect it's not true." At that moment, Mariska looked as though she would rather be anywhere but in the room with him. Still, she held her tongue. "Speak your mind," he bade her.

"Eldest Hunter," she said formally. "Please forgive my voicing what you already are aware of, that questioning the histories of our people is akin to blasphemy."

Yako nodded before she'd finished speaking. "Only those with something to hide forbid the questioning of their wisdom. If the history of Elder Massius is true and complete, why would there be offense for anyone to seek out this knowledge on their own? The solidarity and security of every coven is dependent on the lineage and history of its leaders. Lycan packs throughout the world that we vampires so look down upon know this as well. Ignorance is a risk I will not entrust my life with."

Mariska watched as he perused the many rows of books. Some looked older than the castle itself. "What do you intend?"

"There is a personal historical account of every Elder, living or dead."

"Yes," Mariska agreed. "But this knowledge is more easily available in the library above, is it not?"

"Perhaps, perhaps not."

"You think we'll find more here?"

Yako stopped at a brown tome simply entitled, Vein. He carefully removed the thick book and placed it on a nearby desk, blowing a layer of dust from the cover. The spine crackled as he gingerly opened the book to the table of contents. Mariska appeared at his side, glancing from him to the book as he scanned the various names and attached page numbers. Many of the names were familiar, Lemanda and her two sisters, Juliana and Lorayne. After the three names was a large bracket, after which was written, The Sisters.

Interested as he was, Yako moved on. There wasn't a great deal of time available before their absence would be noticed. There were the names of the other High Council members: Vicken, Alicia, Stavros. Massius's name was included, but he was further down the page, and there was an asterisk after it. His was not the only name with such an affix, and the notes at the bottom of the page indicated that those names with the symbol attached had incomplete personal histories and/or broken branches in their genealogies. Yako stared at the name as though scrutinizing the Elder himself.

He carefully flipped to the corresponding page, read the text referencing Massius's history alongside the other Elders. Some had died during conflicts with the lycanthrope packs in ancient times, and others had risen to power as a result of their victories. Vicken's exploits were legendary, and Stavros proved to be nearly as powerful. Yako had felt that when he'd seen the Elder earlier. Alicia had been capable enough, physically, but had used her cunning to begin the trend that would lead to the end of the conflict. Lemanda had stood by Vicken's side through countless hunts and wars, not only stalking and killing the most powerful of the werewolf pack leaders, but also defending against rival vampire covens who sought to attain greater power through toppling the Romanian coven.

It was a detailed and fascinating history that Yako wished he had more time to explore. What he did take note of, was that Massius's name failed to appear in a single battle or skirmish of any kind. It was not until later, after the Elders—only several hundred years old at that time—had established a powerful coven, that the serpentine vampire had made his appearance.

"The history books in the libraries of our coven do not list these exploits in such detail," Mariska said, devouring the information.

"Nor do they list that Massius was not an original member of the coven at that time," Yako replied. "I would be interested to know how he could attain his current position without having contributed to its base of power."

They read on, and the answers trickled through. Long before Massius had appeared at Peles Castle as an outsider, the fifth seat of the Council was occupied by none other than Denry Ordine, the Elder who had been killed during a skirmish with a pack of lycans.

Massius had expressed great interest in the inner workings of the castle and its leadership, desiring the opportunity to obtain a seat in the Council. But every seat was occupied, and the laws stated that only one born of the coven and having proven themselves worthy through deed could ever have the possibility of attaining a position of power or influence.

Decades passed and apparently, through his expertise in architecture, Massius had secured his welcome. He assisted in creating more defensible additions to the castle and had a large hand in reworking the inner architecture to make it more easily defendable should an attack occur. And those attacks did come, and frequently. After one incident when Peles Castle had been attacked by a coordinated effort of three growing packs of lycans, Massius came before the Council with an offer. What came next was as shocking as it was unbelievable. Yako's lips parted, and beside him, Mariska took in a sharp breath.

Once again Massius came before the Council, this time, with a plan that would sway the conflict heavily in their favor. The vampires had warriors, but this alone was not enough. They needed better organization and leadership. They needed to do more than simply fight or defend against the wolves. They needed to go out and meet them in the woods and forests. They needed to counter the superior lycanthrope strength with skill and precision.

And so Massius created the Hunters.

CHAPTER 18

The irony fell heavily on their shoulders. Mariska looked at Yako, but his disbelieving eyes were fixed to the page. Massius had created the Hunters.

"Impossible," Mariska whispered. "Never have I seen one who is so far removed from being a warrior. How could he create and train the first of our Order?"

Yako didn't reply, but read on. Massius had beseeched the Council to allow him to form a group of specially trained vampiric warriors that would be instrumental in finally putting a stop to the attacks.

Then another thing happened, and as he read on, Yako's hands balled into fists.

The Elder had not personally created and trained the Hunters. Instead, he had asked that the Council allow him to contact an associate of his. Jiro Shimamoto. The vampire warrior's prowess was a thing of legend among every ninja clan in Japan, as well as among the human population. Since ninjas operated at night, and only those few who trained with them in their reclusive villages knew their identities, it was not looked at as unusual that he was only seen after the sun had set.

The assassin had never failed a mission and there had not been a politician or emperor alive whose blood did not turn to water at the mention of that name. Jiro Shimamoto had three pureblood children; his only son, Ichiro, and two daughters, Amaya and Hisako. Mariska's eyes went from Yako's calm face to his trembling fists. She read on.

The book did not go into much detail about Jiro or his family, but there was mention of Hisako bearing a child, Katashi Shimamoto. Katashi's lineage reached all the way to present day, and his descendent had gone on to become the best Hunter on the North American continent.

Mariska's eyes widened and she looked at Yako, whose features were a little too controlled. He continued reading, his eyes darting rapidly from left to right as he devoured the text. Jiro had come to Peles Castle at Massius's behest, formed the clan that would become the Order of Hunters, and trained them. In a manner of one year, they had decimated an entire pack of werewolves and beaten back the other two. It was not until later, after Denry Ordine had been killed during a skirmish with the wolves, that an exception was made and Massius had been allowed to become a member of the Council.

Mariska watched the Eldest Hunter. The more he read, the more Yako's rage became apparent. As with every craven who attained power, Massius had felt decidedly vulnerable and in need of better protection. He brought the proposition before the Council that there be the creation of one more clan, an elite clan that served only the members of the Council. After tirelessly pressing his point, Massius had finally convinced the Council, and he once again commissioned Jiro Shimamoto. This time, the legendary warrior was to train only the best Hunters of the coven with the best *talents* to become elite warriors and personal guardians.

Each vampire warrior would be required to take a series of tests that would push their physical and mental abilities to their limits and beyond. They would require the maximum use of every *talent* they possessed, and even the leaders of the coven, the most powerful Council members themselves, would offer the final tests. These series of challenges became known as the Trials of the Ancients.

Yako closed the book, having read enough and, Mariska figured, wary of lingering any longer. He carefully replaced the tome in its rightful slot and checked the room to be sure nothing was out of place.

"What does this mean?" she asked as Yako pushed open the door.

"That you know more than you should," Braggus's voice answered from outside the door.

THE THREE STARED at one another. Mariska's looked from left to right, quickly assessing that there was no one else present. Yako held the giant Reaper's gaze, watching a smile creep across Braggus's face. With a baritone laugh that caused his heavily muscled torso to bounce, Braggus unfolded his massive arms and reached forward to give Yako a pat on the shoulder. The motion gave Mariska a chilling view of the large scythe strapped across the huge vampire's back. She'd never seen Braggus in battle, but every Hunter knew of his exploits. He could rip that scythe off his back in an instant and cleave them both in two, if they weren't fast enough to avoid it.

"May I assume you are not here to dispatch us?" Yako asked evenly, not sharing Braggus's laughter.

The Reaper shook his head, causing his long, straight, black hair to slide back and forth over his broad shoulders. "It's a testament to your character that you have any friends at all with such a persona, Eldest Hunter. Yes, you may assume my appearance here does not involve yours or your Second's uncreation." He gave a half bow toward Mariska, who returned it uncertainly.

"I know of no other who can claim the fear of an Elder," Braggus continued.

"The fear of a coward is not so difficult to attain," Yako replied.

Braggus laughed again. "We must surely be on very familiar terms for you to speak of an Elder such, in my presence. But your words are true, and our familiarity was what led me to find you here."

"Did he send you to spy on me?" Yako asked. He couldn't quite bring himself to speak Massius's name just yet.

"Not exactly. But he asked me to keep an eye out for your whereabouts. I don't know what he fears in you, but he wants to know where you are at all times before the hunt."

"I'm sure he does," Yako said, and Braggus frowned at the venom in his voice.

"What did you find here that lends such irascibility to your tone, Yako?" Braggus asked, folding his arms again and leaning against the opposite stone wall in the narrow corridor.

"I have discovered a number of things regarding a certain member of the High Council that makes me unable to decide whether to remove his head from his shoulders or his heart from his chest."

"Hmm." Braggus's frown deepened. "I'd be interested in knowing more, but this isn't the time." His normally jovial face grew serious. "Have a care with your actions, Yako. I needn't tell you that you are being watched. If you misstep even a bit, it could mean your end."

"Duly noted," Yako replied.

Braggus nodded at the Hunter and turned his gaze to Mariska. "See that you do not allow your Eldest to cause that beautiful little head to become separated from that beautiful body of yours, hmm? It would be a shame to lose you."

"Thank you, Eldest Reaper," Mariska replied.

"So formal, even in the depths of the castle's underbelly."

Braggus snickered. "You two are truly a pair." He turned and strode further down the corridor in the opposite direction Yako and Mariska had come. "Take care, little Hunters. The worst way for a warrior to meet their end is at the command of a craven."

Yako got the message. Massius may not be able to directly order that he be executed, but there were other methods. Standing in the dark corridor, Yako considered the death of Elder Denry Ordine and Massius's subsequent rise to power. He thought of how several of his own ancestors had simply disappeared some time after Massius had become a member of the Council that would one day become the High Council of Elders. He thought about how Remy coveted his own position as Eldest Hunter, and how he was certain that the ambitious Hunter and Elder might actually be related.

Had Massius arranged this hunt that Yako was ordered to lead? It made sense. If the accounts recorded in that little known volume were to be believed, Yako had no reason to doubt that the scheming Elder was plotting his death.

Had Massius already arranged for him to fall in the upcoming hunt, regardless of whether he could reason with the wolves? In Yako's mind, the question was a rhetorical one.

"Come," he said, walking past Mariska.

"What do you intend?" Mariska asked, falling into step beside him.

"To assemble a team."

CHAPTER 19

F lashlight in hand, Jelani trudged uphill through the snow,
climbing over fallen trees and the giant roots of the endless
world of towering vegetation that surrounded them. Beside him,
Daniel also struggled. Jelani had received the call about an hour
before sundown. Though the original plan was for him to meet
with Remy alone, Daniel had insisted on coming along. Since the
Hunter planned to kill them both anyway, and saw the two humans
as not much of a threat, Jelani had consented.

The drive to Grouse Mountain had been a quiet one as both
men thought about what was to come. Despite the situation, Jelani
felt less fearful than before. There was something about heading
into a perilous situation rather than running from it that was calm-
ing, in a way. If he was going to die, he would face his death rather
than have it catch him from behind. The stony features of his best
friend beside him hinted at similar thoughts.

Of course, Wen and Alisha had not wanted them to go. Wen
had pleaded with Daniel to find another way.

"Are you sure?" Alisha had asked him in a surprisingly steady
voice while crying silent tears. But there was nothing for it. Jelani

would have to meet with the vampire and hope that Remy would hold up his end of the bargain, releasing a still living Melinda in exchange for his life. Now that exchange numbered two. At least, that's what the Hunter believed.

Through some of the most unusual bargaining Jelani had ever done, he had convinced Saaya to aid him. At least, he believed he had convinced her. For all he knew, the *dampeal* had simply agreed to help him out of feelings no deeper than boredom. On top of that, he still wasn't sure exactly what it was he had agreed to in exchange for her help.

Saaya had been right about one thing, though. Whatever she wanted of him mattered little if it meant seeing Melinda safe again. He wondered where the *dampeal* was. She was somewhere out there in the woods, unseen to them, as well as their enemy. Saaya had assured him impatiently that when the time came, she would put a swift end to the Hunter, and this business would be over.

Jelani reached a gloved hand into his coat pocket and felt the familiar shape of the plastic water gun. He didn't know whether or not he'd get close enough to use it, or how strong an effect it would have. Even Saaya was not much help. Apparently, though, most vampires were susceptible to the concoction of water and garlic, not all were, and it might not have as debilitating or lethal an affect as it did on those vampires in the Skyride car. Saaya had told Jelani they were definitely newly turned vampires. A pure-blood, she'd said, would have reacted much faster and probably snapped his arm or his neck before he could bring his knife or water gun to bear.

What chances did that leave them here, now? The fact that there were two of them was at least something. They wouldn't be able to overcome the Hunter on their own, but the couple seconds it would take for Remy to dispatch one of them would at least give the other a chance to put a silver knife in his back, or at least spray a stream of garlic water in his face.

The more Jelani thought about the little water gun in his pocket, the more ridiculous it felt to him. Still, it worked. He may feel foolish, but he was alive to feel foolish.

Tiny white flecks fell on his face. Jelani looked up, scrunching up his features at the dark, starless sky. Snow. Any other time, he would have welcomed it. Having grown up in southern California, he'd only seen snow once in his life, and that was after a two-hour drive to the mountains. Snow could make anything look beautiful: buildings, houses, even an old rusted car falling apart in a lot overgrown with weeds could look like art under a nice layer of snow.

But at the possibility that he may have to fight for his life, and the low visibility and difficulty of movement that came with snowfall, was not something he welcomed. "Great," Daniel grumbled, a few feet to his right. "It's already dark, and now we've got snow. I guess it's too much to hope that the snow might make it hard for him to see us as well."

"I seriously doubt it," Jelani replied. "They can already see in the dark. What's a few snowflakes?"

"He's probably been watching us scramble up the side of this mountain for the past half hour now anyway," Daniel said. "He couldn't have chosen a more out of the way place to meet."

Jelani remembered the news footage of the fallen Skyride car and the car operator's broken body, found further down the mountain. The mountain was closed down and the whole place had been turned into a crime scene. The last thing the vampire would do is meet with them too close to the site.

"Oh, he knows what he's doing," Jelani said. "He wants to meet with us a safe enough distance away from where the cops are surveying the area where the Skyride went down, but he also wants to keep it close enough so that when our bodies are found it might look like a related incident. That's my guess, at least."

"Nice hypothesis," Daniel said dryly, climbing over a fallen tree already coated with snow. "It's not like it'll be hard for him to find us, what with all the light we're shining with these flashlights."

Jelani didn't disagree. He imagined the Hunter, perched in a tree somewhere with Melinda under a firm grip, snickering to himself as he watched the two beams of light, turning this way and that, as the helpless humans below struggled up the endless slope.

The cold was starting to nip at him. They were dressed for the weather, but in the mountains it was a different kind of cold than what drifted through the streets of the city. Up here, breathing was more difficult, and the air frosted in front of their mouths with each breath.

He hoped they weren't pointlessly throwing their lives away in coming to meet with the vampire. After all, what would stop Remy from simply killing Melinda right before he killed them? Daniel had verbalized that same thought, but Saaya had disagreed, assuring them that the combination of needing to keep the bait as long as need be to snare the prey, and Remy's own astounding arrogance, would assure Melinda's safety. At least for a time.

"At the very least," Saaya had said, "he'd kill your female, then use the two of you as bait to get to your other two females, then kill you all."

Comforting.

They heard a wolf howl in the distance and Jelani froze. Daniel stopped as well, the two men looking at each other, then glancing around at the dark woods. A second howl answered the first, but Jelani found himself relaxing. He nodded to Daniel to continue. When his friend gave him a questioning look, he waved a hand.

"Those howls aren't werewolves. They're just regular wolves."

"How do you know that?" Daniel asked. "You speak wolf?"

"Believe me. You'd know the difference."

"Guess I'll have to take your word for it," Daniel said. "It'd be ironic, though, if the guy led us all the way up here to be taken out by werewolves."

"Always thinking on the bright side," Jelani remarked.

Daniel shrugged.

They continued on in silence to conserve their energy for the climb. The terrain was getting steeper, and with the added difficulty of the snow, their progress was more slow going. As the incline became more extreme and the ground more slippery, they moved in closer together, able to quickly lend a hand when one or the other slipped. They navigated between the trees, making straight paths in front of the large trunks so that there would be something to stop them, should they lose their footing and slide downward before one could reach the other.

The wind intensified and with it, the snow. Instead of falling around them peacefully, now the large white flakes were blowing in their faces. The wind whispered ominously through the darkened woods and the two friends jumped at the slightest sounds. They tried to take comfort that Saaya, and possibly Kafeel, were nearby, but with the siblings nowhere in sight, it was a hard lifeline to hold on to.

"Still wish you hadn't spent that extra money on waterproof hiking boots?" Daniel asked.

Jelani smirked, remembering the conversation as he crunched through the snow. "Yeah, yeah, fair enough. I owe you one for that."

"Let's hope either of us is still around after this for you to repay me."

Jelani wanted to say something reassuring. He wanted to say that of course they would be all right after this. As long as they kept their wits about them, they'd come out of this fine. But he couldn't. The truth was that there was too much against them. They were alone, on the side of a heavily wooded mountain at night. No lights, no people, no witnesses. On top of that, they were going all this way to meet with a vampire.

Their lives dangled by the thread of hope that was Saaya. The *dampeal* said she would be out there somewhere, but she had to remain at enough of a distance that the Hunter wouldn't smell her. Though vampires had a much more acute sense of smell than a human, it was nothing compared to a werewolf, so she could be reasonably close. They hadn't appreciated the joke when she told them that if they had been coming out here to meet with a lycan, there would have been no way she could be close enough to help them unless the thing had a severe cold or the flu. She'd told them to loosen up when they'd failed to find the humor.

Jelani shined his flashlight farther up the hill and saw what looked like an opening in the trees. "Not much farther," he said. "We're supposed to be at a place where the slope levels off. I think that's it."

"Well then," Daniel said. "I guess let's get this over with."

Jelani took a deep breath and continued to put one foot in front of the other. Once the ground leveled off, the trees thinned into a small clearing. Jelani and Daniel stopped just short of the clearing, feeling the need to remain concealed.

After a few minutes, Jelani was about to suggest they step into the open when his gaze fell on a figure lying on the ground on the other side of the clearing. His heart skipped a beat. Melinda! He looked at Daniel, who saw the alarm in his face, and they stepped out, ready to draw their long silver knives at any sign of a threat.

They crept out of the trees, eyes darting this way and that. Jelani faced forward while Daniel moved backward behind him, watching their rear. Something about this didn't feel right at all. The vampire, Remy, was nowhere to be seen, Melinda was lying face down on the snowy ground, clearly dead. Jelani's heart sank lower and lower as they approached. Her disheveled light brown hair blew gently in the moaning wind. Jelani shook his head regretfully, fighting back the lump in his throat.

He turned her over and … saw that it was not Melinda. It was a woman he'd never seen before. She had the same body type as Melinda, and the same long brown hair. Lying face down in the snow that had begun to cover her body, Jelani would never have been able to tell it wasn't her until he turned her over. "Why?" he whispered.

"What?" Daniel backed closer till he was beside Jelani. He shined his flashlight on the body. "Who's that?"

"Hell if I know," Jelani said. "Some poor girl that he killed."

"Why would he leave—"

He stopped when he heard a whimper from a dozen feet away, and they turned to see Melinda tied to a tree. They ran to her, and Jelani drew his knife. He stopped and spun at the sound of a voice behind them.

"Well, you came after all."

They shone their flashlights in the direction of the voice to see Remy step out of the concealment of the trees, casually striding across the clearing. He stopped several dozen feet away and smirked. Jelani and Daniel looked at each other. They knew he could close that distance quicker than they could get away. He was toying with them.

"Looks like we have a little dilemma, don't we?" Remy said.

Jelani and Daniel just stared at him.

"Nothing to say?" Remy asked. He placed a hand to his ear and leaned forward. "Come now, I know you have some witty remark waiting to counter my words. No?"

They still didn't respond.

Remy snarled at them, "You know, for two people who are about to die, you don't seem to be making much of an effort to stall for those last few precious minutes. Don't you want to engage me in some kind of conversation to prolong your insignificant existence just a little longer?"

"Why are you playing games with us?" Daniel asked while Jelani knelt over Melinda and began cutting at the rope binding her arms. She moaned again. Had Remy been starving her?

The vampire spread his hands. "I have to admit that my method in all of this has been grossly inefficient, but we should find the fun in life wherever we can, shouldn't we?"

"You didn't have to kill her," Daniel said, nodding his head at the dead woman a few yards away.

"You took too long, and I got hungry," Remy teased.

"You didn't have to involve Melinda either," Daniel continued. "She had nothing to do with any of this, and she didn't even know about vampires."

Jelani sawed at the thick ropes as Melinda moaned again. Her head lolled to one side and Jelani recoiled, scooting backwards. He heard laughter from farther behind.

"Ah ha! And now things become more interesting."

Daniel threw a questioning expression over his shoulder at Jelani, who just continued to stare at Melinda, at her neck, where two puncture marks were visible. Daniel needed only to see the look on his friend's face to guess what had happened.

"So what to do?" Remy said, pacing back and forth, tapping a finger to his cheek. "I confess that this girl," he indicated the dead woman, half covered in snow, "didn't completely sate my hunger. I think she may have been anemic or something. Since I was still hungry, poor little Melinda there had to serve as a snack."

Jelani ground his teeth. Never had he ever wanted to kill another person, but he would have killed this man without a second thought.

"While I was enjoying her thick, rich blood, and I assure you it is very sweet, a thought occurred to me. Since you've been hiding out and making things more difficult than they needed to be, I thought I might add some flavor to the situation by giving you a choice."

He nodded past Jelani. "Our damsel in distress over there has been bitten by the big bad vampire, and will soon turn into yet another demon-spawned creature of the night." Jelani narrowed his eyes at the sarcastic tone. Hunter or not, Jelani would find a way to kill him.

Remy's smirk turned into a snicker. "Before I kill you, I'll give you a choice. Do you take the moral high ground and kill your friend, thus preventing her from becoming a bloodsucker? Or do you allow her to live and be forever turned from the sun's embrace? Can't you see the beauty in this?" Remy gestured as if he was an artist explaining a painting to his viewers. "You, two doomed souls, have a chance to do the right, yet difficult thing, by killing your friend to prevent her from becoming a vampire. Or you can *not* kill her, not having the heart to do it, and die knowing that because of your weakness, she will rise again and stalk the night."

Jelani looked back over his shoulder at Melinda. Her head lolled from side to side and she moaned as if in pain. Her mouth fell open to reveal slightly more pointed canines than was normal. Her eyes opened lazily and there was a gently pulsating red hue in them. Her skin seemed to move, as though tightening. Her chest rose and fell dramatically as she gasped. Jelani closed his eyes and breathed a curse. The sound of the Hunter's voice intruded into his thoughts.

"Tick-tock," Remy taunted. "Let's get on with it, shall we?"

"He's telling the truth?" Daniel whispered over his shoulder.

"Yes," Jelani croaked. His heart felt like it was about to split. He lifted his knife and closed his eyes. Better to kill her than doom her to vampirism.

"Your actions are shameful, Remy."

Jelani's eyes snapped open. Saaya.

"Would the leaders of your coven approve?" She stepped out of the trees, barely six feet from where they stood. How long had she been there?

Remy looked at her, unimpressed. "The job will be done. It matters little."

"The deleterious effects of your arrogance could easily affect your coven, Hunter. Your job is to prevent the human population from discovering our existence, yet you take so many chances. If I were your leader, I would dispatch you in favor of someone more competent."

"You are in a more perilous situation than you understand, *skiek*," Remy said. He looked at Jelani and Daniel. "I admit that I hadn't actually expected you to come without help. There is little a simple half-breed can do to help you, but you're more intelligent than I gave you credit for. I didn't see or smell her at all." Remy raised a hand, and six vampires stepped out of the trees behind him.

Saaya eyed the newcomers. From the way they moved, she took them all to be Hunters. "You brought a lot of assistance to deal with a simple half-breed, no?"

Remy's lips curled, revealing a pair of elongated fangs beneath a pair of glowing red eyes. "As you said, no need to take unnecessary chances." The vampires started forward, then stopped. A tall, cloaked figure materialized from the trees and came to stand towering behind Saaya. She grinned, revealing a pair of elongated fangs of her own.

"You know, Remy. If this were under different circumstances, I might actually like you. Look how much fun you've brought!" Her tone was so light, she might have been talking about going on a vacation. "So much fun! Will you take turns, or shall we all dance at once?"

In answer, Remy let out a loud hiss. The six vampires behind him flew past, quickly closing the distance. What followed was a blur of eight shadowy figures in the night, darting around the snow-coated clearing in a dance of death that Jelani and Daniel's eyes could barely follow. Remy watched on the far side of the clearing as Saaya and Kafeel met the charge of the six Hunters. One of the vampiric warriors, a thin, pale-skinned blond male with glowing red eyes launched himself at Saaya.

He never reached her. His body stopped just several feet away and was thrown aside as though by a giant unseen hand. Figuring Saaya to be the least threat of the two, the other five Hunters had charged in at Kafeel, leaving the other vampire to deal with her alone. They could not have misjudged their enemies any worse.

Jelani saw Saaya easily toss her enemy aside with her mind, while Daniel steadily backed away, watching in horrified amazement at the six snarling figures tearing at each other. Or rather, five figures tearing at one other.

Never had they seen Kafeel move so quickly. Kafeel leaned back away from one vampire as she slashed her clawed hands at his face, ducked another slashing claw from behind, and spun away from the tip of a thrusting sword. He reached out his own hand, nails now elongated into claws, and ripped out the throat of a male vampire nearly as tall as him. Before he could fall, Kafeel punched through his chest and snatched out his heart. The dying Hunter thrashed on the ground, gurgling as his lifeblood stained the white snow beneath him.

Kafeel kicked out, landing his foot in the midsection of a female, and grabbed her by her long red locks. With barely a grunt, he yanked his arm outward and sent the shrieking vampire across the clearing to land at Saaya's feet just as she finished dispatching the blond Hunter.

"What have we here?" the *dampeal* asked in that same playful tone.

Remy watched in disbelief as the fight took an impossible turn against him. These were only a pureblood male and a *skiek*. How could this be happening?

Kafeel spun and ducked, leaped and whirled. None of his enemies could lay a hand or sword on him. One of the Hunters hissed at him in the vampire tongue.

Kafeel responded by spinning away from a sword slashing at his back, and in the same motion, thrust his elbow at the speaker. The vampire's head snapped sideways and he staggered. Just as he'd completed his turn, Kafeel reached behind his back, grabbed the stunned Hunter by the arm, and hurled him into the air.

"Oh, shit!" Daniel said, seeing the vampire flying backward toward them. On pure reflex, he flipped the blade in his hand and launched it in an overhand throw. The resulting scream of pain told him that he'd hit the mark, and the vampire crashed into the snow between them, thrashing as he reached behind his back attempting to extricate the silver weapon that burned his skin. They heard a sickening, hissing sound, as though steam was seeping from the wound.

Jelani had no intention of getting anywhere near the dying vampire, so he flipped a blade in his hand and launched it into the Hunter's chest, silencing him. As soon as the vampire had gone still, he started to decay, death rushing to claim him.

"Okay, let's get the hell away from here," Daniel said. He collected their weapons and tossed Jelani his. "What are we gonna do about her?" he asked, pointing with his knife at the still moaning Melinda.

"Maybe Saaya can do something for her," Jelani said, as he cut the last of her bonds.

"You think that's wise?" Daniel asked, glancing back and forth between the limp woman and the combatants. Kafeel had killed all but two of his enemies, and Saaya seemed to be playing with the other female vampire.

"No. But she's still unconscious, so maybe after all this is done, we can do something. If not ..." Jelani shook his head, not able to speak the words. "Let's just get her and us out of here."

"You really think you can carry her all the way down?" Daniel said, helping Jelani lift her.

He slung her sideways over his shoulders. "All I can do is my best."

He'd barely taken a few steps before he heard Daniel curse.

"Shit! That fucking Hunter is looking right at us! He's coming this way!"

"COME ON NOW," Saaya said as the redheaded vampire picked herself up off the ground. "Fighting like this is so unladylike.

184

Should you not be sitting in some coven leader's lap, pleasuring him?"

The female hissed and lunged. The tiny bells of Saaya's *paayal* jingled as she avoided the attack. "I know you can do better than that," she said, smirking at the seething Hunter.

The woman leapt at Saaya again, slashing at the air as she tried to tear the half-breed to pieces. The female Hunter clearly could not fathom why this lowly half-human was able to so easily match what should have been her superior speed and dexterity.

Saaya continued to slash at the other woman, who avoided her efforts with such grace, it appeared that she was dancing around her. With an evil grin, the Hunter continued to press the attack, letting the half-breed have her fun. After another round of one-two slashes, she reached to her hip and grabbed a dagger, which she launched at the other woman. With speed that surprised even the redheaded vampire, Saaya turned her head away just in time to avoid the missile.

The redhead narrowed her crimson eyes. "Looks like I almost got you that time. You're not as fast as you think you are."

As soon as the last word left the woman's lips, Saaya was standing right in front of her. Before the Hunter could react, she slapped her across the face. The woman staggered back, making a choking sound. She reached trembling hands up as if to touch her still sideways head, a head that was turned a little further than was natural. Saaya waited until she heard the clicking and popping sound of bone repairing itself and cartilage pushing it back into place.

Finally, the woman managed to slowly turn her head back, and just as her lips drew back in a hiss, Saaya slapped her again, sending her head almost completely around. Before the vampire could fall to the ground, the *dampeal's* hand snapped out, burrowing into the other's chest. She snatched her hand back and tossed the Hunter's heart aside. The redheaded Hunter fell to the ground, death greedily claiming her lifeless body.

Saaya looked down at the grisly object and then at her bloody hand in disgust. How she hated getting her hands dirty. She looked around for Jelani and Daniel as she cleaned her hands in the snow. When she failed to locate them, she looked for Remy, and just caught sight of him as he disappeared into the woods, no doubt pursuing the two humans. She started toward them, not bothering to even glance in Kafeel's direction. Her brother was more than a match for five—she noticed four rapidly decaying bodies—one vampire. Hunter or not.

Curiosity got the better of her, and just before she entered the woods, she looked over her shoulder to see Kafeel holding the remaining Hunter aloft. He held the struggling vampire by the neck in a one-handed grip.

"Be done with him, Kafeel," she called out. "There is more."

The only audible response was the loud cracking sound of Kafeel snapping his victim's neck. He dropped the body and started walking away. Just before he reached his sister, his hand lifted over his shoulder and he snapped his fingers. The remaining vampire burst into flames.

THEY MOVED AS QUICKLY down the slope as Jelani could manage, carrying the unconscious woman over his shoulders. Daniel kept a constant eye on the woods behind him, shining his flashlight in every direction. It didn't make sense that the Hunter had not caught them yet. Even if they had been moving as fast as possible, they shouldn't have made it more than a few dozen yards at most. That guy seemed to have a propensity for playing games, so this might be another one. Daniel stopped worrying about it. They'd already survived an impossible amount of time considering the circumstances.

Jelani spared no such thoughts as he concentrated on the downward slope in front of him, carefully placing one foot in front of the other as quickly as he could. His legs nearly buckled a few times when his foot slipped on a root concealed by the snow. The sounds of fighting were beginning to drift away. Whether because the fight was over or they were putting more distance between themselves and the conflict, he didn't know.

Hopefully Saaya and Kafeel would be able to kill all those Hunters. If they were really lucky, one of the siblings would get their hands on that sadistic Hunter, Remy, and put an end to him. If Jelani could have one wish, it would be to kill the bastard himself. "How's it look back there?" he asked Daniel.

"Still nothing," came the reply. "I don't know whether to feel encouraged or terrified."

"Feel terrified," Jelani said. "It'll keep you on your toes."

"I've got a bad feeling about this."

"That's because vampires are killing each other behind us."

"No, man, I mean right now. Why hasn't that guy caught up to us yet?"

Jelani was about to respond when he heard a soft hiss behind his ear. His instincts were in sync with his reflexes, and he thrust his body outward from underneath Melinda. She dropped heavily to the ground, and Jelani immediately regretted dumping her. She rolled down the hill but stopped herself and came to her feet.

As soon as she was upright, she launched herself at Jelani and grabbed hold of him. They flew a dozen feet and were stopped by a tree. Blunt pain shot through Jelani's upper back, and stars blinked in his vision. His sore ribs gave complaint, as well.

She held him in a steely grip just under his jaw. Jelani heard Daniel sliding down the hill after them, and just as he came in to stab her in the back, Melinda kicked out, connecting her foot with his stomach. He doubled over and fell, gasping for air. Jelani's eyes flicked down to his friend, then back to Melinda's face.

A hungry red glow crept into her eyes. She turned his head sideways with her thumb, giving her a better view of his neck. She opened her mouth to reveal elongated fangs, and lowered him to the ground while maintaining that vice-like grip on his throat. Her fangs had just touched his neck, when she stopped. Suddenly, her crimson eyes were in front of his face again, and though the glowing orbs were a frightening sight, he saw a flicker of recognition there.

He forced himself to look into those inhuman eyes. "It's me, Melinda," he said in a strangled voice. "It's Jelani." She opened her mouth again, then stopped. In an instant, her hand fell away, and Jelani dropped to his knees, coughing and gasping. Behind Melinda, Daniel was just recovering. He hoped his roommate wouldn't try to kill her again. He might be able to talk their way out of this.

"Jelani?"

"Yeah, girl; it's me. You all right?"

"No," came the answer, and he felt stupid for asking. "I ... I want to kill you," she said in a tiny voice. "But I don't. It feels like my blood is on fire, and I'm hungry and thirsty at the same time." She took a step toward him and stopped. "I can smell it. I can practically hear it flowing through your body. I need it, Jelani. I *need* it!" She hissed through her teeth and turned her head away.

"Just hold on, girl. Hold on. Try to think about what you're doing."

"I can't think. It's too much. I feel like all my insides are on fire." And in an instant, she had him pinned to the tree again, her face inches from his. Her warm sweet breath clouded in his face as she gasped, struggling with herself. Jelani saw Daniel regain his feet, and he lifted a hand, signaling for his friend to hold still. Daniel looked at him as if he'd lost his mind but stopped advancing.

"Just try to think this through, Melinda. You don't want to do this."

"I don't ... I don't know if I have a choice. It's like," her voice deepened, "it's like breathing air. You just do it." She leaned in close, and Daniel took another step. "I can't help myself, baby," she whispered ever so softly in his ear. She might have been a lover, whispering words of desire in the heat of passion. "I want you, I want all of you. I can smell it in you." She looked into his eyes and the primal hunger was unmistakable.

"I can hear your heart beating so rapidly, pumping so much of what I need, baby. Don't you want me to have it?" She forced his head aside, and Daniel raised his knife, ready to drive it into her back.

"You know you've always been special to me, Melinda." Jelani was thinking fast. "Even though we couldn't be together, you know I've always cared for you. You know that, don't you?"

"You cared about me until that bitch came along." He'd managed to distract her and piss her off at the same time. Great.

"You know that's not true. I was always truthful to you. I never took advantage of you, Melinda. I would have done anything to protect you."

"Then why didn't you protect me from that thing that turned me into this?" she shrieked. "Why did you let him do this to me?"

"Why do you think I'm here?" He said. "Why do you think I climbed all the way up here and was trying to carry you back down? Because I was trying to protect you, girl."

She hesitated, and he took that moment to look into those terrifying eyes again. "If I could've stopped him, you know I would have ..." he trailed off and dropped to the ground when she released him. In less time than it took him to look up, she was gone.

Daniel was quick to his side. "Holy shit, she's fast." He offered Jelani a hand and pulled him to his feet. "For a minute there, I thought I was gonna have to jump on her."

"You might have gotten lucky, or she might have killed us both." Jelani ran a gloved hand over his face. "I can't believe what just happened." A howl sounded in the distance to their right. It was a deeper, throatier sound than any they'd heard earlier.

Their heads whipped around in the direction of the sound, then Daniel looked back at Jelani. "I know that wasn't a normal wolf."

"Hell, no, it wasn't!" Jelani said, and they half ran, half stumbled down the slope, using the trees to keep from tumbling all the way down. As they bounced from one trunk to the next, Jelani couldn't help but feel like a ball ricocheting down a pinball machine. His ribs vibrated with pain with every impact.

"Can this get any worse," Daniel huffed beside him.

"Can you think of any other mythical monsters that could show up? A dragon, maybe?"

"I could almost believe it," Daniel replied.

Another howl rent the air, followed by another. They were closer. Jelani glanced up at the dark sky and saw the half-moon in the break in the clouds. "How can they be out hunting now?" he jumped over a large root and almost fell. "It's not a full moon."

"Maybe that's another one of those myths," Daniel offered.

"I'd like to find the guy who thought up all these myths and kick him in the ass," Jelani said, using his hands to soften his impact with a tree and slip around it. Behind them, they heard heavy, raspy breathing and hard footfalls.

"I think one of those things is behind us," Daniel said.

"Keep running."

"We're like beacons out here with these flashlights," Daniel growled.

"You think we should ditch them?"

"We can see the trees."

"But not the holes in the ground," Jelani said. "We're also the only ones who can't see in the dark."

"Right."

They heard more grunting, and Jelani glanced over his shoulder. A massive four-legged monster was pounding down the slope after them. "SHIIIIIT!" he hollered, quickening his pace.

Daniel didn't need to look, he just increased his pace with Jelani. "Think we should try to climb a tree?"

"Not if you saw how big that thing was," Jelani replied. They were almost running downhill now, heedless of the fact that if they fell, they would likely tumble to their deaths.

"Was it as big as that?"

At the sound of Daniel's terrified voice, Jelani looked further down the slope ... at another giant four-legged figure tearing up the path toward them.

CHAPTER 20

J elani and Daniel fell back and slid downwards as they desperately tried to avoid the monster coming up at them. Jelani threw his hands back, scrabbling for an exposed root or branch, any handhold to stop him from practically sliding right into the jaws of the monster that was less than twenty feet away. Though the darkness of the night obscured its features, Jelani knew it could be nothing else but a werewolf.

Several feet to his left, Daniel had turned on his side, also reaching for something to stop himself with. They continued to slide, and the werewolf drew ever closer. When it was no more than a dozen feet away, it leapt into the air, and Jelani knew that he and Daniel were about to die. He turned on his side in a last desperate attempt to get out of the way, but there was nothing he could do.

The airborne monster was falling upon them when a humanoid figure bolted through the trees and slammed into the werewolf, sending it tumbling head over heels to collide with a tree. The beast was quick to its feet and shook its head, growling deep in its chest. Closer, now, Jelani got a good look. The giant wolf turned onyx-black eyes on the newcomer who, judging by his height and that cloak, Jelani guessed to be Kafeel. Its lips wrinkled back to reveal an upper and lower set of elongated fangs, along with rows of sharp, jagged teeth.

It stalked closer, moving toward the vampire. Then, to Jelani's terror, it stood up on its hind legs, closer to eight feet tall than seven. It flexed its claws open and closed as it took its time drawing nearer to Kafeel.

As carefully and slowly as he dared, Jelani quietly scooted upward, away from the face-off. He backed into a tree, and pulled himself around to hide behind it. A couple of dozen feet to his left, he saw Daniel lying flat on the ground, a few feet behind Kafeel. His heart nearly stopped when he saw his friend wasn't moving, but then Daniel's head turned toward him, and Jelani knew he was trying to remain unnoticed during this new encounter. Jelani was afraid to hope they might make it out of this alive.

The werewolf barked at Kafeel, who stood still as a statue, waiting. Jelani reached behind his back, and gripped the hilt of his foot-long knife. It felt like a toothpick in his hands compared to the giant monster with its snapping jaws closing in on Kafeel. His grip tightened. Toothpick or not, it was silver. If worse came to worse, he knew they couldn't outrun that thing, so he would at least make a fight of it before he died.

The werewolf charged, barking a spitting, then leaped the last dozen feet at Kafeel. Jelani watched as he stood there, motionless. Then, just as the beast was nearly on top of him, Kafeel side-stepped and punched it in the side. There was yelp that seemed hugely inappropriate, coming from that thing, then it turned and growled, swinging a claw out that Kafeel easily ducked.

Again, he punched the wolf in the side, then in the midsection. It shrugged off the heavy blows and lunged forward, snapping its jaws at his face. Kafeel leaned away and slapped it on the side of the head, causing it to stumble sideways. That split second of vulnerability was all he needed, and Kafeel was instantly beside the monster. With a right-handed roundhouse punch, Kafeel knocked the wolf from its feet. It did a full horizontal turn in the air before falling heavily to the ground, where it slid down the slope.

As it slid away, Jelani could hear the sickening popping sound of bone and cartilage reforming and snapping into place as the lycan reverted to its human form. He didn't know whether it was dead or unconscious, but it was no longer a threat.

"There will be more." Jelani's attention was drawn from the now human lycan male to Kafeel. The tall, dark-skinned vampire was looking directly at him.

"Gotcha," he replied, stepping from behind the tree. He remembered the other werewolf that had been chasing them earlier. "There was one—"

"It's gone," Kafeel cut him off.

Jelani didn't want to think what the towering man had done to the other monster, and instead looked over and saw Daniel, already having regained his feet. "You all right?"

"I will be once we're out of here," his roommate answered.

"Thanks, man," Jelani said, but when he looked back to where Kafeel had been, there was only an empty space. "Dude's fast," Jelani muttered under his breath.

They started down again, giving the unconscious naked man a wide berth. After a few minutes, Daniel asked, "Do you think that guy's still out here somewhere?"

"I don't know," Jelani said, climbing over another fallen tree. "It might be safe to say that Saaya and Mr. Congeniality are still lurking around here, so he might have just booked it."

"Hey, chill with the sarcasm!" Daniel hissed. "You know they can hear everything."

Jelani didn't argue.

Another howl sounded in the distance.

"I'm really starting to think we're going to die," Daniel said.

"You didn't think so before?"

"That was before we were almost eaten."

"Well, we're still breathing, so let's get out of this mess."

They were silent for the rest of their descent. Finally, after what seemed like the rest of the night had gone by, they reached the base of the mountain and made their way through the last half-mile of woods before coming into the open. The moon was less than half visible through the occasional breaks in the drifting clouds.

After taking a few minutes to get his bearings, Daniel pointed west. "My car is that way, about a mile."

"Then let's get going."

They set off at a jog, ignoring the complaining muscles in their legs and arms. They occasionally encountered the random jogger or couple out for a night stroll. They glanced at each other. If only these people knew what was out there in the woods, less than a few miles away.

When they reached Daniel's Lexus, they hopped in and he turned on the car and threw it in reverse. He backed out, then threw it in drive, and the tires screeched as the car took off.

"I really thought we were dead," Daniel said. "Did you see how big that thing was? It was huge!"

"Yeah," Jelani said. "It was big enough on all fours, but when it stood up?" He shook his head. "I'll be great if I never see anything like that again." He looked out the window, watching the scenery pass by in a blur. "Poor Melinda," he finally said. "There were several ways I imagined all this might play out, but her being turned into a vampire wasn't one of them."

Daniel glanced at him a couple times. "Don't go blaming your-self about this. You did the best you could."

"Which isn't looking like it's enough," Jelani said. "We've got to get proactive about this, Daniel. He's working his way through people we care about, and he's getting closer and closer to the people we care most about. First your friend at EA, now Melinda.

We need to figure out how to put this guy down before he gets to—"

"Don't even say it." Daniel held up a hand to stop him. "Don't finish that thought. I know what you're saying, but I don't want to hear it." A few minutes passed. "So what do you have in mind?"

"Maybe if we can get Saaya to work together with us, we might figure out a way to lure him out."

"It would have been nice if Saaya and her brother could have just killed the guy a long time ago."

"Actually," Jelani said, "they did try. Saaya told me that this guy, Remy, is pretty elusive. She said where the other Hunter, Yako, was highly skilled and more dangerous and all, Remy is dangerous in a sly way, like a fox. They haven't been able to get the drop on him. In fact, tonight was probably the first time they've gotten this close to him."

"That doesn't make our prospects sound any better," Daniel said. They passed the last few houses in the residential area at the base of the mountain, and Daniel turned left on Highland Boulevard, making his way to Marine Drive.

"I'll feel better when we've crossed the bridge," Jelani said, referring to the Lion's Gate Bridge that separated North Vancouver from downtown.

"I'll feel better when it's daylight," Daniel replied.

"Can't disagree with that. I hope—"

A heavy weight crashed on top of the car and dented it inward. The car swerved, but Daniel quickly regained control. "Son of a bitch!" he swore, looking up at the inward dent in the roof of his car. Jelani thought fast. Reflectively flinching away from the impact, he reached under the seat and pulled out his knife.

They heard a pounding sound, and then metal being ripped apart. Daniel swerved left and right, trying to dislodge the attacker.

"Come on now," they heard Remy's voice from outside. "You can do at least a little better than that!"

Daniel slammed on the brakes, then hit the accelerator again.

Jelani's eyes were fixed on the roof, knife ready. The pounding and ripping continued, and Daniel swerved again in an attempt to distract their attacker. When they had reached the busier part of the street, he began weaving in and out of traffic, sideswiping a pickup truck, then swerving away. All around them, horns blared and cars parted to get out of the way.

They reached the end of the street, and Daniel turned right at Marine Drive in a sideways drift.

"Impressive," Remy yelled from outside. "It's gonna be a shame to have to rip your throat out, you know."

The pounding resumed, and then a large portion of the roof tore out, and a hand reached in at Daniel. But Jelani was fast; he slashed his knife out and scored a cut along the vampire's forearm. They heard a cry of pain and the hand recoiled.

Daniel continued to swerve, but it did little good. Not knowing what else to do, he turned left at the bridge. The sound of screeching tires and the smell of burning rubber assaulted them, and through the hole in the ceiling, Jelani caught a glimpse of Remy's hand. The veins were not only visible, but looked to actually be moving beneath his skin.

"You know you two aren't going home tonight, right?" He seemed to be having fun with this.

"Just stick your hand in again," Jelani answered.

"Oooh. The prey has a little spunk in him. Okay. I'm game." The hand did indeed reach in again, but this time, it was Remy who was faster. First he reached in and dealt Jelani a painful slap to the shoulder, knocking him sideways. His head hit the window and stars flickered in and out of his vision. Next, the hand reached over and elongated claws bit into Daniel's right shoulder.

Daniel screamed and swerved again. Remy only laughed, not the slightest bit off balance. "How about some fun?" He pulled his nails out of Daniel's shoulder, then grabbed hold of the steering wheel and forced it left. The car leaned on its right tires, and went left, into oncoming traffic. Howling horns filled their ears and bright lights blinded them.

Daniel tried to fumble for the knife under his seat, but the wildly turning car kept him off balance. "Woohoo!" Remy yelled, and he pulled at the wheel again. "How about a swim, guys?"

Daniel's gaze shot up ahead at the line of orange construction cones, and he had a brief moment to look at the equally horrified expression on Jelani's wide-eyed face before he was thrown right, as the car swerved left. Daniel's foot went for the break.

"Oh, no, you don't!" Remy said in a playful tone. He slipped in through the gaping hole and clamped his hand on Daniel's leg, forcing it over the accelerator, then down.

The engine roared, and the car blasted through the concrete barrier, across the bike lane, and burst through the rail. "Woooooohooooooo!" Remy shouted, laughing as the car and bits of debris plummeted toward the water below.

Jelani and Daniel screamed, unable to do anything but watch as the ocean rushed up to meet them. Suddenly, their seat belts were ripped away, and the vampire clamped down on Jelani's arm and hauled him out of the car, which was turning sideways in the air. Daniel managed to get his wits about him and grabbed hold of the hole in the roof. He started to pull himself out, but the car continued to turn, and he found himself falling out instead.

"Don't worry," Remy said playfully. "The impact won't hurt. I'll make sure you're dead before we hit the—" his words were cut short by the slash of Jelani's silver knife across his throat. Remy gasped and released him to clamp a hand to his throat.

Jelani tucked his knees in and kicked the vampire away from him. Turning over and over, he caught a glimpse of Daniel struggling around the side of the car just as it hit in an eruption of water. Jelani only had a second to hope for the best for his friend, as he barely got his feet under him before he hit the water.

The shock of the impact and the cold of the water nearly

blasted all the air from his lungs. Jelani opened his eyes, ignoring the burn of the salt water and searched for Daniel. A short distance away, he could barely make out the headlights of the sinking Lexus, surrounded by bubbles and on its way to the bottom of the ocean. Daniel was nowhere to be seen, and Jelani was running out of air, so he forced his mind to calm, and swam for the surface.

He breached with a big intake of sweet air, and looked around. A few dozen feet away there was a crimson stain in the water, likely from where Remy's wound had bled out.

"Jelani!"

He turned this way and that, searching until he finally spotted Daniel, who was swimming toward him. Once Daniel reached him, he only stopped long enough to tell Jelani to keep going.

"C'mon," he gasped. "He's not that far away. His neck is cut and he was sinking with the car when I saw him, but his eyes snapped open and he looked right at me! I'm guessing you cut him somehow. He looked really pissed off!"

Jelani didn't say anything. He turned, and they threw all their strength into swimming for the shore. Flashlights shone on the area where the car had hit the water, and people screamed down from the bridge. Jelani and Daniel dipped below the surface and swam as quickly as they could, coming up for air and submerging again. While help would have been nice, they needed time to figure out what to do about all this.

They had barely made it halfway across the bridge when the car went over, so it was a long swim. Daniel, being the stronger swimmer of the two, paced himself with Jelani, who was beginning to labor.

"Come on, bro," Daniel said. "Not much farther."

"Told you not … to call me bro," Jelani coughed.

Once they were under the bridge, they figured they wouldn't be seen, so they swam above the surface. They made faster progress now, swimming with the ripples of the ocean as they continued toward land, which seemed mockingly close, yet far away. Several times Jelani was tempted to rest and float on his back, but the thought of Remy swimming after them, and the possibility of a shark or transient male orca taking an interest in them gave him the extra strength he needed. *When did my life become a series of attempts at not being eaten?*

After what seemed like hours, they finally reached the shore. Following Daniel's lead, they came to the rocks on the other side of the bridge.

When the water became shallow, they crept over the rocks and skulked alongside the Stanley Park seawall until it was low enough for them to climb a boulder and get on the jogging lane.

"You swim so slow, I can't believe we made it," Daniel said.

"Yeah, well, don't jinx it," Jelani replied, shivering. "Meet me on the track and we'll talk about slow."

"I'd love to if we survive this."

"You want to take a chance and run through the middle of the park? No one will see us."

"Where were you when all this mess first started?" Daniel reminded.

"I get your point, but when all this hits the news, and you know it will, it'll be easy to remember a Chinese guy and a black dude, soaking wet and jogging around Stanley Park."

"Not too many people jog around the park at night," Daniel argued, "and it's dark anyway. If someone sees us, it'll be too dark for them to make out that we're wet if we blow past them fast enough." He also went through a fit of shaking.

"Maybe," Jelani replied. Cold and wet was a bad combination. They had to get moving.

"I like our chances better out here than in the trees where he could take us out easily," Daniel said.

"Then let's do it your way." Jelani started off. "I'm freezing. We can work up some body heat at least."

They took the path away from the bridge, heading in the direction of English Bay. It was farther away from home, but it was also farther away from the scene of the accident. Jelani felt a pang of paranoia when he realized that his knife was likely at the bottom of the ocean. He pulled out his phone and touched the screen. It came on, showing the manufacturer's logo, then a line flashed across the center of the screen and it went black.

"Looks like my phone is done," Jelani huffed.

"Use one of the girls' blow dryer when we get home, then seal it in a bag of uncooked rice."

Jelani smirked at Daniel. "Oh, yeah?"

"You make a joke about rice and Chinese, and I'll slap some barbeque sauce on you and drag you back to that vampire," Daniel said. Despite the situation, Jelani laughed.

They rounded another corner, just as a solitary figure came running in toward them. Before they could react, he launched himself at them. With inhuman strength, the man grabbed them by the neck lifted them off their feet. Jelani and Daniel grabbed hold of his wrists to give some support to their necks.

"Remy said you might be slippery little mice." The voice might have come from a snake. "And so the game ends ..."

Another figure glided out of the trees to the left and landed behind him. Quiet as this new person was, the vampire heard, and dropped the two humans. He spun with a backhanded slash with his elongated nails.

Jelani heard Saaya's telltale snicker, and relief washed over him. The vampire slashed at her so viciously, Jelani glanced at Daniel, wondering if they should try to help. But what could they do? Those two were moving almost too fast for them to follow.

"That's about enough," Saaya said, and grabbed the other vampire's arm. With a sickening crunch, she twisted his forearm in her iron grip, grinding the bones to dust. When the vampire opened his mouth in a silent cry of pain, she drew her hand back and slammed it through his chest. Jelani and Daniel flinched at the sight, and the squishing sound that was no doubt the unfortunate vampire's heart being crushed.

He crumpled to the ground, and seconds later his body started rapidly decaying. Jelani and Daniel looked from the decaying corpse to the *dampeal* standing in front of them. They backed up a step, seeing the lavender glow of her eyes and the blood dripping from her tiny hand. She noticed their hesitation and smiled.

"I know, boys. It's very unladylike and off-putting to see a girl with a bloody hand like this, but it was either that, or watch you two beautiful men be ripped to pieces."

Daniel glanced over his shoulder as if expecting more monsters to appear out of the darkness. "Oh, believe me. Right now, the last thing we're worried about is you being ladylike."

Saaya grinned at him, then raised her hand and examined it. "I hate getting dirty like this." She looked over the seawall at the water below. "You'll have to excuse me for a moment."

Before they could say a word, she was over the side, dropping the fifteen feet to land on the rocks below. They watched her gracefully hop from rock to rock until she made it to the water. She crouched and dipped her hands into the water, scrubbing her left hand clean. A few moments later, she rose and hopped back to the seawall, jumping the fifteen feet back up to them as if it were nothing.

"Man, what I wouldn't give to be able to do that," Jelani said.

"Careful what you wish for, *jaan*," Saaya replied. She turned and started away, the tiny *paayal* around her ankles tinkling with every step.

"You think maybe we should move a little faster?" Daniel said as they fell into step beside her.

"No. You'll not have any more trouble, this night."

"Oh?" Jelani said. He wrapped his arms around his torso but still shivered. "A group of vampires, Remy, a couple werewolves, and another vampire right here, and you don't think someone else might come around?"

"The wolves have been persuaded to leave off of hunting you."

"How many of those things were out there?" Daniel asked.

"Oh, six or seven," Saaya replied casually. "Actually, they may have saved you."

"I thought that was your job," Jelani said, trying to tone down the sourness in his voice.

"Ah, love. Do not be angry with me. Kafeel and I were waylaid by another five Hunters while Remy pursued you. I give him credit. He expected us to be near and planned for it. If that lycan pack hadn't come along and caught your scent mingled with the vampires, things might have ended differently."

They passed the public pool along the seawall, still dry since it was early spring. A family of raccoons scampered across their path from the beach into the trees.

"You said the werewolves were persuaded?" Daniel asked.

"Mm-hm. After Kafeel had his little scruff with Ryss, back there, the others took it to be a fight and attacked every vampire in sight. Lycans can be impulsive."

"So you and Kafeel stepped back and let the werewolves do the work?" Daniel surmised.

"Yes and no," Saaya answered. "We avoided the lycans and helped them decimate the Hunters while making our way to you. What we hadn't counted on was how swiftly they killed all but two of them: Remy and another."

"So that guy you killed back there was the other one that got away?" Jelani asked.

"Actually, no. As I said, Remy planned well. He had an entire force of Hunters to aid him against Kafeel and myself, but also had more to stay on the other side of the bridge just in case."

"So there are more of them," Daniel said, glancing around. Normally, the open grassy mounds and large trees were beautiful even at night, but now they looked like hiding places for living nightmares.

"There were," Saaya admitted. "But I dispatched two more

before that third one where I found you. I counted another two, but they fled. I doubt you'll be bothered for the rest of the night."

"Saaya. We've got a big problem," Jelani said. "Daniel's car is beyond destroyed, and once they bring it out of the water, the police are gonna trace it back to him."

"I care little about your car, handsome boy." She fluttered her eyelashes at him. Despite everything, Daniel managed to blush. "But I wouldn't worry about the police. The reason you've never heard of a vampire before now is because they are interwoven in your societies." She saw the horror on their faces and giggled.

"Oh, yes. There are vampires in every facet of your society. Politics, law enforcement, science, art. There are some professions that are less desirable than others, such as those that require daytime hours, but you get my point. The coven will likely reach out to their contacts in the police department and find a way to explain this all away."

"Wouldn't it make more sense for them to have the police after us?" Jelani reasoned. "Maybe have them shoot first and ask questions later?"

"Not necessarily," Saaya responded. "Killing you in such an official manner would lead to more inquiries and investigation than handling this as an accident."

"Well, I guess some good comes out of this, however little or indirect."

They were nearly to Jelani and Daniel's condo by then. Having forgotten the cold during the night's events, they were starting to shiver again in their damp clothes. Saaya looked them both up and down and *tsked*. "Foolish boys swimming in the cold night. I have a mind of taking you home right now, stripping those clothes off you and sending you to the shower." Jelani and Daniel glanced at each other, the latter's mouth twitching.

"Um—"

"I'm just toying with you, silly boy. I know your little human girl is waiting for you at home, no doubt biting at her little finger-nails awaiting your arrival."

"You're so considerate," Daniel responded dryly.

"Your heart still beats, does it not?"

"Good point. And thanks, by the way."

She reached up and patted him on the cheek. "Such a polite one, you are. A shame you're promised to that child up there." Saaya looked up to the tenth floor of their building.

"Um, thanks. I think I'm flattered."

Saaya grinned at him as if she wanted to pat him on the head, then addressed them both. "There is more here than we know, but I have an idea. It makes little sense to pull a Hunter of Yako's skill and replace him with one who is less capable, conniving though he may be. There is something going on in the coven, and I believe this new Hunter, Remy, stands to gain in some way if he manages to kill you. I expect he may become more aggressive."

"Vampire politics?" Jelani said. "Is there no species that's free of it?"

"Maybe those werewolves," Daniel offered, opening the front door for Saaya, who stepped in.

"The wolves have their own form of politics, though more simple."

Jelani noted the subtle derision in her tone. "I've always found that if it's not simple to understand, you're not doing it right."

"Really?" Saaya replied. "How so?"

"To me, it just stands to reason that it you truly understand something, you should be able to structure or explain it in as simple a manner as possible. Think about—" He trailed off when Daniel rested a hand on his shoulder.

"She's playing with you, dude. Do you really think she doesn't know all this already? Or care?"

Jelani looked at Saaya, who smiled at him as though he were dull-witted. "Right," he said. "Nice to know despite everything, you manage to hold on to that shining sense of humor, Saaya."

She placed her hands on his chest and rose up to her toes. Her lips brushed his ear as she whispered, "Walk in the light."

When she backed away, Jelani thought he might fall over. "M'kay," he mumbled. She strode gracefully to the door, and Jelani found he was unable to avoid admiring the twitch of her hips as she drifted away.

She glanced over her shoulder at him, then down at herself and back up at him again. "Careful, *jaan*. You wouldn't want to tempt me." A glimmer passed over her eyes, and her voice floated in the air to caress his ears.

Once she was out the door, Daniel slapped him on the back. "You done, or should I give you some alone time?"

"All right, all right," Jelani said. "You don't know what it's like, dude. She can say things in a way that seems like the words just, I dunno, just caress your mind, or something."

"It's called dazzling, buddy. I suspect if she were ever planning to kill you, she would just hold you entranced and then have her way."

"And there would be nothing I could do," Jelani agreed.

"You're weak," Daniel said, pressing the button for the elevator. The soft *ding* sounded, followed by the doors opening.

"Yeah, you say that," Jelani said, "but it's not always pleasant. I told you what that guy Yako did to me. He commanded me to stop, and I did. It's hard to explain, but it was like his words just forced every part of my being to cooperate. It was impossible to move, regardless of the fact that a part of my brain was screaming at my body to run."

The elevator stopped on the tenth floor and they exited, turning left and walking down the hall to their condo. "You know Wen is going to be freaked out, right?"

Daniel sighed. "I wonder if the news has already covered the accident."

"Probably," Jelani said.

Daniel shrugged. "Well at least we're alive."

"I'm sorry about your car, man." Jelani squeezed Daniel's shoulder. "I'll help you replace it."

"It's not your fault," Daniel said. "We've been lucky that nothing worse has happened until recently."

"Yeah. Still, it would make me feel better if I help you replace it."

"Maybe later," Daniel said. "I'm more worried about living."

CHAPTER 21

A knock on the door pulled Jelani from dark thoughts. "Come in," he said, and the door opened to admit a hesitant Alisha.

"I figured you'd want some time alone, but I also figured I'd better check up on you."

"I'm good," he lied.

She crossed the room and stood next to the bed. After a moment, he slid aside and she sat down next to him. "You tell the truth way too much to be good at lying," she said.

"Or maybe I lie so much that the truth seems insincere."

She smiled at him. "Sure." They sat in silence for a while. Alisha lay a hand on Jelani's leg and let her head fall back against the wall. "I'm sorry about your friend," she finally said. "I really am."

"Thanks. Me, too. I'm not gonna lie. It bothers me a lot that this happened to her because of me, whether indirectly or not. This whole thing has me in a really bad place right now."

"I know." She didn't try to say anything to make him feel better, or tell him that everything would be all right. She knew him well enough that those would be the wrong things to say. Instead, she asked him the right question. "What are you going to do about it?"

Jelani was silent for a while as he pondered the question. What would he do? What could he do? How could he strike against Remy, who was not only a vampire, but a Hunter on top of it? He looked at his bare hands. Hands that would be considered fairly strong by human standards, but pathetically inadequate under these circumstances.

"Put him down before this gets any worse."

"You think she'll help you?"

Of course Alisha was referring to Saaya. The exotic woman had always been there to when he needed her the most. As the situation grew messier, she'd become more and more involved. Perhaps she was committed to see this all the way through?

"She might," he answered. "Doesn't really matter if she does or doesn't. "I need to figure out how to put a stop to this before that guy works his way to you and Wen." She started to speak, but he turned and looked at her. "I can't promise that everything will be okay, or that this guy won't get to you. But what I do promise is that if he does get to you, it'll be because I'm already dead. I will never let anything happen to you as long as I'm alive, Alisha. You understand?"

She looked back into those eyes and saw that he meant every word, that he would die protecting her. She looked at him and knew this was not the typical guy declaring he would protect a woman as if she was a damsel in distress. He had accepted that the vampire would come for them all because of him, and that he would do whatever it took to make it right. Whether he was right or wrong to blame himself, he would do what he had to do.

"I understand, baby." And then she kissed him. It was a gentle, tender kiss. When they pulled away, Jelani studied her eyes. They had kissed before, but this was different. Those hazel eyes were not playful or teasing. They were hungry. She licked her lips. Whether unconsciously or intentional, the action drew his attention to her round, soft lips. Lips that he desperately wanted to kiss again.

He forced himself to look back into her eyes, and she leaned in and kissed him again, then again, and again; each kiss longer and deeper than before. Her hand touched his cheek, and his heart leapt. In so many ways, a kiss and a woman's gentle hand on his cheek was more sensual than the act of sex itself. Not that he wished for it to stop there.

She squeezed his leg and leaned closer into him, pressing her body into his. He slid down on his back and she climbed on top of him. Her hair fell down to cover both their faces so that it was just the two of them in their own private canopy, shielded from the rest of the world. Her hips fell against his, and she sank into him, kissing his lips, his forehead, his cheeks and neck. She lifted his shirt and gently kissed his torso while his hands explored her body.

Then her lips found his again. He let out a gasp when her fingernails slid up and down his bare skin. Jelani forced himself to remain under control as he slid her top over her head. She sat up, straddling him and waiting patiently while his eyes explored her tiny waist, the subtle impression of her stomach muscles every time she exhaled. Then his eyes rose above her stomach, and she smirked at him.

"You admiring the details of my bra?" she whispered.

"Yes," he said, and she laughed softly, grabbing his hand and guiding it up her waist, stopping it just under her left breast.

"Should I leave it on, then?"

"No."

His eyes devoured the smile on those beautiful lips as she reached behind her back and released the hooks of her bra. And then it fell onto his bare chest. He lay there, admiring the shape of her slightly small yet full breasts, half a shade lighter than the rest of her skin. His hand slid up her stomach and the middle of her now heaving chest, and then his other hand came up, exploring every curve.

She arched her back and his body responded when her hips rocked forward. She let out a tiny sound of pleasure and arched an eyebrow at him, her lips parted in a hungry smile.

"Found something you want?" he whispered.

"Yes."

SAAYA SHIFTED AND SQUIRMED, her body tangled in the sheets of her bed. Her mouth opened in a sigh of ecstasy, revealing her elongated fangs. Her back arched and her hips thrust upward. She clenched the sheets in a grip that could crush concrete. Her nails extended, ripping and tearing the fabric. Damn that bloody human! He was making love to that female!

She knew it was not Jelani to blame, but herself. She felt another wave of pleasure, and her back arched again, only the back of her head, her buttocks, and the tips of her toes touching the bed. So desperate had she been to taste his blood, that she'd punctured that bruise she'd put on his shoulder when she had knocked him away from her on the couch, some time ago. True, she had taken away the swelling from the bruise as promised, but she had also sampled his blood. It had been sweet and delicious, and she had since formed a connection with him that the human male had been oblivious of.

It had been so long since she had formed a blood connection with another, that she'd forgotten the consequences, such as what she was experiencing now. With even just a small bit of his blood in her, she experienced all of the passion and lovemaking without the physical passion and lovemaking. Jelani was in his home, merging with that girl over and over and over again, while Saaya squirmed and writhed in her bed, doing her best not to rip it to pieces and destroy her house. Such passion! Such *stamina*! She wanted him. She wanted him right then and there. Her mouth flew open and she squeaked.

"Stop it. Stop it!" she breathed. Her hands went to her breasts and she forced them away. How long could they keep this up? How long had they been at it? She had first felt his blood quickening in her while she was still near his building. Kafeel had known. He'd lifted an eyebrow at her and told her to go. And she went. He was right. She had to put some distance between herself and the two of them or she might have been overwhelmed and broken into his room and ripped them both apart.

She'd barely staggered through the door of her condo when they had taken each other in earnest. In the midst of her sexual delirium, she had to admit that Jelani and the girl fit well together. She met every motion, every thrust, with a twitch of her hips here, a rocking of her hips there, a squeeze of the thighs at just the right movement every time.

Saaya rolled back and forth on the bed, then, flat on her back, she dug her nails into the mattress at either side of her body, holding herself down. They were almost done; they had to be. She quivered as spasms of pleasure coursed through her body. Her breath came in hoarse grunts, then she gasped. Her back arched again, and her head and feet were the only part of her touching the bed, besides her hands, that still dug into the mattress. Her lavender eyes flew open and a thin piercing scream seeped from her throat. The distant pained moan of dogs in the nearby vicinity preceded the shattering of hers and several other windows in her building and some next door and across the street.

There was a thick, tearing sound, and her hands flew out at her sides, ripping out two large chunks of the mattress. She fell limp, lying on her back. Her bright eyes smoldered with spent passion.

For a while, she lay on the bed, chest heaving. Her lidded eyes stared at the ceiling, heedless of the broken glass carpeting the floor and some of the bed. After some time, her breathing finally slowed. Saaya closed her eyes for a while, then opened them and sat up. She looked around at the glass-strewn floor and the destroyed bed. Cold night air drifted into the room and caressed her skin, still sensitive from indirect pleasure.

She sighed. "That was interesting." She closed her eyes again, and lay still for a long time.

"It's getting early, brother," she said, opening her eyes to see Kafeel standing just inside the broken window. Despite the glass on the hardwood floor, he hadn't made a sound. That didn't mean she couldn't feel her older brother whenever he was near. A blood connection of a different sort. "Are you not planning to sleep through most of the day?"

"I found her," he said.

She sighed. Kafeel referred to Jelani's other female acquaintance. It was a shame the girl had been pulled into this, but there were worse fates. She could be dead, after all.

"What of her?"

"He has her."

Saaya looked at him uncertainly. "He can have her anytime he wishes, Kafeel. You know that. He has her blood, and she is bound to him, since he is her re-creator ..." she stopped, Kafeel's words taking root. "He's planning to use that girl to get to Jelani," she reasoned.

"There's more," he said.

Saaya looked at him and sighed again. Whether he was talking about the weather, or the end of the world, his tone was always the same. "And what might that be, loving brother?"

"The wolves."

CHAPTER 22

Hunter's Moon. Humans referred to it as a blood moon, when every so many generations the moon would shine a brilliant reddish color in the night sky. To vampires, the moon also shone brilliantly, but it was orange. During a Hunter's Moon cycle, the thirst became nearly undeniable in all but the oldest and most disciplined of them. Every existing Hunter was ordered to patrol the night and ensure that chaos did not erupt in the human population as a result of the undisciplined *shaquora*, in many cases driven mad by bloodlust.

Even most purebloods were subject to the maddening blood thirst that the orange orb in the sky caused. In ancient times, it had been called the Moon of the Hunter, then the Lunar Hunt, until finally it had come to have its current name: Hunter's Moon.

Darren, his unlikely lycan ally, and the closest anyone other than Mariska could come to calling Yako a friend, had teased that in all their snobbery, vampires were just as susceptible to the moon as was his own species. As he knelt at the edge of the plateau, Yako found he couldn't dispute the lycan's logic.

Nine vampires knelt atop a hill overlooking the nearby woods.

Yako had been ordered to assemble a team of nine Hunters including himself, and so he had.

Nine Hunters.

Of the other eight, he trusted one implicitly. On his left, Mariska peered into the dark forest. Though vampires as a whole could remain still indefinitely, her level of focus and patience rivaled his own. She could remain here for hours, staring into the woods below without moving.

Of those eight Hunters, there was one that he trusted well enough. On his right, Nikko frowned in the direction of the distant trees. Yako could tell he was spoiling for a fight, anxious for some kind of action to offset the failure of their mission in Vancouver and the subsequent loss of Steja. Yako didn't doubt the other's loyalty, but he doubted his level of control, and that could be troubling.

Of those eight Hunters, six he trusted not at all.

"They know we're coming." It was Reed who'd spoken. The statement brought to light his level of experience being the least of the group. Only a stupid lycan would believe the Hunters would not come for them during a Hunter's Moon cycle, if only to ensure they had their pack under control.

"Lucky for Eldest Hunter that Massius insisted he bring you along, eh, kid?" Barakus teased. "If we didn't have you to state the obvious, this might get boring."

Reed narrowed his eyes at the large Hunter, and the corner of Yako's mouth twitched. Reed's threatening glare practically shattered off of Barakus's massive frame. Although size was not necessarily a major factor in a conflict, Barakus—who was by far the largest of the group—would tear the smaller Hunter apart. Whether chosen by himself or Massius, Yako had taken careful measure of every member of his group. He gauged Barakus to be the strongest, while Reed was inadequately skilled for this mission, but possessed uncanny speed.

Then there was Lydia, a stocky, flame-haired woman with giant freckles and thick shoulders. She was by and large shaped like a woman, just a large one, whose strength was second only to Barakus in this team. Yako had selected her immediately. There was something in her eyes that spoke of loyalty and honor that Yako had recognized.

Ratrik and Korck were another matter. The two kept stealing glances at him and everyone else in the group whenever they thought he wasn't looking. Of the six that he didn't trust, he trusted those two even less.

And however much he didn't trust Ratrik and Korck, he trusted the one named Mikelroy the least. The vampire had volunteered to join the team, and had been insistent that he knew the lay of the land better than any, and that his knowledge would prove invaluable should they come to blows with the lycans.

Since his inclusion, Mikelroy had made a constant effort to befriend Yako. The more he tried to show his loyalty and devotion to the mission, the less Yako trusted him.

"What course of action, Eldest Hunter?" Even the sound of his voice made Yako want to drive his sword through Mikelroy's heart.

In answer, the Eldest Hunter stood and stepped from the edge, falling the sixty feet to the ground and sprinting silently across the grassy field. The others landed just as silently and were behind him. Yako's hand was over his shoulder, hovering over the hilt of his sword as he glanced left and right for any signs of trouble.

Behind him, he heard the sounds of automatic weapons being drawn. At first, all remained quiet as they sped across the moonlit field. Then Yako heard the first thuds of the heavy footfalls of lycans in their lupine forms. Seconds later, three giant wolves burst through the wall of trees and came running toward them. Yako peered across the several dozen feet between them, directly into the lead wolf's black eyes, and saw that there would be no reasoning with it. This one had no intention of treating with him.

The wolves came at them straight, and Yako slid down to one

knee, bringing his sword to bear and slashing it downward from right to left. He scored a deep gash in the werewolf's torso that sizzled its fur and flesh, then followed through as he passed the other two lycans, rolling back to his feet and trusting that the agonized sounds of the remaining wolves told of their deaths.

Yako hadn't wanted the night to go this way, but there was nothing for it. The pack that had—according to Mikelroy—attacked and slaughtered a group of thirty local humans, frequented these woods. Yako wished Darren was here. His lycan friend might have mediated the situation. For whatever reason, Darren had chosen to return to North America himself, despite having a trusted second in command to lead the pack in his absence.

They dashed headlong into the woods, past the ambush that had been waiting for them. Yako dove into a roll and brought his sword over and down, severing the head of a wolf that had lunged out of the brush from the side. Its head hit the ground with a heavy thud, jaws half open.

Behind him, the sounds of roaring and howling, growling and hissing filled the air. A wolf appeared in front of him, and Mariska glided over his shoulder and stabbed her two silver knives down into the top of its head. She turned and braced her feet on the back of its neck, pushed off while extricating the knives, and glided away in a backward somersault. Mid-somersault, she drew a semi-automatic handgun and shot it in the back. The werewolf was dead before her feet touched the ground, and she darted off into the trees.

A scream rent the air, followed by a curse from Korck. Silencer-muffled gunfire mingled with the sound of snapping jaws and roaring, growling monsters.

Yako dove aside just as a smaller werewolf dropped out of a tree and landed where he'd stood a second earlier. Another lycan lunged out of the darkness of the woods to his left, and would have bitten his head from his shoulders had he been any other Hunter. But Yako was Eldest Hunter.

He launched himself forward under the snapping jaws, at the same time drawing a silver dagger, and driving it into the monster's neck. It jerked back, gurgling, and Yako brought his sword around, disemboweling his enemy. He turned back to his left and drove his sword through the chin and out the top of the head of the first lycan, holding it upright for a second before yanking the weapon free. By the time the dead wolf started to revert to its human form, the Eldest Hunter was already gone.

As suddenly as the assault had started, it ended, and Yako called for the Hunters to regroup.

"We lost Korck, Ratrik is dead, and Reed is wounded," Mikelroy said, coming up beside Yako.

The Eldest Hunter didn't respond, but instead turned to the waiting Mariska, who was still scanning the trees. "Report, Second," he said, sending what he hoped to be a direct message to Mikelroy that only Mariska was to give a report directly.

"It is as he says, Eldest. Ratrik is dead, and Reed has lost a lot of blood."

Yako narrowed his eyes over his shoulder at the younger vampire, who was holding his right arm. A large crimson splotch stained his shirt from where he'd lost a good deal of blood before the wound sealed. That one was a sacrifice, whether he knew it or not. "As Eldest Hunter, you are responsible for the lives of your team," Massius had said. "Then do not place inexperienced Hunters in my care," Yako had argued.

"How else would our warriors gain this precious experience if not in the field?" Massius had countered. Oh, how Yako would have liked to further widen that jackal grin with his sword. "Reed is a newly appointed Hunter. Who better to learn from than the most capable Eldest Hunter Yako, hmm?"

Yako looked away in disgust. It wasn't Reed's fault, but life wasn't fair, and he was Yako's problem at the moment. "You!" he pointed at the injured Hunter. "With me, now!"

Reed gathered himself and moved to face him.

Yako studied the boy's face. How old was this child? Twenty? Thirty years old? Hardly old enough for a normal lycan hunt, but on Hunter's Moon? Ridiculous. He looked into the boy's eyes. He was shaken. A shaken enemy had one foot in death's door. This one had little hope.

He surveyed the rest of the team. Barakus sported several slashes on his torso and legs, and his long red hair had been cut loose from its tie. Aside from those visible signs of injury, the big Hunter was fine. Korck reappeared and stood off to one side, glancing at the trees and everyone else. That one had a conniving look that made Yako wary. He wondered what the diminutive vampire would do now that his friend had been killed.

Yako looked at Lydia who held a double-sided axe in each hand. The big woman looked no worse for wear than Barakus, and seemed no less concerned. Mikelroy sported a few cuts to his clothes where Yako guessed there were supposed to be wounds he'd suffered during the conflict. He didn't believe it for a second. Yako didn't know what standard Hunters were held to here in Romania, but he never would have granted this one the rank.

"Looks like there will be no parley today, hmm?" Barakus said, hefting his claymore over his shoulder. "Although we might be able to come to some agreement, if we throw that one to the wolves as a peace offering." He nodded at Reed.

The young Hunter bared his fangs and hissed at him, drawing a round of laughter from the big Hunter. Yako turned his back on them and started forward again, Mariska and Nikko falling in step. The latter came up beside Yako and made a show of checking the magazine of his gun, while he spoke using hand gestures. Though he was pointing at his own stomach, the angle that Nikko pointed was in the direction of Mikelroy. Yako kept his head facing forward, but his eyes were on Nikko's fingers.

As he'd suspected, Mikelroy had disappeared into the woods once the conflict had started, only reappearing after the battle was ended sporting only the visible cuts to his clothing. He next pointed in the direction of Korck. He suggested that although he wasn't certain, it looked like Korck had actually aided in Ratrik's death somehow. Odd.

The smell of lycan stopped Yako mid-step, and he bared his fangs in a snarl. The others went into a defensive position and scanned the trees. Yako looked in every direction as he slowly drew his sword from over his back. A mobile pack usually constituted no more than five to seven lycans. There were more than that.

All uncertainties melted away in his anger, for now there was no doubt that Massius had plotted with the wolves. Unlike Yako's genuine friendship with Darren, and his general civility with several other packs, Massius had sided with them for more devious reasons.

"There must be about ten or twelve of them out there," he heard Mikelroy say. Bad move. The direction his voice came from told Yako that he was at the back of the group, behind everybody else, and in a position to disappear when the opportunity arose.

Yako signaled to Mariska, then to Nikko to kill Mikelroy as soon as possible. They nodded. "We come to talk, not to fight!" Yako said into the gloom of the woods. There was no response. "The High Council of Peles would speak with you openly and without conflict—" that was all he was able to say before the attack happened. Calm turned to chaos, as werewolves of varying sizes burst from the dark woods and dropped from above.

Nikko went down under the weight of a lycan that dropped from overhead. Yako hadn't the time to help him, as he was forced to duck and hop, sidestep and roll as three large wolves came at him with slashing claws and snapping jaws. He dropped into a squat and hamstrung one beast, then continued the turn and drove the tip of this sword into the belly of another. He withdrew his sword and turned to deal with the third, but Mariska was there. She landed on its back and unloaded a dozen pure silver rounds into the back of its neck.

She jumped away, and another lycan attempting to tackle her

from behind, crashed into the dying wolf. She glided over its head, unloading another burst of silver bullets into its back while upside down. She completed the flip and landed on the ground just as another wolf burst through the trees and tackled her.

Yako ducked a slashing claw, brought his sword in an overhead chop and severed the claw. He spun away from the snapping jaws, drew a silver dagger, and launched it into the side of the monster holding Mariska to the ground. It let out a pained grunt, and then Nikko was there. He wrapped his arm around its neck and struggled to pull it up. He forced it away just enough for Mariska to free her gun, and she unloaded the rest of the magazine into its midsection.

Yako turned to see another wolf bounding toward him. He lowered his stance, ready to sidestep and attack, when a spinning axe caught the werewolf in the side of the head. It was knocked sideways, but got to its feet just as Lydia came in with her other axe, which she buried in the monsters chest. When she yanked her first axe free, the wolf head-butted her in the chest, and she went down on her back. It jumped on top of her, snapping its giant jaws at her face. The big woman growled and threw the wolf off of her and scrambled to her feet.

Trailing blood from its burning wound, the stubborn lycan leapt at her. "Come on then!" Lydia brought both of her axes together in a sideways swing and knocked the beast away. A lycan dropped behind her and bit down on her shoulder. She let out an open-mouthed hiss, and her fangs elongated as she tried to dislodge the wolf. It suddenly released her and howled as it was lifted from the ground.

"Filthy mutt," Barakus growled, and with a mighty heave, he threw the monster against a tree and followed, driving his silver claymore through its chest and into the trunk of the tree behind it.

Korck was a blur of movement, stabbing and slashing, and in some cases, biting his enemies. It seemed the paranoid and calculating eyes were due to the fact that he knew he was also ill-suited for this hunt. It took him twice as much effort as the others to bring down one of the beasts. Still, despite wounds in a dozen places, he fought and killed.

Reed dropped to the ground and unloaded the rest of the clips of his semi-automatic handguns. The lycan in front of him fell to the ground, and another replaced it. The younger vampire quickly regained his feet and skittered away as he reloaded.

The wolf crashed into Reed and sent him flying sideways into a tree, then swatted him aside. Through the dizzying impact he managed to hold on to his guns and sent a round of bullets into its face. The lycan dropped to the ground.

Yako had just felled yet another enemy when at least twenty more appeared, dropping out of trees and bursting from the dark woods. *And so you win after all, Massius.*

The eight Hunters were surrounded and pushed to their limits. Barakus and Lydia were now back-to-back, twin axes and claymore leaving blood, death, and evisceration in their wake.

Korck flew over Reed's head to bury a dagger in the eye of an approaching wolf, then shoved his handgun into its maw and unloaded a barrage of silver bullets. Yako drew another silver dagger strapped to his leg and let fly. His aim was perfect, and the dagger flew straight into the maw of a lycan creeping up on Reed and Korck from behind. He spared a brief glance at Korck, but the wiry Hunter was occupied with yet another monster.

More werewolves appeared, and the group of Hunters was being pushed closer together. Nikko swiped a horizontal cut with his sword but missed. He brought his other arm around to shoot, but the werewolf was faster and stronger. It bit down on his arm, crushing bone and causing him to holler in pain. His finger reflexively pulled the trigger, loosing a spray of silver bullets, lethal to vampire and werewolf alike.

Mariska dove to the side, but was not quick enough, and a bullet caught her leg. She screamed as the flesh around the wound sizzled. The wolf behind her was even less lucky, as the bullet that wounded Mariska passed through her leg and into thigh of the beast behind her.

It staggered, and that was just enough time for Reed to put it down with several shots to the head and torso. Another lycan was stalking toward her, and Mariska struggled to rise, then fell again. On Yako's other side, Nikko was losing his struggle with the wolf that had bitten his arm. He would not have time to help them both. Making a decision, Yako called to Nikko and tossed a dagger to the struggling Hunter, then launched the last of his throwing knives at the werewolf on top of him as he sprinted toward Mariska. He didn't look to see if Nikko was to be saved or not. He would live or die. Yako had given him a chance to save himself and it would be enough, or it wouldn't.

Sword in hand, Yako stood over Mariska and held the wolf back with a flurry of stabs and cuts until he found an opening and drove his sword into its neck. He pulled the blade free before its knees gave out, and reversed his grip to stab backwards and impale the lycan bounding up from behind. In the span of a heartbeat, both beasts were on the ground, reverting to their human forms in death.

Mariska struggled to her feet and held her gun ready. A wound inflicted by silver took longer to heal. Reed fought with surprising ferocity. His hands were a blur of motion as he shot every lycan that came into his line of sight, buying Nikko the precious seconds he needed to finally kill the wounded wolf on top of him and regain his feet.

Yako took a quick moment to survey the scene and saw that Mikelroy was nowhere to be found. Korck was the farthest away from the group, which would have seemed like suicide if not for the fact that Yako saw through the ruse. The small Hunter shot and stabbed and avoided halfhearted bites and claws in his direction. The wolves he shot staggered away, but it was a show. Yako was certain that neither the bullets in his gun nor his knives had an ounce of silver in them.

A wolf lunged out of the trees, grabbed hold of him, and

snatched him from view. Lydia yelled and tried to go to his aid, but was tackled from the side. His back now exposed, Barakus suffered a bite to the shoulder, and the giant wolf forced him down. The big vampire gnashed his teeth and stabbed a dagger beside his face. He plunged it to the hilt in the monster's eye, then grabbed the wolf by the neck and threw it over his shoulder to crash into another of the beasts loping toward him.

The two wolves collided mid-air and crashed to the ground. Mariska fired on the wolf as it extricated itself from the transforming corpse.

The battle seemed endless. For every wolf they killed, two more took its place. It seemed like every lycan in the world converged upon them. Yako never knew this many of the things even existed.

Reed went down, and Nikko pulled the monster off him and shot it in the back, then shoved it aside. It didn't look good. The rookie suffered a broken arm and his leg looked like the bones had been bitten to pieces, which they probably had. Nikko took a swat to the side of the head and went down. Mariska turned and unloaded half a clip of silver bullets into the wolf. It went down under the assault, reverting back to its human form beside the unmoving Nikko.

Three wolves turned and regarded Yako, and there was too much focus in their eyes for him to have been a random choice. They snapped their long maws and barked. Yako lowered the tip of his sword to the ground behind him. There were only so many ways a werewolf could attack. Teeth and claws. They may be smarter than a normal animal, but they were no less equipped. A lycan could not kick, or hold a weapon. They couldn't easily duck an attack to the head, or lean backward.

They stalked forward and Yako held his ground. Two of them bounded forward and leaped a full fifteen feet to close the distance between them. Yako tightened his grip and waited, but a huge figure shot through the trees and slammed into the two wolves. In all his experiences, Yako had never seen a lycan knocked unconscious, but those two lay in an unmoving tangle of fur and limbs. He backed away from the new wolf, which was easily over eight feet tall, with blue-black fur.

More of the blue-black wolves crashed through the woods, tackling and tearing into the others. The other pack members were not nearly as big as the one in front of Yako, but were still larger than the werewolves the vampires had been fighting.

The battle became a chaotic blur of fur and claws and jagged teeth, and at times it was difficult to tell one beast from another. A lycan leapt out at the big one, that Yako surmised to be the pack leader, and it turned and reached out a claw, caught the wolf in mid-air, and snapped its neck. It hurled the dead body away to crash into another wolf.

After that, none of the other werewolves challenged the big one, and soon they retreated, the howls and carnage ended, and the woods were quiet once more. Broken and bloodied, but alive, Barakus aided a similarly haggard Lydia to her feet.

What was left of Nikko was rapidly being claimed by death, and Reed lay groaning beside the remains. Yako wondered if the boy was worth the life of the experienced Hunter he'd just lost. If he survived this, Yako would make a claim on him.

To his left, Mariska's eyes took in every werewolf in the vicinity. The big wolf let out a loud growl, and they heard the sound of popping cartilage and reforming bone as the pack began reverting to their human forms. The leader turned to face Yako, as it transformed into a big human. Darren.

"I have a gift for you," the lycan leader said without preamble. He held up a hand, and there was a ripping sound, followed by the head of Mikelroy bouncing out of the woods to roll to a stop near Yako's feet. It started to decay immediately.

Yako looked down at the disintegrating trophy, then back at Darren. "You have my thanks," he said, bowing in respect.

"Ever so formal, my friend. I would have made a similar

trophy of the sneaky one," he said, no doubt referring to Korck, "but he's slippery. I'm afraid he fled and we were unable to catch him."

"No matter. Your help here is appreciated," Yako replied, sheathing his sword. "They are too many to be one pack." He indicated the dead men and women that had been their lupine enemies only minutes ago.

"They are," Darren confirmed. "This is the coordination of at least three packs. I won't know until I gather more intelligence tomorrow."

To Yako's side, Mariska snorted. Darren looked her up and down and favored her with a lewd smile. She snarled at him. He blew her a kiss.

"We are now in your debt," Yako said, moving over to take a closer look at Reed. His coat and shirt were ripped to shreds and the scratches and bite marks littering his body were slow to heal. He was paler than usual. Yako doubted he would last much longer. Better to end his suffering.

The young Hunter must have seen the doubt in Yako's eyes, for he coughed and whispered, "I will live, Eldest, if you will but give me a chance to heal. I will rise and serve."

Yako looked into his flickering pale red eyes and nodded, then stood and turned back to see Darren watching from a discrete distance. "Compassion from a blood?" Darren said, incredulous.

"Recognition of continued usefulness," Yako said. He glanced at Barakus and Lydia, who were fast on the mend. Those two were strong. Aside from their natural weaknesses, being savaged by a werewolf was one of the few things a vampire could not quickly heal from.

"Of course," Darren said. "And as for your debt, I only require your Second's hand in marriage, as is our custom.

Yako turned just in time to see Mariska draw her gun and point it in Darren's face. The other members of his pack bristled, but Yako just watched and said nothing. After a tense moment, Darren burst into laughter, followed by the rest of his pack. Barakus and Lydia joined in, and despite himself, even Yako smiled at the jape. Mariska's eyes narrowed, but she lowered the gun. Yako knew she would like nothing more than to put a silver bullet between Darren's eyes. He hoped she wouldn't be so foolish. There might not be enough silver bullets in the magazine of her gun to kill the powerful lycan.

"Seriously, though," Darren said, his muscled shoulders bouncing with suppressed mirth. "We've been friends for some time now, have we not?" Yako nodded. Darren nodded back. "Then simply have my back when I need you, and that will be enough."

"So it is," Yako replied

The smiling werewolf walked up to him and extended his hand. Knowing Darren as long as he had, Yako reached past the proffered hand and they clasped forearms.

"From the looks of this," Darren indicated the scattered bodies, "one pack has been decimated and another seriously crippled. I'll have a long talk with the leader of the Blood Pack. They've never let go of their hatred of you bloods, and this attack, I'm positive, is mostly their doing." He glanced at the listening vampires. "Though I believe there is more to it than that."

All things come to light, and the treacherous will soon walk in it, Yako thought. "I would be interested in the outcome," he said aloud.

"Right back atcha," Darren said. He turned to Mariska. "You know, you might enjoy it, little blood. I would make a good mate for you."

Mariska looked as if she had suddenly tasted something foul. "I would sooner embrace the sun's light, mutt." She looked him up and down. "Are there no expanding clothes you could wear?"

Darren looked down at his naked form and chuckled. "Still playing hard to get. I understand. I understand." He started off into the woods and his pack fell in behind him, and soon they disappeared into the night.

Yako stood where he was for a time, still surveying the scene, until Barakus came beside him. "Eldest Hunter," he began, "you stayed your hand when they presented Mikelroy's head, and so I stayed mine." It was more question than statement.

"Because he was a traitor," Yako answered.

Barakus frowned down at him. "A traitor? How is this?"

"Did you see him kill a single lycan?"

"The heat of battle offered me little chance to view my comrades' exploits," Barakus answered.

"You killed eight. Lydia also killed eight." Yako turned to indicate where Nikko had once lain. "Nikko slew four, and Reed, two. Second Hunter Mariska, seven." He turned back to Barakus. I saw Mikelroy in a well-choreographed attack-and-retreat dance that would be well received in a performance or a fool's eye for battle, but what I did not see, from him or Korck, was a kill." There was silence for a while as each of them digested his words.

"You remind us of why you are Eldest Hunter," Barakus said with a bow of his head. "What now?"

Yako regarded each of the remaining Hunters. "I have openly declared that Mikelroy was a traitor. I also declare that Korck is a traitor, and is now making his way back to the coven where he will concoct his own version of the happenings tonight. If anyone opposes my view of this, let them speak now."

"I might not be able to doubt that either of them were traitors," Lydia said, "but I doubt that either one of those two had the intelligence to orchestrate this little attack."

Reed finally regained his feet. He was still weak, but he was standing. Yako gave a curt nod in approval of the small Hunter's resilience.

"I will explain my reasoning, but I require that all here listen to the situation in its entirety before you draw a weapon against me."

"And should you move against the Eldest, you move against his Second," Mariska added from behind.

Barakus harrumphed. "No one is attacking anyone, girl. Unruffle your feathers. I have known of Eldest Hunter's exploits for many years and Hunted beside him on occasion. There has never been a more ridiculous candidate for treachery than he."

"I appreciate your confidence, but save it until after you have heard what I have to say."

"Are we not still here to treat with the lycans or eliminate them?" Reed asked. "An entire pack just left us."

"Still a rookie," Barakus said.

Reed glared at him.

"Learn to think," Mariska said as she retrieved throwing knives from the ground and the bodies of the dead men and women. She tossed those that belonged to Yako back to him. "There's no need to speak with the pack that just left. They aided us against the rogues."

"And they are off to speak with the leader of what remains of the two surviving rogue packs," Lydia said, strapping her axes to her hips. "Or so that big muscly one said." Barakus raised his eyebrows at her.

They retrieved their weapons and Yako led them to another small clearing. Everyone found a place to sit, and cast expectant looks to the Eldest Hunter.

He looked at each of them in the darkness of the night, his vampire eyes easily seeing the details of every face.

"So," Barakus said. "I would hear this tale, Eldest Hunter. Then we can return to the coven and rip out the flicking tongue of our little traitor."

Yako stared down at the ground in front of him. "There is more than one tongue that needs removing."

CHAPTER 23

The animosity between vampires and lycans has not existed in full for well over two hundred years," Yako began. "There are those of each of our species that find the other distasteful, but we are not in conflict, and there is certainly not as much need to monitor their level of discretion among the human population as some would have us believe."

"Your words skirt a traitorous tone, Eldest," Lydia said. Yako studied her eyes. It was not a threat, so much as a warning.

"The words I am about to speak will cross well over that line," Yako replied. "But if we are to survive this situation, we must all know the facts.

"Though it is generally frowned upon by our kind, I have had a lasting friendship with one of the strongest lycan species in the world, and as such, have a measure of respect with his pack."

"So we gathered," Barakus said.

"My intentions were and always have been to continue good relations with them. There is another who has fostered a relationship with them, whose intentions are less beneficial to us. After tonight, I'm sure of it."

"You're not talking about Korck or Mikelroy," Lydia said. It wasn't a question, but more a disbelieving statement of fact.

"No."

"Then who?" she asked. "Who would, or could, establish a relationship with several packs of lycans and enlist them to kill us? And why?"

"Their primary targets numbered only three," Yako said.

"Three?" Reed frowned. "It looked like they were trying to kill us all to me."

Yako thought about how he'd seen the wolves attack. True, they had attacked everyone, but their primary efforts were focused.

"If I remember correctly," Barakus said, "Lydia and I have the highest number of kills."

"Because a lot of them were focused on getting past us," Lydia said. It was like a light went off in her eyes as comprehension dawned. She looked at Barakus. "They attacked us all, but more than half the ones I killed so easily were focused on attacking one of them." She pointed at Yako, Mariska, and Reed. "And I didn't once see Mikelroy in the thick of it. He was always on the outside. I didn't have time to think about it before."

"Absurd," Barakus said. "Why would those two side with a pack of lycans, near maddened by the Hunter's Moon cycle?"

"Did Darren's pack seem maddened to you?" Mariska asked him.

Barakus opened his mouth to speak, hesitated, then fell silent.

"That still leaves the question of who wants you three dead," Lydia said.

"I hand-picked each of you to have on my team with four exceptions," Yako stated.

"Korck, Mikelroy, Ratrik, and me," Reed said, and Yako nodded.

"What of Ratrik?" Barakus asked, still skeptical. "We can't know, since he was killed."

"Not by a lycan," Reed said, and everyone stared at him. "I

heard them talking," the young Hunter continued. "I heard Korck and Ratrik before we left the coven when they thought no one was around. They kept talking about staying out of the way and that they would be well rewarded when this was done. Ratrik seemed less at ease about it than Korck, though."

"Well rewarded to stay out of the way." Barakus's voice went low and angry.

Reed nodded. "When we were attacked, several times one of them would move out of the way just as a lycan was bearing down on them, and it would attack me instead. The first time, I didn't think about it, but it happened several times. Then I heard Ratrik complaining about betraying a fellow vampire to the dogs, and later, out of the corner of my eye, I thought I saw Korck stab him in the back of the neck. That's all I saw, since I was trying not to be eaten."

"So you four were not selected by Eldest Hunter," Lydia said. "Who ordered you to hunt with us?"

Reed frowned. "Elder Massius."

Barakus gnashed his teeth.

"To speak against the Elders is disloyal and traitorous," Lydia said.

"I didn't speak against the Elders," Reed argued. "I said who selected me to hunt with you, as you asked."

"Your answer implies that Elder Massius is involved in this attack."

"Not because I say he is," Reed clenched his fists and looked from Lydia to Barakus. "I didn't say Elder Massius did anything other than select myself, Korck, Ratrik, and Mikelroy to hunt with you."

He was right, of course, and that truth hung in the silence.

"We still have no answer to why this is," Barakus said. The big Hunter looked on the verge of exploding with anger, though Yako was unsure who his ire was directed at.

"Of the four Hunters Elder Massius placed in my command,"

Yako stated, "he was adamant that Reed was to learn the way of the lycan hunt, his first lycan hunt. I was told directly that his survival was my responsibility."

"I remember those words," Lydia said. Her curly red locks bounced as she nodded her head. "The Elder was adamant about that more than anything else."

Mariska spoke up. "Massius enlisted the wolves to kill the two of us," she said, indicating herself and Yako. "If that failed, they would at least kill him," she pointed at Reed, who narrowed his eyes at her offhanded wave. "Everyone heard the Elder's decree that Reed's death would mean Yako's as well. It was his excuse, and Reed was extra insurance of that. Korck, Ratrik, and Mikelroy were here to see that everything went as planned, though Ratrik must have had a change of heart, and Korck killed him for it."

The Second Hunter looked at Lydia and Barakus. "In Massius's eyes, you two and Nikko were no more than necessary casualties to see his will done."

Barakus glared at his boots. "And so I ask once more, plainly. Why?"

"Elder Massius has desired my uncreation for longer than I've been aware of. I'm just now learning the truth of it."

"I'm finding all this difficult to believe."

"Yet the truth is what it is."

"How well do you know Elder Massius's history?" Mariska asked the big Hunter.

"As well as any of the others," Barakus answered. "What do you imply? And choose your next words carefully." Yako never took his eyes off of Barakus. Could he be trusted?

"The only choice I make with my words is truth, Barakus," Mariska said. "And I'm speaking them to you because I have faith in your ability to think for yourself. The histories we have learned and that are available to us only tell a part of the story. One of our High Council of Elders has secrets he would have die with our Eldest Hunter."

Barakus's expression darkened. "What do these secrets have to do with you, Eldest Hunter?"

"Betrayal," Yako answered. "Whether you would hear it from my mouth or not, it is a personal matter that I will deal with directly. Every crime must be answered for."

"You would speak against the Elders?" Barakus stood, his voice growing louder. "I do find that parts of this tale hold a ring of truth, but I cannot readily accept that one of the Elders would scheme in such a way. To betray you? To what end?"

"His personal history indicates his insatiable lust for power. Is this story not typical of most betrayals and coups, Barakus?" Though the big vampire was on his feet, Yako remained seated. "He is not originally of this coven or its lineage. He was an outsider who attained his seat through opportunism and plotting."

In the blink of an eye, Barakus had drawn his claymore and was in front of Yako, the giant sword arcing downward. Yako's hand snapped out and slapped the flat of the blade aside. He came to his feet and thrust his knee into Barakus's midsection, and when the larger man doubled over, he spun one step away, drawing his sword, and brought it around and down.

With perfect control, Yako stopped the killing stroke. Beneath the cutting edge of the naked blade, a thin red line dripped a tiny stream of blood. Yako had stopped the blade the instant it touched Barakus's neck, which was now sizzling from the burn of the silver.

Barakus remained kneeling, likely realizing the next few seconds could be his last. The moment passed and Yako withdrew his sword and replaced it in its sheath across his back. Barakus stood slowly and turned to regard him. The tiny cut struggled to heal as soon as Yako had withdrew his sword, but Barakus still reached back and touched sensitive the area.

"I spoke and struck against you, yet you did not kill me?"

"I see no enemy here," Yako replied, "only a Hunter whose loyalty is to an undeserving leader." Everyone had gotten to their feet, but relaxed when the confrontation, lasting little more than a second, ended.

"What do you intend, Eldest Hunter?" Lydia asked. Her hands had been clenching the axes at her sides, but now she released them.

"Nothing that involves you," Yako answered. "I have business to deal with across the ocean, and I will see it done before I return."

"You would return?" Reed asked.

Yako looked at him. "There are those in my family that cannot right the wrongs done to them. It is for me to do in their stead."

"To kill an Elder is unheard of," Lydia said. "Supposing you could best any of the Reapers that protect them, each of the Elders is stronger and more powerful."

Yako nodded. "You speak of the true Elders, yes. One who has gained his position of power through favors and deeds is not necessarily an Elder. I know what I propose is against the coven itself, and our highest laws, but I assure you there is a viper in the nest that is waiting to strike. I will deal with it."

"I don't like this," Lydia said. "But I especially don't like the possibility of someone undermining the Elders. How do we know your words are true, Eldest?"

"Search for yourselves and you will find your answers," Mariska said. "You'll find things in the histories some would prefer kept obscure."

"There are no laws against reading the histories, Second," Lydia said. "Every pureblood is well versed in our history."

"Have you been to the ancient library?" Yako asked. He sat down again. Barakus rubbed his neck, now sporting a tiny scar, and bowed to the Eldest Hunter. He returned to his seat as well.

"The ancient library?" Lydia repeated. "Many of the books in our libraries contain ancient books, but I was not aware of an ancient library."

"Because you were never told it existed," Yako said. "The

Elders knew full well that the best way to ensure that others took an interest in the ancient histories was to openly discourage reading them. Instead, they took the oldest books containing undesirable information and buried them deep."

"And you are suggesting our Elders have done this?" Barakus asked. His tone was more subdued, but still had a shade of anger in it.

"I do not know whether or not the Elders of the High Council know about the lengths to which Massius has gone to achieve his own ends, but I am certain that he is a poison." His words were greeted with silence. Lydia, Barakus, and Reed sat looking at the ground, thinking his words through. He didn't blame them. What he was saying was directly against one of the Elders of the High. It was unthinkable

"I'll ask you to answer this question. Given what has happened tonight. Do you have any doubts that Massius wishes me dead?"

"You still have no proof that those wolves were acting at his behest," Barakus insisted.

"I do not," Yako agreed. "But I do know that I was pulled from my mission in North America before I could complete it and brought here. Massius has been the only member of the High Council who has insisted on my uncreation because of my failure and has refused to hear my testimony. He has been insistent that no one hears what I have to say."

"And so we have this dilemma." Barakus spread his hands. "I've served the Elders for over four hundred years, and in that time I've never had reason to doubt their integrity. Now you come to tell us this."

"You have had no reason to doubt because you haven't been targeted," Yako replied. "If Massius had not been so vehement in his call for my death, I would have gone on believing him to be nothing more than a craven."

Barakus's nostrils flared.

"Set aside your unyielding devotion for a moment and think,

Hunter," Yako said. "Every Elder of the High Council has detailed accounts of their exploits in the creation and protection of the coven. What do you know about Massius?"

The big man thought for a moment. "He was a genius in regards to designing the fortifications during the conflicts, centuries ago. There was a time when he led the Hunters against the wolves during the times of conflict. He was the best of the Hunters, and passed along his skill and knowledge to us." He spread his hands. "Much of what we are and have become is because Elder Massius had a hand in it." He leaned forward and placed his hands on his knees. "You would deny this, Eldest Hunter?"

"There is some truth woven in the lies," Yako replied.

"And you would tell us your truth?" Lydia said. "You've never given me a reason to doubt you, Eldest, but this is dangerous talk you're asking us to buy into."

"All I ask is that you hear me, and think for yourselves."

"Well let's get to it then," Barakus said. "Dawn is not far off."

And so Yako spoke of their findings in the ancient library, how Massius had come with no ties or status with any coven. He told them of the Elder's relationship with Yako's ancestors and how he'd used it to his gain by having Jiro Shimamoto create the two classes of warriors to protect the interests of the immortals. He told of Jiro's oddly timed fall in addition to that of Elder Denry Ordine, whom Massius had ultimately replaced. He finished, fell silent, and waited.

"That is quite a tale," Barakus finally said. "If even a small part of this is true, I have to wonder why the other Elders wouldn't have been suspicious of why this history is so difficult to obtain."

"I do not pretend to know the answer to that question," Yako said. "But I will have it from Massius's own lips."

"Before you rip out his throat," Lydia said. "Is that what you mean to do?"

Yako considered her. She was fairly quick for her size, quicker than Barakus, and nearly as strong. But she was not very dexterous. She would lead with her left axe, then the right, constantly pressing the attack. Barakus would likely aid her. The sound of her laughter broke through Yako's thoughts.

"Be at ease, Eldest," she said. "I've no intention of doing battle with you. Two hundred and forty-two years of life have I seen. I'd like to see another Two hundred, maybe another two thousand."

Barakus snorted, and she shot him a warning look.

"You have something to say?" she asked. "He would have us both dead before we could pose a suitable threat. And even if we did get the upper hand, you can be sure his little curvy tart of a Second, there, would be on us as well."

Barakus looked to consider her words, then looked at Reed. "And what say you, boy?"

"Me?" Reed looked at every member of what remained of the team. "I would say that by himself, Eldest Hunter could take us all. With his Second, there is no doubt—"

"Yes, yes, our Eldest Hunter's prowess is the stuff of legend," Barakus interrupted, waving his hand for the young Hunter to get on with it.

"—and since this is the case," Reed continued, "they could have betrayed us to that pack of big lycans, or simply attacked us on their own. To concoct such an elaborate lie about this situation would be pointless.

Barakus nodded. "My thinking, too." He looked back at Yako and Mariska. "I don't like your words, but I will not stand against you. In fact, if I find your words to be true, I will stand beside you and bring the wrath of the *Ancestor*s down on that bastard's head."

"Sounds like you've already made up your mind about Elder Massius," Lydia observed.

"Never liked him much. Truth be told, I think he's a craven also. But we are Hunters, are we not? It is not for us to judge our betters."

"Even when our betters turn out to be lesser?" Reed asked.

"That thinking can lead to a quick death," Mariska commented.

"Or a slow one," Barakus added. "Careful, boy. An illegitimate Elder, Massius might be. Maybe even a craven. But he is far older than any of us, which still makes him dangerous. A little stripling like you would still find yourself in trouble. Remember that."

"So," Lydia said. "Now that we've established the possibility that one of our Elders, a member of the High Council, no less, could be an outlander and a traitor, what do we do about it?"

"A fine question, Lydia."

They were on their feet, weapons drawn and trained in the direction of the woods from where the voice came. Barakus opened his mouth to speak, but it hung open when he saw the Reaper emerge from the brush.

CHAPTER 24

Jelani lay awake, his arm draped over the sleeping Alisha, who was pressed tightly against him. A day and a night had passed since the situation with Remy. Whenever he was not vigilant, his thoughts would fly to Melinda. The woman who had been his friend, sometimes an intimate friend. Now, because of him, she was a vampire.

Jelani only knew as much about vampires as he had recently learned these past weeks, but he suspected that when Melinda had had him cornered in the hills, it had taken a great deal of restraint for her not to drain every last drop of blood from his veins right there. Because of his situation, she had been turned into a monster, but despite the fact that he had been unable to protect her, she had spared his life.

"It's not your fault, Jelani."

"Hmm?" He lifted his head and looked down at Alisha. She smiled up at him with smoldering hazel eyes. "How'd you know I was awake?" He asked.

"Baby, you wear guilt like a coat. It's practically wafting off of you."

"Well, it's a hard thing to deny."

"You ever been to Las Vegas?" she asked.

"Yeah, why?"

"It's owned by the mafia. They kill people. You wear athletic shoes? Foreign facilities that pay poverty wages are where they're made." She turned onto her back and looked up at him. "Coffee? Clothes? Electricity? In fact, anything to do with society in general? All of it is having a negative effect on someone somewhere."

"That makes me feel a lot better," Jelani said.

She tapped a finger on his forehead. "My point is that all you can do is the best you can with what you have. You can't be responsible for something that is not in your control, any more than you can be responsible for selling your car to someone who might drive away and hit someone with it later."

"It's not so straightforward as that," Jelani said. "If that's the case, what if he wipes out everyone I know, or turns them? Would I not feel guilty about that either?"

"Life is rarely ever straightforward," Alisha replied, "and I've never known any good to come out of what-iffing the future. We'll figure something out, love. But you're as good as dead if you let guilt take you over."

Jelani sighed. "I know you're right. It's just not easy to let something like this go."

"I know, and you wouldn't be a good or normal person if you didn't feel something about all this."

"I really wish I knew what to do about it."

"Talk to that girl," Alisha suggested.

"Why can't you say her name?" Jelani asked, smirking.

"Because the last thing I want to do while lying in bed with you is mention the name of a woman who would sooner have you in hers."

"Whether she wants me in her bed or not doesn't matter. I'm here with you."

"I told you before," Alisha said, slipping out from under the covers. "You don't lie very well. I know that if she really wants to, she could make you do whatever she wants. I'd just rather not be reminded of it, if that's okay."

"Fine, fine. I'm sorry I asked. Really, I am." Jelani lay there, admiring every smooth curve of her body as she slipped into her silk robe and tied it at the waist.

She glanced over her shoulder at him and frowned. "I don't know what you're staring at. You're not gettin' any."

Jelani made a disappointed face. "You don't know what you're missing. Gurl, I'll put you on a biscuit and sop you up!"

"Ugh!" Alisha said, wrinkling her nose. "Will you stop saying stuff like that?"

Jelani climbed out of the bed and wrapped his arms around her when she tried to run away. "Gurl, you know you like it." She giggled, fighting halfheartedly to get free of him. "Don't fight it," he said in an exaggeratedly suave voice. "You can't."

She suddenly stopped struggling and looked over her shoulder at him. "Jelani."

"Mmhm?"

"Get off my booty." She glanced down over her shoulder and back up at him.

"Oh," he said. "Oh, no, I was just—"

"Uh-huh," she cut him off. "I can feel what you were just about to do, and it ain't happening now. I have to get ready for work."

"Okay, fine." He heaved a big sigh and let her go.

She sniggered and he watched her walk to the bathroom. "And stop staring," she said, never looking back.

"Geez." He threw up his hands. "Fine, then. I'll just brush my teeth while you're in the shower."

"You can brush your teeth when I'm done, love."

"What? What sense does that make—"

"I'll never be able to get ready for work, and we'll never get anything done if you're in there while I'm in the shower." She closed the door.

After a few minutes, he heard the water running. Unable to resist any longer, he walked over to the door and opened it just enough to peek inside.

"Jelani! I already told—"

"By the way," he interrupted. "The mafia hasn't owned Vegas since the eighties."

"I TOLD Wen to hold onto her vacation time," Daniel said.

They stood on the same boulder that Jelani and Melinda had rested on after the same hike. The last hike before he had told her that he had only wanted to be friends. The last hike of her human life. Jelani shook off the thought. "Why so?"

"Because when this whole thing comes to a head, and you know it will, I want her to be as far away as possible, and someplace where the sun is hot and takes up most of the day."

"That's impossible," Jelani said, gazing out at the city below. "She can go someplace hot, or she can go someplace where it never gets fully dark this time of year, but not both."

"Yeah, yeah. Right. I guess twenty-four hours of daylight is more important than it being hot," Daniel said.

"So you told her to save her vacation time so you can send her to Alaska?" Jelani asked.

"There's also Iceland."

"Iceland? They get the same summer there?"

"Just as high on the map, bro."

Jelani tipped his head. "Didn't know that. And while we're on the subject, why the hell is Iceland green, and Greenland ice?"

"It's because when the Vikings—"

Jelani waved him off. "Yeah, yeah, I know that old story. The Vikings called the icy one Greenland and the green one Iceland so that people wouldn't come and bother them on the green one."

Daniel frowned at him. "Well why'd you ask, then?"

"It sounds like an old wives' tale or something. Is it really true?"

"Look it up on Wikipedia."

Jelani rolled his eyes. "Now there's an information source I can trust." They were silent for a time before he spoke again. "Maybe I should suggest the same thing to Alisha."

"Wen will have probably done that for you already."

"When do you think we should try to get them out of here?"

Daniel shrugged. "The sooner the better. Maybe after we've spoken with Saaya again. If she chooses to continue helping us, that is."

"Now that's just rude."

Jelani and Daniel nearly jumped out of their skin at the sound of the woman's voice between them.

"Damn, girl!" Jelani said, looking around to see if anyone was around. "You having fun giving a guy a heart attack?" On her other side, Daniel's chest was heaving as well.

"Walk with me," she said, emerging from behind them and hopping down from the boulder.

"What brings you all the way up here?" Daniel asked when they caught up.

As usual, the *dampeal's* clothing was altogether inappropriate for the weather. She wore a dark purple top with beautiful sparkling swirls embroidered in the front. It was made of light material that stopped at her navel, and a thin, transparent sash was draped over one shoulder. The matching skirt sported equally impressive embroidered patterns, and hung just above her feet. It was the type of exotic and beautiful outfit that no one would wear in mid-fifty-degree weather at such an altitude atop a hiking trail.

"Did you not just say that you wished to speak with me, while questioning whether or not I would keep my word?" She lifted a thin eyebrow at him. Those eyes were rich light brown pools a man could drown in.

"But how did you know that before now?"

She gave him an impatient look. "You barely survived a Hunter ambush only to almost die at the fangs of a friend who now walks the night. It wouldn't take intellect quicker than the speed of a sloth to determine that you might wish to speak with me about it."

"So you waited up here for us?" Jelani asked.

She laughed at him. "Oh, sweet boy. That is exactly what I was doing. Waiting impatiently for my adorable helpless companions to happen across my lonely boulder as I desperately wished to speak with you on how I might keep you alive."

Daniel snorted.

"Cute," Jelani replied.

"Thank you," Saaya replied back.

"So, what now?"

They came around the back of the lodge and made their way up the hill toward the woods. "Do we have to go in there?" Daniel asked. The two exchanged a glance, and Jelani couldn't have agreed more. If he never went into another patch of woods again in his life, it would be fine.

"I assure you there are no wolves stalking these woods right now. Besides, if there were, I would protect you." She said it with a playful chirpiness to her voice. The effect was almost mocking. "What?" she asked, seeing the sour looks on their faces.

"Having a girl tell a guy she will protect him kinda goes against nature," Jelani said carefully. "We're usually the ones that do the protecting."

"Ah. The bastion of male chauvinism endures through the ages."

"What?" Jelani's mouth fell open. "How did we get there? This isn't chauvinism! I was just saying …" he trailed off and sighed when she started sniggering at him. "Okay, so we're in the woods where you'll protect us from the boogeyman, or anything else out of myth that tries to do us harm. Let's have it."

"Boogeyman?"

They looked at her, trying to decide if she was serious. She was. "Never mind," Jelani said. "So what do you have for us?"

"As her re-creator, your friend is bound to Remy."

"Then why didn't she kill me the other night?" Jelani asked, dread creeping up his spine.

"His concentration was elsewhere, but it takes a great deal of fortitude for a newly turned vampire to resist the thirst, no matter who they attack. It isn't uncommon for new *shaquora* to attack their own families and drain them all."

Daniel was horrorstruck. "Are you serious? Don't they have any memory of being human?"

"You have never experienced the thirst," Saaya answered. "It can be maddening. As a half-blood, it was a powerful urge, even for me. Imagine your blood being on fire and a parching thirst that is like hunger. A thirst no water can quench. A hunger no food can sate."

"You said it *was* a powerful urge," Daniel said. "It's not that bad for you any longer?"

"It's different," Saaya said. "Purebloods have better control over the thirst and can subsist on infrequent feedings in younger life. As they get older, purebloods need to feed even less frequently, and can survive by other means that exist within the medical industry." She sat on a log and crossed her legs, patting the spaces to her left and right. Jelani thought she looked so tiny, so frail, sitting on that giant log.

"For me," she continued once they'd taken their seats, "it's more different, still. The thirst is strong, but not so strong as a full-blooded vampire. If you were to bleed in front of me, I wouldn't be crazed by the sight and smell of it." She winked at Daniel. "Though I cannot deny I might want a little taste."

Daniel's lips pursed and he made an apologetic. "Um. Sorry."

Saaya looked disappointed, but shrugged. "Should you meet your friend again, you would most likely die." She gave them both a heavy look. "Make no mistake about this. If you should meet her again, she might not want to kill you, but if the thirst is upon her, or if Remy compels her, she will. There would be nothing at all your friend would be able to do to stop herself."

"Thanks for the heads up," Daniel said. "So what are we going to do about this guy before all this gets worse?"

"Kill him," she said simply.

"Oh!" Jelani replied. "I wish I'd thought of that! Yeah if we kill him, he might leave us alone." His face brightened in sarcasm and he looked at Daniel with an open-mouthed smile.

"Careful," Saaya said. Her smile was sweet, but there was a warning in her tone that Jelani couldn't miss. She ran a finger along his cheek, studying his face. "The worst thing that could have happened has happened to him," she said, looking into his eyes. Jelani looked back into those hypnotic light brown orbs. He visually traced the shape of her eyes, admiring how they ended in an upward slant. It was impossible to tell where the lightly used mascara ended and the actual shape of her eyes began.

Saaya slowly opened her mouth, ever-so-slightly, and the tip of a fang peaked below her upper lip. "Remy has led a handful of Hunters to their deaths, yet none but himself and you two survived. It was an historic failure. Can you imagine the shame he faces, having led six Hunters to kill two humans, a half-blood, and her brother? And all he has to show for it is a newly turned *shaquora*?" She closed her eyes and laughed softly. "A failure of this scale is something that he will never be able to escape."

"So he's going to be coming after us fast," Daniel said.

"And hard," Jelani added.

"Fast and hard?" Saaya repeated, favoring each of them with a seductive glance.

"You're really something else, you know that." Jelani tried to lighten the suddenly sultry energy in the air. "Let's be focused here, can we?"

"Mm hm." She offered a lazy blink in response. "I believe Remy has only waited this long to attack again because he wants to find another person close to you to draw you to him. When that happens, he'll kill all of you. He won't play games to enjoy the moment as he did the other night. That was a foolish mistake he won't repeat."

Jelani felt a sense of alarm growing in his stomach. Again, Saaya looked at each of them and sighed. "Right now, you're probably thinking you shouldn't let either of those fine little girls of yours out of your sight. You would be right, if there was anything at all you could do to protect them." She stroked his cheek again. "Of course, there are alternatives, should your delicate flowers be tragically plucked from this life prematurely."

She studied Jelani's face and saw the reaction she likely expected but didn't desire. "Oh fine," she said, pouting. "Kafeel has been hunting him since the attack and has been unable to find where the Hunter sleeps. We are left only with the option of waiting till the slippery worm finds his way back to you. The next time will be the last. If Kafeel doesn't put an end to him, I will."

"You seem pretty determined," Daniel observed.

"As I said. The worst thing that could have happened has come to pass. Questions will be asked, and answers will be sought. I doubt Remy knows of the existence of my kind, but if he discovers my true nature, and that of my brother, he will go to a great deal more trouble to prepare himself than he had before. There is no need to allow this to be any more difficult."

Jelani resisted the urge to point out that this could have been avoided if she'd simply killed that first Hunter instead of playing games. The thought of the events that led up to this point seemed to have happened years ago, yet only several months had passed.

"So what part do Jelani and I play in all this?" Daniel asked.

"Unfortunately, the only thing you can do is bait him out while trying not to be killed. And you must trust me." The way she said it implied that she knew they were having trouble doing just that.

She stood. "I've enjoyed our walk today, boys, but I must leave. Kafeel sleeps today, and the night will come."

They stood and started back toward the lodge. "So what do we do in the meantime?" Daniel asked.

She craned her neck and looked up at him. Her response couldn't have been simpler. Her response couldn't have been more difficult.

"Survive."

CHAPTER 25

Tara slipped out of the brush. She was not alone. Clasped in her left hand was Korck, held by what must have been a powerful grip. It was an odd sight. Korck was smaller than the average man, and Tara was a good deal smaller than him, standing no taller than five feet three inches. One thing every Hunter knew was that size made no difference when the other person was a Reaper.

Yako looked from Tara to Korck, who was struggling to extricate himself from her grip around his neck. "I see you have found our missing party member," he said, bowing in deference. "We figured him for dead."

"You figured no such thing," Tara said. "He's a traitorous little flea, and you knew it." She eyed the others. "The question is, does everyone here feel the same?" The moment grew tense as six sets of eyes all darted from one to the other.

"Eldest Hunter has shared his suspicions with us, Reaper," Barakus said. "It is a disturbing possibility that we must take time to consider."

Tara looked at Yako, but it was to Barakus that she spoke. "Your Eldest Hunter suspects nothing. He is certain of the facts that he has presented to you, and he is correct." Korck squirmed in her grip and she tightened it, giving him a rough shake. "Hold still, or I will snap your neck." Korck hissed, but let go of her hands.

"This one," the diminutive Reaper nodded her head down at her captive, "is not only undeserving of the rank of Hunter, but has been working directly for Massius for more years than any of you would believe. That is why he was given his rank."

They looked at him. He seemed utterly pathetic, held so helplessly in her hand. Yako had known at first sight of Korck that he was no warrior, but it wasn't his place to question the Elders.

"Can't say that's much of a surprise," Barakus muttered, speaking Yako's thoughts aloud. "About that one not being a true Hunter, I mean. Truth is, I would've been surprised if he'd ever been in a fight at all."

Beside him, Lydia snickered.

Tara looked down at Korck. "Looks like you've fooled no one. And now you will tell them the truth." She loosened her grip just enough for him to speak.

"It is forbidden to speak against the Elders," Korck said, trying unsuccessfully to sound sincere. "There is no betrayal here, and I was returning to the coven to get reinforcements. That is why you found me—"

"You were returning to the coven to alert Massius of our survival against his allies," Yako interrupted. He stepped away from the others and into the open space in their camp.

Mariska looked at Lydia and Barakus and signaled for them to fan out and block any would-be escape route. She knew what was coming, having served beside Yako for so many years. There were two things one did not do under his command, exhibit cowardice or betrayal.

Yako leveled his gaze at Korck. "Whether your rank was given or earned, you were a Hunter under my command and sought to undermine me. Apparently, you believe I have lost my ability to lead." He reached over his shoulder, and slowly drew his sword.

The metal sang a steady, ominous tune as it slid from the sheath. "Apparently, I must be relieved of my command."

Yako stepped sideways, eyes narrowed and focused on the other Hunter, still gripped in Tara's hand.

With an amused smirk, Tara gave Korck a little shake. "Hold your stroke, Eldest Hunter," she said. I promised him he would be released if he told you the truth." She looked down at him. "Are you feeling more forthcoming, Korck?"

Pale as he was, Korck looked as if he could be even more pale than usual. "Yes," he said. "But I beg that you leave me out of this. I was doing as ordered by Elder Massius. I want no part in any of this."

"You will play no part in the events that proceed after tonight," Tara assured him. "Now speak."

Korck ground his teeth, clearly not wanting to say what he was about to. "Elder Massius has wanted to kill you for more years than I can say," he began, looking at Yako, then at the naked blade in his hands. "When he had his eyes set on becoming an Elder of the Council, he knew the only way to do it was through two courses of action. First, he would have to perform deeds in favor of the coven that would be of immensely great benefit, placing him in their highest esteem."

He stole glances at the other four Hunters, each looking more angry with each word he spoke. "He also would need to create a vacant position in the High Council."

"And Elder Denry Ordine met his end," Barakus growled.

"Elder Denry was killed by a lycan," Lydia said, shaking her head. "That is known."

"And who told the tale of his demise?" Mariska countered.

"Save your debate," Tara said. "I don't have a lot of time here." She gave Korck another shake. "Continue, and be quick about it."

Korck wisely glared at the ground in front of him instead of the Reaper at his back. "Elder Massius will personally see to my uncreation if he finds out about this," he pleaded.

Tara shook him again. "By the time Massius finds out about this, it will be too late for him to do anything about it. Speak. I won't tell you again."

"Elder Massius has many contacts, and is good at forming the most unlikely alliances. Before he arrived at Sinaia Coven, he had already formed a favorable relationship with the Silver Pack."

"The most powerful lycan pack in the country," Mariska said.

"Likely several countries," Yako added, his eyes still on the treacherous Hunter.

"Yes," Korck agreed. "They've been the dominant pack for over three hundred years. When Elder Massius formed an alliance with them, the Woodland Pack, and the Ghost Pack fell in with him easily enough. In exchange for the numbers they would lose in the aftermath of the Battle of Hunter's Moon, Massius promised them free roam of the lands unchecked, so long as they were discrete."

"Which explains the rise in their numbers that I've been receiving," Barakus said, "and the fact that my reports have been met with silence and inaction."

Korck glanced at him nervously. "Yes, well—"

"What of my ancestors?" Yako demanded in a quiet, calm voice." Mariska glanced at him. Korck was not going to live much longer.

"Your ancestors—Jiro, Ichiro, Amaya, and Hisako—were all very loyal. They were—"

"Did I ask you to recount their loyalty? Speak of their dealings with Massius, or I will remove your tongue."

"They were unaware of Elder Massius's plans," Korck spoke up. "I'm guessing you've already figured that out by your questions. They were the ones who trained vampire warriors to become the first Hunters, and later, the elite Reapers. Jiro was Massius's closest friend. Or so he thought. Jiro trained the first Hunters, who aided in the staged Battle of Hunter's Moon, and that is how the event got its name. Jiro was not a man given to the trappings of ego, so he didn't care about the credit that Massius claimed for himself."

"After Elder Denry's demise, Elder Massius was offered the vacant station. After that," Korck shrugged. "Elder Massius thought it necessary to create one more class of warriors. An elite class that would serve only the Elders."

"Reapers," Reed said.

Korck nodded. "Reapers."

"Why does Massius want me dead?" Yako asked.

"I can't say I know absolutely. The only reason I know what I do is because I would not have been able to perform certain tasks for him had I no information to aid me."

"Like being eaten by a pack of lycans if you did not bear some information proving you were in Massius's service?" Lydia asked.

"Yes," Korck replied. "Among other things, yes. I might have snooped a little, too." He looked back at Yako. Upon seeing the tip of the Eldest Hunters sword pointed at the ground, he relaxed a bit. "All I can say is that it's my guess that when you refused to take the Trial of the Ancients, Elder Massius became suspicious." He tilted his head and smirked. "I mean, of all the Hunters in all the covens of the world, *you* would be the last one he believed would refuse the test, given your history."

Yako didn't know what that meant, but he wasn't about to ask in front of this group. "I see," he said. His hand tightened on the hilt of his sword.

Korck glanced around nervously at the group. "That is all I know."

Tara looked up at Yako. "Satisfied?" When Yako nodded, she gave Korck a shove with her foot, and he stumbled away from her.

Korck looked at the statuesque Yako, then back at Tara, then at the other members of the group, who formed a circle around them. "What is this?" he said, looking back at the Reaper.

"Draw whatever weapon you have," Yako said.

Korck visibly trembled. "You go against your word! We had a deal!" He looked back at Tara. "You said I would be released!"

"Am I still holding you, fool?" came the reply.

"Draw whatever weapon you have," Yako repeated.

Korck studied the Eldest Hunter. He stood at what looked to be at-ease, with the sword held in his right hand, tip hovering just above the ground. His mind went to the nine millimeter handgun with the silver rounds tucked in his pants at his back. He knew Yako was fast. But who was faster than a bullet?

Yako knew Korck had the gun at his back. He waited. With speed only a vampire could possess, Korck drew the gun and pointed it at him. Yako flew forward. The faint whipping sound of his sword slicing through air, flesh, and bone came an instant later, and Yako slid to a stop several paces past Korck. He was leaning forward, sword in both hands, and a thin line of blood ran down the edge of the blade to drip off the tip. Korck stood motionless, staring straight ahead with unseeing eyes, his finger poised to pull the trigger. He never did. *Who could be faster than a bullet?* It was the last thought Korck had before his head slipped from his shoulders and fell to the ground with a heavy thud.

After the headless body fell over, Reed collected the gun from the curled fingers and tucked it in the back of his pants. "You won't be needing that," he said to the decaying corpse.

Yako wiped his sword off on Korck's shirt. "You've taken a risk in coming here," he said to the Reaper.

"I have," she agreed. "But I took the Trials of the Ancients and swore the oaths. I am bound to their service, and cannot act against them. The power of the *Ancestor*s is strong and far reaching." She turned away. "Mind how you step, all of you. With his two informants dead, and his lycan contacts as well, Massius will be sniffing around you all." She disappeared into the woods.

For a while, they stood in silence, digesting what they had just learned. "You wanted your proof," Lydia said to Barakus, "you just got it."

"How so?" Barakus asked. "The words of a craven boy, desperate to save his own doomed life, bear no weight with me."

"Then how about the account of a Reaper?" Mariska said.

"And a Reaper is above plotting?"

"Yes, they are," the Second Hunter replied. "In fact, of all our ranks, including the Elders, Reapers are the most trustworthy."

Barakus snorted. "And how do you figure that, little flower?"

Lydia gave him a shove. "Is there not a brain in that massive skull of yours? That girl practically told you she cannot move against an Elder."

"And she just moved against Massius," Barakus said, finally catching on.

"Through the Trial of the Ancients, a Reaper is bound in service to the Elders," Yako stated. "The *Ancestor*'s reach is far and powerful." After he said those last words, a thought came to him, and its weight crashed on his shoulders, nearly buckling his knees.

"What is it," Mariska asked.

Yako sheathed his sword. "Nothing I will speak of here." He retrieved the last of his throwing knives.

"So what now?" Reed asked. "What are we supposed to do?"

Yako looked at the four who remained of the original eight under his command. "You," he pointed at Reed, "were sent to die under my command. Massius will not be happy that you survived, but there is nothing he can do about it. When I return, I will have you placed under my command permanently. You owe me blood for my protection and Nikko's sacrifice." He looked at the other two. "Lydia, Barakus. You will take him with you and return to the coven and give a full report of the events, minus the most important ones, I'm sure I need not tell you."

"Of course, Eldest," Barakus said. "And while I'm at it, I want to have a look at that library."

"I would recommend you wait a while on that," Mariska said. "Massius will be suspicious." Barakus nodded.

"And what of you and your Second?" Lydia asked.

Yako started toward Sinaia. "Mariska will remain here." He looked at his Second and she nodded in obeisance, though he saw in her eyes that she would rather have remained at his side. "You," he said to Mariska, "will tell them I went after the wolves."

Barakus looked from the Eldest Hunter to the woods in the opposite direction. "The wolves are that way," he said, pointing away.

Yako never stopped walking. "I know."

CHAPTER 26

J elani finished his business at the urinal and went to wash his
hands, then held them under the hot air dryer as it turned on.
He chuckled silently. Humorlessly. His life had been a dream
that had turned into a nightmare overnight. One evening jog had
flipped his life upside down, and now he was being hunted by
vampires and had barely survived two encounters with werewolves. What was next? Bigfoot? Chupacabra? *Maybe I could go
to Scotland and swim in Lock Ness,* he thought. *Get eaten by the
monster.*

He heard the door open and looked in the mirror to see the
same technician guy that he'd run into before. Jelani's blood went
cold, and he turned around just as the vampire closed in on him.
Before he could reach into his pocket for his small water gun,
loaded with garlic infused water, the vampire restrained his arms.

"No need to go reaching for whatever is in your pocket, my
man," he said, leaning in far too close. "I just wanted to say hi,
that's all."

Jelani was thinking fast. "Hi."

The vampire laughed, then inhaled deeply. "The smell of a
skiek is all over you. It's like you've been wearing one like a robe."

He leaned back a little and looked Jelani up and down. "I don't know if the smell is mouthwatering or offensive."

Jelani struggled, but that only caused the vampire to strengthen his grip. "Well," he grunted when the grip tightened, "I would feel disgusted if I were you, since it is another dude you're holding here in the bathroom." He focused his breathing as waves of pain shot up his arms. "You know, if someone comes in and sees us like this, it's gonna look a little, intimate."

The vampire cocked his head and regarded him with a questioning look.

"Not that I have anything against that," Jelani continued. "I just don't get down like that is all."

The vampire snickered, and his eyes shifted from light blue to pale red. "I should make a meal of you right now," he said. "It wouldn't hurt for long, I promise."

"That wouldn't be a good idea," Jelani said, mind racing. "You know how gossip travels through this place. There's always somebody who knows what you're doing, no matter where you are. You think there's no cameras right outside this bathroom? We're all on a fifteen-minute break, dude. If I go missing, they will find me in here and track it down to you."

"What do I care what humans discover?" the vampire hissed in his ear. "They are nothing but food."

"Okay, so you're not scared of a whole building full of people finding out what you are," Jelani said. "Let's forget for a minute that that's not too smart. I'm sure the Hunters would see things differently." That got a reaction. "You know I'm right."

"Too late," the vampire said, recovering. "You already know about me."

"I've known about you for a while now, and wish I didn't," Jelani countered. In his mind, he wasn't so sure about that last bit. It was always good to know where one stood on the food chain. "Believe me when I say that I know firsthand how much you all don't want people to know you exist and to the lengths you'll go to keep it that way. And with that in mind, just remember that despite me knowing what you are, no one is passing by you in the halls looking at you funny."

The vampire technician seemed to consider that for a moment before the sound of talking outside the restroom made up his mind for him. Before Jelani knew what was happening, the vampire had released him and moved away.

"You be careful now," he said.

"I'll do that," Jelani replied.

After the vampire left, Jelani took a few minutes to let his pounding heart settle. He wished he could have gotten to his water gun and sprayed that guy. All he would have needed to do was wait a few minutes and then sweep the evidence onto a paper towel and flush it, then toss the clothes in a dumpster somewhere.

This was getting out of hand. Even if he did manage to get this Hunter off his back, any vampire nearby could smell Saaya on him. He wondered how likely it was that he could cease with the occasional visits from the *dampeal* and go back to what his life used to be. He shoved his tongue into his cheek at the thought. Not likely.

He sighed and pushed the thoughts aside. He needed to get focused on the project. Whatever happened, he would enjoy his work, at least.

He left the restroom and returned to the studio, where the small crew and a couple of actors were waiting. "Ah, there he is!" the director said. "All right, Jelani, let's get going, then."

"Let's do it," Jelani said.

"YOU SURE ARE BEING HELPFUL," Jenny Grey said.

"I've got some extra time on my hands so I thought I'd help you clean everything up," Jelani said.

"Really, we've got it," she said. "Actors don't usually stick around to help the crew out. Even on a small set like this, it's just a little unusual."

"Yeah, I know, but I don't see anything wrong with helping folks out. I appreciate the work you all do." It wasn't a lie. He did appreciate what the film crew did behind the scenes, on large sets and small. What made him feel a little guilty was that he wouldn't be here right now if he wasn't trying to avoid running into that vampire technician in the parking lot. Safety in numbers.

"Hey, if Jelani wants to help out," the director said, walking back into the studio, "I'm not gonna stop him." He pointed at several cases containing equipment that likely cost more than any possession Jelani had ever had in his life. "Hey, Lani. You mind if I call you Lani?"

Jelani tried not to growl his response. "Lani sounds like a girl's name."

"Aw, come on, be a good sport. Hey, if you could grab those cases, there, it would save us a couple more trips."

Jelani eyed the cases filled with the ridiculously expensive equipment. "Um. You sure you want me to carry those?"

The director waved his hand away as if it were nothing to worry about. "Oh, don't worry about it. Just don't drop the stuff or we'll have to make you work for free for the next hundred years." He sniggered. Jenny tittered. Jelani laughed nervously.

Everyone shouldered the equipment and headed down the hall. Jelani turned away while the director typed in the access code and opened the door. After they stored the equipment in the locker, they waited outside the restroom for the cameraman, a short stocky guy that was always there, and the four of them made their way to the parking lot. The three crew members chatted idly while Jelani scanned the darkened surroundings just outside the lit areas. Normally, he found the dark and quiet grounds peaceful, but now they felt ominous. He hoped the vampire wouldn't attempt to dispatch them all just to get to him.

They continued down the long, snaking walkway, then turned

the corner. A lone figure rounded the corner on the far end of the walkway and was moving toward them. Jelani's pulse quickened and he thought maybe this was a mistake.

"Hey, Officer Boyd!" Jenny said, waving.

Jelani let out an audible sigh when he saw that it was a police officer walking toward them. Since the murder of poor Claire McMahon, security had been increased, and there were at least two armed police officers patrolling the grounds at night until the last employees left for the day.

"You're all working late tonight," he said.

"Yeah," the director said. "We're running on a tight deadline, and the E3 is right around the corner. They want to have a demo of this new IP ready to show by then."

The officer's eyes glazed over, and he gave a huff. "Well, I won't pretend to understand what you just said, but good luck with your deadline. Is anybody else in the building?"

"I think we're the last," Jenny said.

"Okay. You folks have a good night."

"Thanks," they said, waving politely as the cop continued past.

"Seriously," the director said once they were out of earshot, "it's not like I was speaking some technical jargon ..."

"Yes," Jenny said, "but people who don't play video games don't know that the E3 stands for 'Electronic Entertainment Expo,' and that an IP is simply an 'intellectual property.'"

"Whatever," he said. "It's still funny when they get that dumb deer in the headlights look."

"Either that," Jenny said, smirking, "or they just don't understand geek-speak."

"People like to look down their noses and call the people that provide their entertainment nerds and geeks," the director snapped, "but they still pick up the damn controller."

"Not everyone," Jelani said. "I'm not a techie, but I grew up on video games. We're all big kids about something, I think."

They reached the parking lot, and everyone parted ways to find their cars in the empty parking lot. "You guys have a good night," Jelani called from over the roof of his car.

"You, too," Jenny said, waving. The director and cameraman just waved and jumped in, starting their cars and pulling out. Not wanting to be in the parking lot alone, Jelani hopped in and started the engine. He waited till Jenny started out, then followed. He didn't stop glancing in his rearview mirror until he was on the highway. Finally, he relaxed, and let out a long sigh of relief.

He nearly jumped when his phone rang. Glancing around to make sure there were no police cars around, he answered. "Hey man. I'm on the road, so I have to put you on speaker."

Daniel's voice responded on the other end of the line. "I know I must sound like your mother or something, but I just wanted to make sure you're all right."

"Quite all right, man. Given the situation, I appreciate it. I'm guessing everything is okay at home?"

"Yeah. The girls cooked tonight. Good stuff."

"Can't wait," Jelani said. "I should be home in about fifteen. Let me get off this phone before I get a ticket."

"Gotcha. See you then."

Jelani ended the call and glanced in his rearview mirror again. "I gotta stop stressing like this," he said to himself. "I'm going to drive myself crazy." A tune sounded on his phone indicating a text message was received. He glanced down at the lit screen and saw that it came from Melinda. Or at least, Melinda's phone. "Can't have one friggin' night of peace," Jelani mumbled, trying in vain to push down the dread that was creeping into his stomach. The road was fairly empty and curiosity got the better of him, so he picked up the phone and opened the message, glancing back and forth from the phone to the road.

"Guess who?" it said. Jelani groaned just as another message came in.

"Not in the mood? Okay. Well I'll just keep this short. You needn't worry about your little friend. I'll take good care of her."

Another message came in. *"Oh, and I'm going to kill you very soon. Have a good night."*

Jelani wondered if he should respond. What would he say, anyway? *"Okay, thanks,"* he typed, then tossed the phone on the passenger seat.

He reached into the side pocket of the car door and assured himself that the silver knife was there. Since Jelani lost his in the woods while trying to outrun death, Daniel had loaned him his silver knife since he had to work late.

He exited the freeway and navigated the downtown streets until he finally arrived in Coal Harbour. The sight of his building couldn't have been more welcome. He pulled into the well-lit parking garage, then turned off the engine. Once he got out of the car, he quickly scanned the parking lot while slipping the silver blade in the back of his pants. The car chirped when he set the alarm, and he walked as fast as he could without running.

The minute or two that it took for the elevator to arrive felt like an hour. Finally, it reached the parking garage and there was the soft *ding* that indicated the doors were opening. Jelani went to step in when he saw someone standing in front of him. He looked up, and right into Remy's red eyes. The grinning vampire's hand snapped out before Jelani could react, grabbed hold of his shirt, and snatched him into the elevator.

He whipped Jelani around and pinned him to the side closest to the buttons. "Now let's see," Remy said as he ran a finger up and down the buttons. "If I counted correctly, you're little fox hole is on the tenth floor, right?" He pressed the button, and the number ten lit. The elevator started upward. He turned his attention back to Jelani, who was growing limp.

"Oh, you can't breathe with my hand clamped on your throat, can you? Well, how about this." He made a show of thinking. "I'll keep you alive long enough to find out where you live. Then I'll rip out your throat and take care of your friends. My problems are solved, and I might even start my own little harem and turn your girlfriend and the other one." He lowered himself till his face was inches from Jelani's. "How 'bout that?"

Jelani couldn't speak, so he narrowed his eyes at him.

"Ooh," Remy said. "If I didn't know any better, I'd say you're giving me the 'fuck you' eyes. Ah well. I can't say I blame you—"

Jelani had managed to slip his left hand into his pocket and drew out the little water pistol. Moving only his wrist, he pointed it up as far as he could and pulled the little plastic trigger. A stream of garlic infused water hit the vampire's neck. Jelani pumped as quickly as he could, and the vampire's neck tightened.

"Ack!" Remy released him and stumbled back. Jelani gasped for air and reached behind his back for the silver knife. He coughed, doubled over, but holding the knife so that his body obscured it from view.

His neck smoking, Remy straightened and glared murderously at him. "I'm going to take that little plastic gun and jam it down your throat—" Jelani was on him before he could finish, swiping the pure silver blade in fast horizontal strikes. Beyond all possibility, he'd actually caught the Hunter by surprise, and Jelani scored a glancing cut across his chest.

Remy's eyes glowed in that terrible red, and he recovered enough to dodge every subsequent attack. Jelani was fast for a human, but hopelessly slow for a pureblood vampire. "Not bad," Remy taunted. His voice had taken on a lower, almost guttural sound, betraying his anger. The blistered skin on his neck was almost completely smooth again. "This will be all the more gratifying when I kill you."

Jelani slashed outward, then brought his water gun to bear and sprayed another stream of garlic water at the vampire's face. Remy ducked just in time, and Jelani brought the blade down on his neck. The knife sliced cleanly through air, and Jelani spun around, stabbing backward as he did.

Around and around they moved in the tiny box that was the ascending elevator. Jelani forced himself to ignore the terror of being in such close proximity with this monster, and focused on surviving. Remy hopped backward to avoid the knife, then lunged in with a backhanded slap that connected with the side of Jelani's head and sent him spinning into the wall and then crashing to the floor.

Jelani squinted away the stars in his vision and sprayed the water pistol again. As the vampire dodged the poisonous water, Jelani used the time to regain his feet, and kicked outward, connecting with Remy's midsection. The vampire was knocked back less than half a step, and he grinned at Jelani as though he'd told a ridiculous joke.

There was a soft *ding* and the elevator door opened behind Jelani. Acting purely on instinct, he jumped up and tucked in both his feet, kicking outward and connecting with the Hunter's chest. He succeeded not in hurting the vampire, but launching himself backward and out of the elevator. In the same instant he was pushed away, he aimed the water pistol and let fly another stream of garlic water. Having been amused at Jelani's futile martial efforts, Remy was unprepared for the stream of water that hit his neck and sprayed up into his face.

This time, the Hunter did fall back, screeching and slashing at empty air. Jelani was on his feet as soon as he hit the floor, then he hit the down button on the elevator and sprinted down the hall.

Remy shot out of the elevator before the doors closed, and was half running half stumbling after him, one hand clutching his burned face. Jelani glanced over his shoulder and saw murder in those baleful red eyes.

He managed to outdistance the vampire long enough to reach into his pocket and fumble out the keys. In seconds he unlocked the door and was inside, setting the deadbolt.

Having heard Jelani burst in the door, the others were on their feet.

"What is it?" Daniel managed to ask, right before the door was knocked off the hinges, and Remy came stumbling in. The burns on his neck looked slow to heal, and he was in obvious pain, but far from incapacitated.

His water gun nearly empty, Jelani reached for Daniel's weapon, sitting on the counter near the sink, and pumped the trigger. Trapped in the narrow hallway, there was little room for the vampire to dodge, and another stream of garlic water burned into his skin.

Growling through the agony, the enraged vampire leaped forward and knocked the gun from Jelani's grasp. A wave of pain went through his hand, and Jelani was sure some of the bones had been broken. Before he had time to react, Remy grabbed him by the neck and forced him to the ground. This time, there was no toying, no joking or savoring the moment. Jelani was quickly losing consciousness, and he managed to see the Hunter lifting a hand armed with elongating fingernails lined up with his stomach.

But then Daniel was there. His best friend, always prepared, had an extra silver blade sitting right on the couch next to him. With knife throwing skills Jelani had never managed to grasp, Daniel launched the blade spinning across the room to embed itself in the Hunter's shoulder. Remy barked in pain and released Jelani. Daniel leaped over Jelani and planted a solid kick to the vampire's jaw.

The momentum of his airborne, one-hundred-ninety-five-pound body would have broken the side of a normal person's face. But not Remy. The vampire's head snapped back, but he recovered instantly and slashed his hand out, raking his elongated nails across Daniel's chest.

The sound of ripping fabric and Daniel's cry of pain brought Jelani back to his senses, then he heard Wen's muffled yelp. He glanced across the room to see Alisha and Wen pressed against the far wall next to the couch, the latter with her hands pressed over her mouth.

That tiny sound caught the vampire's attention, and Remy's head snapped up. The instant their eyes connected, Wen collapsed to the floor. Alisha crouched over her, looking from her friend to the vampire who had just knocked Daniel across the room to slam into the couch. Daniel sagged to the floor, unconscious.

Remy cursed in an unintelligible language and yanked the silver blade out of his shoulder. He slammed the blade on the floor and stood.

Pain gave way to anger, and Jelani snatched up the weapon and slashed it at the Hunter's feet, scoring a deep cut in his ankle. Remy hissed and retreated. Jelani gained his feet and pressed the attack, but it wasn't enough. Even injured, the vampire was too fast and too strong, and he knocked the blade from Jelani's hand and grabbed his neck.

Remy spun him around until Jelani's back was to him, then forced his head sideways. With a loud, breathy hiss, he opened his mouth to reveal elongated fangs. Just before the vampire could pierce Jelani's neck, Remy flew over his head and across the room. He hit the floor but quickly regained his feet.

Kafeel shoved Jelani aside and stalked toward the Hunter. Behind him, Saaya stepped through the doorway and moved into the room. Any thoughts Remy had of ending this business tonight were dashed at the sight of the two new arrivals, and he searched desperately for an exit. He glanced at the window, then back at the towering vampire that was nearly on top of him.

Remy dove aside just as Kafeel reached for him, grabbed Alisha, and held her in front of him to ward off the bigger vampire. There was an instant when Remy wasn't sure if this would deter the big man or not, but that moment of hesitation was enough for him to cross the room and crash through the window, a screaming Alisha held firmly in his grasp.

Jelani yelled and struggled to his feet. Kafeel silently leaped out the broken window after the Hunter.

Standing near the doorway, Saaya regarded Jelani for only a moment, then seemed to come to a decision. She grabbed up the two silver blades, and the water guns. "Forgive me, *jaan*," she said.

She looked into his eyes, and a flicker of light crossed those light brown orbs. It was the last thing Jelani saw before darkness took him.

She went to Daniel, who was still unconscious, and whispered into his ear. "Follow Jelani's lead." She went over and did the same with Wen. The sound of doors opening and inquiring voices drew her attention, and an instant later she was across the room and out the broken window, disappearing into the cold, cruel night.

CHAPTER 27

Hold on, he's waking up!"
"Did you call the police?"
"Yeah, they should be here any minute now."
The voices were far away and getting closer as Jelani drew nearer to awareness. He opened his eyes to see three sets of concerned eyes staring down at him.

"You all right, son?"

Jelani slowly blinked his eyes open. He studied the face of the man who'd spoken to him, finally recognizing the long salt-and-pepper hair tied in a ponytail and matching mustache as old Mr. Robins. He and his wife were empty-nesters who lived two doors down and were always kind to Jelani and Daniel. Jelani smiled weakly and tried to sit up, but Mr. Robins held him down.

"Don't try to get up, son. You've got quite a few cuts and bruises on your body. Someone try to break into this place? What happened?"

"Stop grilling the boy, already, Tom." Beside him, Mrs. Robins placed a hand on his shoulder. "The young man has been through enough as it is, and he's barely getting his mind back together."

"Thank you, Mr. and Mrs. Robins," Jelani said in a cracking

voice. He touched Mr. Robins' hand to indicate he was fine to sit up, and after a moment of hesitation, the old man relented. They helped Jelani into a sitting position with his back against the side of the kitchen island. He looked across the room to see Wen and a woman in her forties, short, black hair and gentle, green eyes, crouched over Daniel. Wen was holding a bag of ice on Daniel's shoulder. Though she was visibly shaken, Wen seemed more stable than Jelani would have thought.

"So what happened?" Mr. Robins asked again. "We heard a couple of big thumps on the floor and some rumbling. At first we didn't know what to think, but then we heard someone yell, and a few minutes later, the sound of glass breaking." He looked across the room at the broken window where cool air was flowing in.

"At least it's not winter," Jelani said in a weak attempt at humor.

Mr. Robins chuckled while his wife shook her head. She looked in Jelani's eyes, and there was concern there. "Seriously, Jelani. What happened? This is the second time that window has been broken. What's going on?"

Just then, the building manager arrived followed by two uniformed police officers. One of them, a man in his mid-forties, with crew-cut grey hair and blue-grey eyes stopped at Jelani while his partner stepped past.

"Anyone who did not witness what happened here, or did not find the victims can return to your homes, please. Thank you."

The small group of people dispersed, leaving the two police officers, Mr. and Mrs. Robins, and Jelani and his friends alone. The older officer squatted next to Jelani.

"I'm Officer Davidson, and this," he indicated the other officer on Jelani's left, "is Officer Chu." Jelani nodded to each of them in turn. Officer Davidson nodded to his partner who went to check on the others.

"What's your name?"

"Jelani Shaudee, sir."

"You mind if I call you Jelani?"

"Not at all, sir."

"Are you in need of medical attention?"

Jelani shook his head. "I think I'm fine. Just a little beaten up, but I don't think there's anything serious."

"Can you tell me what happened here, Jelani?"

At first, Jelani felt a wave of panic, but it quickly subsided as a flood of information came into his mind. Suddenly, he knew exactly what to say. "We were attacked. I'd just gotten home, and this guy kicked in the door. Do you mind if I get off the floor?"

The officer helped him up and they walked into the living room where Daniel and Wen were already sitting on the couch together. Jelani sat down, and the two officers faced them respectively.

"So you were saying that some guy kicked in your door?"

"Yeah," Jelani said, running a hand over his clean-shaven head. "I don't know who the person was, or why the hell he chose to kick in our door, or even how the heck he got into the building. I just know that I walked in the door, and closed and locked it. I smelled dinner in the kitchen and was looking forward to it. I took a couple of steps and then there was a loud bang, then another, and the door crashes open, and this guy comes flying in and attacked me."

"Did you get a good look at him?"

"No, except that he was wearing all black and some kind of ski mask, or something like it to cover his face. The guy obviously knows how to fight because he handled both of us," Jelani indicated Daniel, "pretty effectively."

"Did he have any weapons?"

Jelani shook his head. "I honestly can't tell you." The words coming from his mouth were barely his own. It was as if he was simply opening his mouth and letting the words flow. "I mean, I don't remember seeing any weapons on him, but as you can see," he held out his arms, "I've got a few scratches. Maybe he just scratched me with his fingernails or something, because all I remember was getting punched and kicked all over the place."

"Do you think you might know this person?"

"It's possible, but whoever it is, I feel like whether or not we know him, he knows us."

"Why do you think that?"

"Because several months ago when we weren't home, someone broke into our apartment and busted the window. They broke a few things but stole nothing. Just broke the window and left." Jelani shook his head, hoping that blending bits of truth in the story made it more believable. "I really don't get it. I don't."

The officer's blue-grey eyes bore into him, and after a very uncomfortable amount of time passed, he nodded. By then, Officer Chu had finished questioning Daniel and Wen.

"I would recommend you find another place to stay for the time being," Officer Davidson said. "Perhaps a friend or family member. Whoever attacked you here, for the second time, is likely to return again. You might want to relocate until we're able to catch him."

"Here," Davidson reached into his pocket and pulled out a card. "This is the number to the precinct and my direct extension." He handed one to each of them, and Officer Chu did the same. "If anything happens or you remember anything else about this, call that number."

"And avoid being out alone at night in unlit places," Officer Chu said. "I know this seems obvious, but people forget. Pay attention to your surroundings. You never know if someone is following you unless you're mindful of the people around you."

"Thanks, officer," Jelani said, and he found that he meant it. "We certainly will give you a call if we discover or remember anything else."

After the police officers were gone, Jelani, Daniel, and Wen sat on the couch for a moment, silent. The Hunter was gone and he'd taken Alisha with him. None of them had mentioned her abduction.

Finally, Daniel asked what had to have been on both his and Wen's mind.

"We followed your lead," he said, "which led us not to mention what happened to Alisha. You mind telling me why that is?"

Jelani spread his hands. "I couldn't tell you, man. All I know is that the details I gave them was as much, and only as much, as they needed to know without this situation getting even more complicated."

"How do you know that?" Wen's shaky voice drew Jelani's attention. She had held herself together long enough to make it through the questioning, but now she was starting to unravel. Daniel wrapped a strong arm around her shoulders and held her close.

"I just know," Jelani answered. "It's like the proper information was just placed in my mind. When questions came, I knew how to answer them and when to stop."

"Saaya," Daniel said.

"Yeah, I'm pretty sure of it."

"And speaking of her," Daniel said, looking out the broken window. "Where is she?"

"I'm guessing she went after the bastard," Jelani said. "I just wish I knew where he was headed." His eyes narrowed. "So help me, even if it means this guy does kill me, I won't let something happen to Alisha if I can help it." He let out a breath. "Which, at the moment, I can't."

"There are a couple places we can look." Both men looked at Wen, who was sitting next to Daniel, knees pressed together and looking straight ahead. Though she was looking at the wall, her eyes were seeing someplace else.

"Wen?" Daniel asked.

"There are three places he's likely to take her," she continued. "The inn that he's staying at in East Van, the docks near there, or Grouse Mountain."

"How do you know that?" Daniel asked, an edge of curiosity mixed with alarm in his voice.

Wen blinked and shook her head. "When he looked at me earlier, he did something to knock me unconscious. I know he did it so that I wouldn't scream and alert anyone else." She shivered. "But when our eyes met, just before I was knocked out, some of his thoughts and memories went into my mind. He was trying to kill us quickly before Saaya and her brother got here, but he hadn't expected the water guns."

Despite the situation, she smiled. "Those water guns really ticked him off, you know. The thought of being so hurt by a child's toy."

"What else did you get?" Jelani said.

"He doesn't want to kill or turn Alisha until he's killed the rest of us. He wants you out of the way first, Jelani, since you've given him the most trouble. Then he wants Daniel, then me, since I'm what he considers the least threat." Her voice was beginning to shake again, and Daniel squeezed her against him.

"Not gonna happen, babe," he said, kissing Wen on the top of her head.

After a moment, she steadied enough to continue. "I really don't think he realized he'd passed all this to me. I know where he's been staying and the usual places he goes. He hadn't decided to take Alisha yet, so that's why I don't know where he went, only where he might take her."

"If I were him," Jelani said, "I wouldn't go back to the inn. He's still got Saaya and Kafeel on his trail, and to tell the truth, I don't know how anyone could get away from those two. Still, I doubt he'll take her there. I'm guessing either the docks or Grouse."

"I don't think he's going back to Grouse," Daniel said. He pointed at the blanket lying on the couch next to Jelani. In dealing with all that had happened and the threat to Alisha, he'd forgotten that cold air was blowing into the room. Jelani tossed the blanket to him, and Daniel wrapped it around Wen, who still sat with her feet on the couch and her knees drawn up in front of her chest. She looked like a tiny ball of blanket next to Daniel, with only her head visible. Under different circumstances, it would have been a charming scene.

"He'd have to be stupid to go back to Grouse," Daniel continued. "That place is crawling with werewolves."

Next to him, Wen shook her head in bewilderment. "I know this is all real, but a part of my mind still can't quite accept that there are werewolves and vampires in the world."

"Well," Jelani said, "we're going to have to suspend our sense of reality until this works itself out. And I don't mind telling you that after this is done, I might move to the Sahara Desert or something." He looked back at Daniel. "So, I agree with you. We can rule out Grouse."

"So no Grouse, and no hotel," Daniel said.

Jelani frowned. "Yeah. He'll try to ditch them first, then make it back to his hotel room before dawn and contact one of us."

"I doubt he's going to try the same thing he did on Grouse," Daniel replied. "That didn't turn out well for him."

"No," Jelani said. "He'll probably try to pick us off on the way to wherever he tells us to meet him."

"So what are we left with?" Wen asked. "My guess is that he'll try to give them the slip and hide out for a while, to make sure they don't find him before he goes back to his room."

They all looked at each other, and Daniel voiced their thoughts. "He's probably going to try to give them the slip and hide out at the docks."

"That sounds like our best bet." Jelani stood. "We need to get over there ASAP."

The others stood, and Daniel looked around. "You seen my silver knife?"

Jelani recalled more of the information Saaya had injected into his mind. "She took them."

"What? Why?" Daniel was alarmed and Jelani couldn't blame him.

"She knew the police were coming."

"And? We're defenseless now!"

"How do you think it would have looked if our neighbors found us with long silver blades lying around? What if the police searched the place; which they did? How would it have looked?"

"Just because we have silver blades doesn't mean anything," Daniel argued.

"Dude, they have Remy's blood on them, and even if they didn't, all it would do is cast suspicion on the situation. Better that we had no kind of weapons around. Cops don't need much to go on before they start sniffing out things you don't want them to find."

Daniel thought about it, then nodded grudgingly. "Yeah, well, I guess we'd better fill up our water guns and head out."

They filled five of the small water guns with the garlic infused water from a large container they had mixed. Daniel and Jelani each took two, shoving them in their pockets, and Wen slipped one into her purse.

"Guess we need to get down there," Jelani said. "Hopefully before he does."

"Hopefully," Daniel echoed.

After they'd gathered their valuables and enough clothes for a few days away, they left the apartment, waylaid several times by neighbors asking questions. They spent a bit of time talking to the building manager who was not particularly happy to have the same damage happen to the same window again.

The ride down the elevator was an uncomfortable one, as Jelani had shared with them his encounter with Remy in the exact same place. When the doors opened, Jelani and Daniel were ready, holding their water guns like real firearms. Feeling a bit ridiculous, they scanned the parking garage for potential threats, then hurried to Jelani's car.

"Hurry up, man," Daniel said, as Jelani shoved the key in the ignition and started the engine.

"Yeah, I got it. Just get your seat belts on." He put the car in reverse, backed out of the slot, and drove out as fast as he dared, but slow enough not to appear in any rush. The tires squeaked on the concrete as he turned the corner toward the exit.

"I don't mean to snap," Daniel said, "It just felt like something was in there with us."

"Yeah. I felt it, too. We're probably just paranoid. It's understandable."

"Poor Alisha," Wen said from the back seat. Her voice started to crack as the sobs came. "I hope she's okay."

"I'm sure she's pretty terrified, but I'm also sure she's alive." Jelani glanced at her through the rearview mirror. "He wouldn't have taken her if he didn't plan to use her as some sort of leverage."

Jelani stopped the car at the street to let a truck pass, then exited the garage and turned right, heading to Georgia Street. A figure stepped out of the concealment of a dark corner and watched the car go around the bend and up the inclining street. An instant later, it was gone.

CHAPTER 28

Traveling great distances, such as that between Vancouver, BC and Bucharest, Romania, was tricky. If he had been traveling from a place that would require twenty-four hours of flight, Yako would have simply booked a flight in the middle of the night and arrived at the same time the next day. The only other precaution needed was to choose a seat at the back of the plane. He never had to worry about a passenger lifting the window shade because he could simply compel them against it.

Travel from Romania to Vancouver was a different matter. It was a twelve-hour flight, which would require him to leave either during the day to arrive in Vancouver at night, or attempt travel when the forecast was cloudy and overcast at one or both locations.

He had found a measure of luck, being able to book a last minute flight while the weather was cloudy and cold, and the sun unable to penetrate the thick canopy of clouds. His mood had already been dark, and having a rather chatty fellow sitting next to him only darkened it further. Being able to focus under any circumstances, Yako had ignored him, until the small man had asked him to open the window shade to have a view of the land below. Yako had responded by compelling the man to sleep.

Now, with only his thoughts to fill his mind, and an hour left on the flight, the Eldest Hunter planned his next move for when he exited the plane. Likely, Massius would have either gotten word that Yako had left Romania to return to Vancouver, or he would suspect as much.

Once off the plane, there would still be roughly seven hours till daylight. Enough time for him to hopefully locate and eliminate Remy. Of course, the troublesome worm would probably have already received word from Massius that Yako was on his way, and planned accordingly. That one was as slippery as they came. Never had Yako seen anyone so adept at avoiding death and capture as Remy. It was this *talent* that had kept the unlikable Hunter alive for so long. Yako meant to change that.

The pilot's voice came through the intercom to announce that they were beginning their initial descent.

After he dealt with Remy, there was still the matter of those four humans, the *dampeal*, and her brother. Given the current circumstances, Yako wondered if it was even worth pursuing. So much had been uncovered because of this situation that Yako found the humans less and less of a concern. Or at least, less of a concern than Remy. There were other Hunters in the coven that could deal with the targets if need be. That left the problem of the *dampeal* and her brother.

There was not a single vampire in the Vancouver coven that could deal with either one of them alone, of that, Yako was certain. It would take a good number of Hunters to bring them down, and even then, the losses would be costly. If only that foolish half-breed girl hadn't interfered, this wouldn't be a problem. Of course, if she hadn't created this problem, Yako would not have known or suspected any of the historical facts he'd discovered during his detainment in Sinaia. It seemed he owed the *dampeal* an indirect debt of gratitude.

Perhaps a deal could be struck with them. Perhaps he could

speak with the girl and an agreement could be reached that so long as she held interest in the human, she would ensure his and the others' silence about the existence of the immortals. If she ever grew bored, she could either dispatch them, or her brother could turn them. So long as they remained silent, Yako didn't care one way or the other.

The pilot's voice came through the intercom to advise the flight attendants to take their seats.

Ten minutes later, the plane made a smooth landing on the tarmac of Vancouver International Airport. All throughout the cabin there were sleepy murmurs of relief, and comments about looking forward to standing and walking again. It was a feeling Yako had never experienced, and never would. Any vampire could remain as still as a statue for an indeterminate amount of time, but a *skiek*, a turned vampire, knew what it was like to need to move and exercise, lest the muscles and blood flow be compromised. As a pureblood, Yako never had that concern.

After filing out of the plane, Yako moved to the side and scanned the terminal. From the way they moved, to the way they smelled, humans were easily identifiable. Vampires were also easily distinguishable, to other vampires, at least.

Almost all of the people walking through the terminal were human, with the occasional vampire flowing gracefully in their midst, and the even less occasional lycan stalking about, glaring at any vampire they happened to spot. Or smell.

Hunters distinguished themselves from their vampire brethren by the way they moved with purpose, the way they took in the environment and watched those around them. Exactly what Yako was doing now. He didn't see any Hunters here, only civilians, human, lycan, and vampire alike. He continued through the terminal and toward baggage claim, where he would reclaim the bag containing his few garments and his sword and knives.

Once he'd recovered his items, he made his way to the parking garage. The smell of a lycan penetrated his thoughts, and he stopped. He heard soft laughter.

"Darren was right about you. No one catches the Eldest Hunter off his guard, eh?" A tall, broad-shouldered Pakistani man stepped out from behind a thick pillar, spreading his arms in a non-threatening manner. "He told me you would be making a hurried trip back and that I should meet you here. I was planning on waiting for at least a couple days, but you didn't waste any time."

Yako narrowed his eyes. "Why?"

"Because you would get in your own car and drive off."

"And this is bad?"

The big lycan nodded. "If I were hunting somebody, and I was patient enough, I would wait for them to drive off in their car."

Yako caught on immediately. Whoever was sent to watch for him would remain hidden, but would set up a watch near his car. Once they'd spotted him, Remy would be alerted. He knew Darren well enough that he would have considered this possibility. Yako silently admonished himself for not thinking of that.

"Mm hm. Looks like you just caught my drift." The big man approached, and indicated that they get back in the elevator. He pressed the button for the top floor of the parking garage, and the elevator started up.

"The bloods ..." he glanced sidelong at Yako, "no offense." Yako nodded for him to continue. "They've set up watch for you. One near your fancy NSX, and one positioned with an overhead view. They would know you're here and which direction you're going."

The elevator gave a soft *ding*, and the doors opened. They walked out into the cold night, and Yako followed the large man toward a gray Range Rover.

"By the way, my name's Imron. Don't bother telling me yours, since I already know it." When Yako didn't respond, Imron glanced down at Yako. "Darren also said you don't talk much." He reached in his pocket and the parking lights of the Range Rover blinked.

"So after I smuggle you back into town, what are you going to do about this Remy guy?"

"Kill him."

"Hmm." Imron seemed to think about the response, and Yako arched an eyebrow at him. "I'm Darren's second-in-command and I lead the pack while he's away. I sent a few pack members to watch your Remy guy. He's a slippery one. Like trying to hold a fish. That girl and her big brother have been after him on and off for days and haven't been able to catch him. And I'll tell you this: they're pretty damn fast, and much as I hate to admit it, I wouldn't want to be on the bad side of that brother of hers."

Yako took it all in. "Any recent news?"

Once at the bottom of the parkade, Imron nosed the Range Rover out and headed east. "Yeah. As a matter of fact, one of the girls I had posted up outside the humans' building saw him go crashing out the window with a black girl tucked under his arm. The Indian girl and her brother went flying out the window after him."

This caught Yako's interest. "Did she see where he went?"

Imron nodded. "Headed east, but he's zigzagging to wherever he's going. I've had constant word of his movements, and that's only because my spies were prepared. They know to stay on the rooftops for a birds' eye view. That's the only way to keep the slinky bastard in sight."

"So the girl and her brother haven't caught him?"

"Last word I got was ten minutes before you showed up. He gave them the slip and was headed toward the docks, of all places. The two following him don't look like they're far off the trail, but they seem to have lost him for the moment."

"That all?"

"Oh, one more thing. The girl still posted outside the building saw your three humans driving out toward the docks, too. Don't seem like a coincidence to me. I know one of those guys is attached to the girl, but it seems like a pretty stupid thing to do." He looked over at Yako. "You want me to take you over there, don't you?"

"Yes."

"You don't let the grass grow under your feet at all, do you? Ready to get this business finished? Can't say I blame you."

"You already knew," Yako said. "That's why we're already heading in that direction."

Imron laughed. "Yup."

SAAYA MIGHT HAVE ENJOYED the view of the lit city of Vancouver from atop her Gastown high-rise if she hadn't been seething at the fact that that cravenly Hunter had eluded her yet again. She had never known of a vampire evolving a *talent* rooted in cowardice, but in this case, it was clear. Saaya now understood Remy's usefulness as a Hunter. The concept of him as an elite warrior was laughable, mildly skilled though he was. No. His value existed in the form of his dexterity and ability to elude pursuit and make himself practically impossible to locate once he was out of sight.

She narrowed her eyes, still looking over all of the nearby alleys and rooftops. At first, she'd thought he was able to bend light around his body the way she did. There had never been a vampire other than an *Ancestor* or their direct offspring who was able to achieve such a feat. It seemed impossible that this coward could do it, but it turned out not to be so. He was simply good at making himself invisible by more conventional means.

Kafeel had nearly caught him twice, but both times the Hunter had twisted or squirmed loose and darted in a different direction, much like a squirrel escaping a fox. The fact that he'd done this with that girl in his grasp was even more impressive, though Saaya admitted it to herself grudgingly. Never mind Kafeel, she would kill the troublesome Hunter.

Her thoughts went from Remy to Kafeel, as her brother drew near. "East," he said.

"He's moving east?" Saaya stared at the city below.

"I picked up his trail in one of the alleys. He doubled back, then turned east again. He's moving toward the docks."

"You're sure?"

"Fairly."

"Then let us greet him there, shall we?"

There was a pause. "He's feeding on the girl."

Saaya blinked and turned to face him. Of course, he cared little enough about that fact, but he'd felt it necessary to mention it to her. "And you tell this to me because you believe I have a special reserve of tears for the plight of a human girl?"

Kafeel's expression remained stony, as always. "The toy that you are so determined to preserve has a vested interest in her condition."

"That doesn't matter. When it is time for him to fulfill his debt to me, her existence is of little consequence."

"Then why not kill him and make love to his corpse." He turned and dropped off the side of the building. Saaya ground her teeth, watching the tall shadowy figure that was her older brother, leaping from rooftop to rooftop.

In all the years she had known him, she couldn't think of a time when he was wrong, and now was not an exception. "This is getting irritating," she murmured, and stepped to the edge of the roof. She hated that Kafeel was right, but he was. If that girl died or was turned, Jelani would be practically useless to her. As compassionate and caring as he was, the fool would be a hollow shell of himself and no fun at all.

"Oh, fine!" She stepped off the roof.

~

JELANI AND DANIEL skulked along the stacked eighteen-wheeler trailers and giant crates forming the maze that was the East Vancouver shipyard. After Wen had shared all the details she had been unwittingly given by Remy, they'd dropped her off at a nearby friend's apartment. She'd argued against it, but in the end, had relented. There was little enough Jelani and Daniel could do for themselves. Having Wen there would only complicate the situation further.

The docks were poorly lit and ominously quiet. "You think he's here yet?" Daniel whispered.

"I don't know," Jelani answered. "Saaya and Kafeel were after him pretty hard when he jumped out the window. He might not have had time to make it here yet."

"Maybe they already got him."

"As much as I want to believe that, our luck isn't that good."

They crept to the edge of a wall of stacked trailers and pressed their backs against it. Jelani leaned sideways and ducked his head around quickly. He nodded to Daniel that the coast was clear, and they continued.

Beyond the labyrinth of trailers, giant cranes stood towering over everything, like shadowy sentries guarding the empty facility. A rat darted across their path, followed by a feral cat. Jelani's heart nearly stopped, and beside him, Daniel swore under his breath.

They skulked along the sides of the trailers until they reached end of the dock, and the silent darkness of the ocean greeted them. They turned back and went around another bend.

"She said he hangs out around this area," Jelani said.

"She was right." Daniel squatted at the base of a trailer, squinting in the dim light at the ground. "Blood," he said.

Jelani was beside him immediately. After studying the evidence, he sighed in relief. "Looks like this happened a while ago. The rain must've washed most of it away. I wonder how long ago it was."

"About four or five days, I think," a woman's voice answered.

Daniel and Jelani leaped backward, bringing their water guns out of their pockets. A lone figure stood in the shadows further down the path. A feminine figure.

Jelani's mind first went to Alisha, but that wasn't her voice. "Melinda?"

"Nice of you to remember me, love." She stepped into the dim light.

Jelani's heart was pounding in his chest. "Um—"

"Oh, baby," she interrupted, closing her eyes. She leaned her head back and smiled. "You tempt me so much. I can practically hear the blood streaming through your veins. You always know how to drive a girl crazy."

"Melinda?"

"Hm?"

"I ..."

"Yes?"

"Do you know where Remy is?" He couldn't think of anything else to say, but he certainly wanted to get her attention off his blood. "We're kinda looking for him."

"Of course you are," she said dismissively. "Why don't we forget him for a moment and talk about us, hmm?" Beside him, Daniel glanced from Jelani to Melinda, not sure what to do. She must have sensed his indecision because her attention snapped to him.

"Hey, Daniel!" she said, eyeing him seductively. "Just as sexy as ever. Has anyone ever told you that you look something like a younger Russell Wong?" She gave him a once-over and smiled.

Daniel watched her carefully, keeping his features neutral. "Once or twice."

"I'm sure you have, sweetie."

"Um, Melinda?"

"Yes, Jelani." She looked back at him.

"We really do need to find Remy. Do you know where he is?"

"Your interest in another guy could really hurt a girl's ego, love."

"It's not that I don't want to talk and catch up," Jelani said, "it's just that we have some kind of urgent business with him."

"You must be referring to the girl you dumped me for," she responded.

Wrong direction. "Melinda—"

She closed the fifteen-foot distance between them before either Jelani or Daniel could react. "No need to explain. I told you before, no hard feelings. Remember?"

Jelani swallowed. "Melinda—" She'd placed a hand on his arm, and though she didn't squeeze, the strength in that grip was many times more than the last time she'd touched him. "Melinda, you know I care about you, and if there was anything—"

"I think you should stop talking now, love." Her fingers tightened on his arm and he winced. On her other side, Daniel slipped his finger on the trigger of the water gun at his side. She turned slightly to regard him, her eyes darting from his face to the gun, and back.

"You know," she smirked at him, "I would normally tell you that you look a little ridiculous holding a water gun as if it was your only protection, but I know what's in it."

Daniel was frozen to the spot. "Oh, really?"

"Mm hm. Now, you know I like you, but if you try to blast me with that garlic water, I may have to kill you."

"You wouldn't do that," Jelani said. "You're not that kind of girl."

Melinda laughed at him, and she caressed his cheek with her other hand. "Things change, love."

"They don't have to."

She released him and moved away. She pressed her eyes shut,

balling her fists. "How do you know? What do you know? You have no idea! You don't have a white hot fire burning in your veins while fresh blood is just a few feet and a few seconds away! It's like nothing you can imagine." Her brown eyes started to glow with that terrible pale red color. "If you were anybody else, you would already be dead."

Jelani was at a loss for words. She saw the horrified look on his face and laughed dryly. "I know that look. Spare me the moral anecdote, love."

Daniel pointed the gun at Melinda, but before he could pull the trigger, she was there. She knocked his arm out wide, and dealt him a backhanded slap to the side of the head that sent him spinning to the ground. Before Jelani could so much as blink, she was back in front of him. Her thin fingers, once delicate and sensual, were now as strong as iron bands and wrapped around his throat. She lifted him off the ground and he was forced to drop his gun and grab hold of her wrist to support his weight, lest his neck snap from the pressure.

"I loved you, you know. I really did."

Barely able to breathe, all Jelani could do was force himself to look into those frightening red eyes, glowing hungrily at him. He looked deep into her eyes, letting her see him, and what he felt. She blinked, and he saw indecision there. After a moment, she hissed and dropped him.

He fell to a sitting position, coughing and gasping for sweet cold air. "Fight it, Melinda," he said between gags. "You don't have to be like him."

She backed away, her jaw clenched. Her fist shot out and there was a loud bang. Jelani looked to see a small fist-sized dent where she'd struck the metal container. He swallowed again and winced. She'd bruised his throat.

"You don't know anything!" she shouted at him. "I've already had to kill a person, or the thirst would have killed me." A flash of regret crossed her eyes and was gone. "I'm sorry baby. If I was able to just turn you, I would. But I haven't been this way long enough."

"You're going to kill me then?"

"I'll make it quick."

"I'll rip you apart if you touch him." Both Jelani and Melinda looked down the path to see a short, delicate-looking woman watching them.

Melinda looked from her to Jelani and back. An instant later she had Jelani pressed against the trailer, but then her hands were gone and Saaya was there. She was facing Jelani, but looking to the side. He followed her gaze to see Melinda rolling down the path. Saaya had thrown her to the ground faster than Jelani could even register the movement. Melinda came back to her feet and hissed, and Jelani's heart dropped into his stomach. He knew she was a vampire, of course, but to see her so clearly as one hurt him deeply.

"So you're the one who has him so uptight," Melinda said. Jelani had not been taken aback by this new side of her a moment ago, but the venom in her voice added to the shock.

"Your re-creator is a fool," Saaya replied. "An inexperienced fool."

Melinda straightened. "How so?"

Saaya tilted her head at the other woman. "To so share his thoughts with one of his own re-creations is simply humorous. I suspect he doesn't even know that you share some of his memories."

A lethal smile sliced Melinda's face. "No, he doesn't know. He's been trying to figure you and your brother out since your first encounter, and he can't figure out how you find him. The bastard is particularly good at escaping confrontation ... ah!"

"Careful," Saaya tsk *tsked* at her, circling the now kneeling vampire. Melinda was clutching her head, hissing through her teeth. "Your master still holds all the cards, girl. You may be privy to some of his memories, but he can sense your ... insubordination, if you will." She positioned herself between Melinda and Jelani. "Right now he's probably compelling you to kill Jelani and Daniel, is he not?"

In answer, Melinda surged to her feet and slapped Saaya across the face, drawing a line of blood from her cheek. She backed away in a crouch, fangs bared.

Saaya's head was turned. She wiped the blood from the instantly healed wound with a finger and licked it. Then she turned her smoldering lavender eyes on the other woman. "That wasn't wise," she hissed, and Jelani didn't see, but heard, the assault. *Slap, slap, SLAP.*

Melinda went spinning to the ground. With an effort she came back to her feet, but Saaya was there, and with an even louder slap that made Jelani wince, she sent the other woman flying into the side of a nearby trailer. Melinda was up again, and lunged at Saaya who easily avoided her attacks. Somehow, impossible as it would seem, Melinda managed to slip in an elbow to the side of Saaya's jaw.

The *dampeal's* head snapped to the side, and then she looked back, her fangs now bared. Jelani had never seen this side of Saaya either, and yet again he was reminded that he'd had no idea who or what he had been dealing with these past months.

Before Saaya could strike out, Melinda was down the path and leaping over a single trailer. Saaya gave Jelani one quick look and was after her. He heard her call over her shoulder at him, "The Hunter is coming and so is Kafeel." And then she was gone. Jelani immediately grabbed up the water gun and was at Daniel's side. He crouched over his friend, about to try to wake him, when he was suddenly yanked off his feet, flying away to slam into the giant container on the opposite side of the path.

The sound of his impact echoed through the dockyard, and he hit the ground hard, the wind blasted from his lungs. A pair of black boots stopped in front of his face, and one of them lifted and crushed the water gun beside him. Then he felt himself being lifted into the air again. He had just enough time to see the ground before it rushed up to meet him. The impact jarred his senses, and his cheekbone felt like it had broken. Jelani gasped, trying to catch his breath. The entire side of his face felt like it was on fire.

"You're not looking so tough right now, human." As if he didn't already know who it was, that familiar cocky voice confirmed that Remy had found him. Jelani tried to rise, but a boot slammed into the center of his back. He groaned, trying not to let his cheek touch the ground.

"I have to admit that although I find you positively stupid for coming here, I am both appreciative of your desire to help your damsel in distress, and also curious to know how you knew to come here."

Jelani thought about the conversation between Saaya and Melinda. *"I suspect he doesn't even know that you share some of his memories,"* she had said.

"Guess I got lucky."

"Nonsense." He picked Jelani up again, holding him by the arm. "This is ridiculous," the Hunter said, shaking Jelani as though he were a toy. "You get thrown around just a little bit and you're completely helpless. I've never understood how your species has endured for so long." He gave Jelani another shake and dropped him.

"I supposed I'll let you see this before your human life ends." Remy leaped atop the trailer and disappeared over the side. A few seconds later he returned with a woman draped over his shoulder.

Alisha.

He dropped her to the ground with little regard, then walked back to Jelani.

"I figured you'd want to have one last look at her while I drain every ounce of humanity out of you."

He picked Jelani up, spun him around so that he was facing his unconscious girlfriend, then sank his fangs into Jelani's neck. The pain was like nothing he'd ever experienced. Through the fire in his neck, he could feel his lifeblood being leeched out of him. Tears welled in his eyes and spilled down his cheeks. He felt the vampire's fangs slip out of his neck, and Remy's voice was close in his ear.

"I could have injected you with a substance we secrete that dulls the pain, but why bother, right?" He sank his fangs back into Jelani's neck, and the flames of agony commenced anew.

Through the muddled thoughts in his mind, his life flashed across his eyes. There was the fun he'd had, the love he'd shared. The heartbreak. His first kiss. There were the years of struggle to build his business, the moment of relief and exhilaration he'd felt when he'd stepped off the plane in Vancouver, knowing it was his new home. The life he'd created for himself, the friends he'd made. Meeting Daniel, Wen, Melinda. As if to dull the agony, his mind lingered as if savoring every encounter with her, the intimacy and playfulness.

She was gone, and then there were the guys and girls at EA, then Alisha. Alisha. The first kiss they'd shared, the way she looked at him with those intelligent, hazel eyes that were impossible to lie to. All of these moments passed before him in little more than a few seconds, and then they were burned away. Not forgotten, but simply placed in a part of his mind that made them more of a distant past to be looked on with detachment.

The fangs were suddenly wrenched from his neck, and Jelani fell to the ground. He heard an angry hiss, then retreating footsteps. Another pair of feet and the tip of a sword appeared in front of his face. The new arrival crouched, and then Yako's face appeared in front of his. Jelani had neither the energy nor the desire to feel anything at all. He just lay there, awaiting the death that was sure to follow.

The stroke never came. Yako's face lifted from Jelani's sight for a second, then returned. He stared in Jelani's glazing eyes for a few seconds.

"You are no longer my concern." He stood and turned away,

walking toward Daniel. Jelani hadn't even the strength or the will to feel alarm for his best friend.

Halfway to the still-unconscious man, Yako stopped and swore in a language Jelani didn't understand, yet felt he should. Then the Hunter turned and leaped over the nearest tractor-trailer, sheathing his sword in midair.

The Hunter had barely gone before Kafeel arrived. The towering vampire took in the scene around him, seeing Alisha and Daniel unconscious, and Jelani's life flickering.

He lowered his head, as if thinking. Through his gradually dimming thoughts, Jelani watched Kafeel stand this way as the minutes passed. Then he heard the jingling of the tiny bells of the *paayal* around Saaya's ankles. She stopped next to him, and Jelani winced when her fingertips touched his neck. He heard her suck in her breath as she stood.

"You're sure?" she said to her brother. He nodded silently.

She squatted back down to Jelani. "It looks like your luck has run its course, *jaan*," she said regretfully. "Your human life is over. Remy has decided to pass his essence into you."

"Can ... you ... he ... help ... me?" he rasped.

"There are some things that cannot be changed, *jaan*."

He felt a wave of regret and loss. "Then ... ki ... kill ... me."

Saaya recoiled as if she'd been struck. "Of course I'm not going to kill you! You still have not fulfilled your end of our agreement. No, my lovely Jelani. I cannot undo what Remy has done to you, but I can alter it." She leaned in so that her lips were touching his ear and she whispered, "I have no intention of letting you belong to him. You are mine, Jelani. I will make you better." Several feet away, he heard Kafeel grunt, and he turned away, walking toward the far end of the path.

"Do not worry, *jaan*," she whispered into his ear. "You will rise again."

And then he felt her fangs enter his neck. It hurt, but she was gentler than Remy had been. He felt only a bit of his blood being pulled from his body, but then a comforting numbness followed, creeping into his neck and flowing through his body. As soon as the pain had completely subsided, the fangs left his neck, and he was turned to lay on his back. Saaya's face hovered over his, her long black hair hanging beside her face.

"My poor Jelani," she purred. "Sleep."

He slept.

CHAPTER 29

Yako had not seen Remy in more than a year, but it took no more than the instant he'd seen him for the hatred to renew. Yako knew Remy better than the *dampeal* and her brother. He would more effectively track and dispose of the slippery vampire and be done with this business.

He glared out at the city below, thinking of how he'd been forced to scurry away like a rabbit when the hawk that was that tall spawn of an *Ancestor* came bearing down on him. He'd hoped those four Hunters Remy had set on Kafeel would have at least delayed him a bit longer. Of course, it would have been nice if they'd managed to kill him, but Yako wasn't fool enough to hope for that possibility.

Despite everything, it seemed as though Remy might have actually made his job a little easier. With the initial target no longer an issue, that half-breed girl would have little or no interest in the three remaining humans, so they should be easy enough to dispose of. Yako thought about that for a moment and decided against that course of action. Against handling it personally, anyway. If the information he'd collected was true, counting tonight, Remy had managed to get at least ten Hunters killed in a short amount of time. He doubted the fool would be commanding anyone again. Ever.

He gave the brightly lit city one last look. He didn't expect to spy out the elusive night crawler tonight, but he would find him. Then it would be a matter of killing him, or taking him back to Elders before killing him and Massius. Either way, Remy was a vermin that Yako meant to exterminate, and soon.

REMY'S EYES glowed hatefully at her. "So how do you really feel about me, pet?" he breathed into her ear, then slapped her against the wall. "You think I don't know the things you're thinking about me? *Do you?*" He grabbed her by the neck and pulled her head away from the wall. His face was inches from hers.

"You are mine. Do you understand?" He slammed her head back into the brick wall. A few bricks and some clumps of mortar crumbled and fell away. "You think you're smarter than me, don't you? How could you think you know anything, *shaquora*?" He spat that last word in her face. "Know this, and know it in the marrow of your stupid dirty little *shaquora* bones. You were created by me. You are mine, and only mine! You will do as I tell you, serve me how I tell you, and kill who I tell you. You are my servant always. Forever!"

He slapped her again and she fell to the ground, huddled against the wall. She wasn't broken, though. It would take more than a little abuse to break this one. She'd loved that human, Jelani, more than she'd admitted to him or herself. She hated Remy for taking away the possibility that she might still have Jelani. He didn't care. She would obey him regardless of how she felt.

He looked down at her with a smug grin, wondering how much she would hate him when she discovered that he'd turned Jelani. Now she would have to suffer having him at Remy's side with her, never able to touch him. How sweet it would be to watch this dirty little *shaquora* struggle with the torment of seeing her former lover every day, forever, and not ever be able to touch him unless Remy willed it.

His thoughts turned to Yako, and the grin fell away. Now that was a problem. He'd thought Elder Massius would have been up to the task of either eliminating the troublesome Eldest Hunter, or at least keeping him detained long enough for Remy to accomplish his task. Now that it was almost done, the Eldest was on his trail, and probably a good deal angrier.

Remy told himself that the Eldest Hunter was a concern that could be handled when the need arose, but there was a flicker of doubt. Yako was Eldest Hunter for a reason, just like he'd been offered to become a Reaper for a reason. Remy didn't doubt his own skills, but he would be a fool to underestimate Yako.

"That's just fine, Eldest," he hissed, drawing a curious look from Melinda. He turned away from the stupid girl. "You go ahead and come for me so I can finally be rid of you. On my terms."

SAAYA LAID JELANI on her bed and looked down at him. Through some miracle, she had convinced Kafeel to help her with Jelani's two remaining friends. Now they were resting in a hotel room together and would not awaken until the next night; she'd seen to that. Kafeel had already gone for the night to find a place to sleep through the day. Saaya thought that perhaps she had pushed her brother too far in expending so much effort in caring for two humans, and he had left to sleep away his disgust with her.

In a rare moment of obligation, Saaya had felt compelled to do this one thing for Jelani's friends. His life was forever changed, so perhaps this gesture would be at least a small comfort.

She touched his face and nodded. His skin was changing, going through the process of hardening and then softening to create the new skin that was both tougher and infinitely quicker to heal.

Everything in his body was changing, from his bones to his eyes, the cells and neurons in his brain. He would think differently, and absorb information differently and quicker. When he awoke, it would be to a world seen through different eyes. She hoped he might come to accept such a world.

"Time will tell, *jaan*," She leaned over him and kissed his still lips.

"Die and live. Sleep and awake."

ALSO BY RAMÓN TERRELL

Hunter's Moon

Darkness of Day

Revenire (coming soon)

Legend of Takashaniel

Echoes of a Shattered Age

Legends of a Shattered Age (coming soon)

Heroes of a Broken Age (coming soon)

The Fairies

Out of Ordure

ABOUT THE AUTHOR

Ramón Terrell is an author and actor who instantly fell in love with fantasy the day he opened R. A. Salvatore's: The Crystal Shard. Years (and many devoured books) later he decided to put pen to paper for his first novel. After a bout with aching carpals, he decided to try the keyboard instead, and the words began to flow.

As an actor, he has appeared in the hit television shows Supernatural, izombie, Arrow, and Minority Report, as well as the hit comedy web series Single and Dating in Vancouver. He also appears as one of Robin Hood's Merry Men in Once Upon a Time, as well as an Ark Guard on the hit TV show The 100. When not writing, or acting, he enjoys reading, video games, hiking, and long walks with his wife around Stanley Park in Vancouver BC.

Connect with him at:

www.ingramcontent.com/pod-product-compliance
Lightning Source LLC
Chambersburg PA
CBHW020225260626
47156CB00002B/548